Serving Pleasure

Alisha Rai

Cover by Kanaxa
Edited by Sasha Knight

For everyone who ever read Glutton for Pleasure (my very first published book!) and asked me, "but what about Rana?", this one is totally for you. Thank you for sticking with me and I promise, I'll never make you wait so long again.

CHAPTER 1

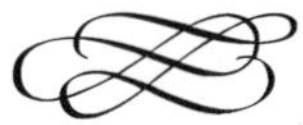

Long, elegant, dexterous. His fingers slid over her curves with the greatest of precision, handling each centimeter with expert care. This was a man who knew his way around a woman's form, from the roundness of her breasts and the dip of her belly, to the arch of her neck and the muscles of her limbs.

Rana Malik tucked her legs under her body, ignoring her aching feet. After a busy Friday night waiting tables at her family's restaurant, a hot bath should have been her first priority. But when she'd happened to glance out her bedroom window, she had no choice but to abandon all of her thrilling plans for the evening and plop down on her bed, enthralled.

Happened to glance? Let's not fool ourselves.

Fine. In the two months and sixteen days since The Hottie had moved in, peeking through her curtains at the house next door had become an admittedly bizarre part of her nightly ritual.

She wasn't always rewarded. There was no rhyme or reason as to when he would be busy at his craft in that brightly lit room, and sometimes it would be vacant and dark. Those nights were tragic.

When he was there, though… Lord. Those nights were the *best.*

She couldn't fully explain her fascination. It might, however—and she was just spitballing here—have something to do with the fact that he was so fucking gorgeous her eyeballs felt like they were being French kissed by angels when she looked at him.

That was only a small exaggeration.

This glorious creature could have been engineered in a secret government lab to take advantage of Rana's infamous weakness for beautiful men. Tall? Check. Packed with muscle? Check. Wide shoulders, narrow hips, strong back, grabbable ass? Check, check, check, check.

Granted, his hair wasn't short like she preferred, but maybe her preferences were wrong, because *damn.* She'd had more than one fantasy about loosening the tie that kept those heavy black strands clubbed back. His hair would skim against his high, sharp cheekbones, framing his face. She'd sink her hands into the rough satin and tilt his head down, and he'd lift one of those fierce, angled black eyebrows. Not both eyebrows. Just one. Super sexily.

Then she'd lick the scar that bisected his full upper lip.

She sighed. That would be her starting point. There were so many places her tongue could travel on that man.

He paused, his pinky resting against a nipple, as if he heard the voyeur peering over his shoulder. Rana pressed her lips together, instinctively freezing.

Surely he couldn't hear her. He had no idea she'd been here night after night, until she could barely remember a time when she hadn't come home hoping his lights would be on.

"Don't stop. Not yet. Keep going," she whispered, like she could will him to continue. Silly. If she could will him to do anything, it would probably entail taking off all his clothes and coming over to her place.

She let out a low breath when instead of swiveling around to glare at her, he leaned back on his stool.

In profile, his expression remained stony. Smiles and giggles were not something this man was familiar with, she imagined. She'd never seen anything on his face except focused concentration.

His arm flexed as he raised his pencil in a smooth glide and threw it across the room, the act seething with repressed violence.

Or frustration.

Aww. He hadn't had one of these nights in weeks, and she'd hoped he was past it. Rana opened the bag of leftovers her youngest sister had stuffed into her hands as she'd left the restaurant, pulling out foil-wrapped cold naan and a plastic tub of chicken curry, her eyes glued to the action. As the sole living expert (she assumed) on the man's solitary painting sessions, she could attest these shows always ended in one of two ways. One was with him working feverishly for hours, until even her night-owl sensibilities had to cry uncle and she fell asleep watching his long fingers dragging a brush over canvas.

Or two…

She flinched when he picked up the X-Acto knife from the table, aware of what was coming next.

Prepared as she was, she couldn't stifle her cry of dismay

when the knife cut into the canvas, sinking through the drawing of the couple entwined in a passionate embrace like it was hot steel through butter. He was thorough, not stopping until the entire canvas was reduced to nothing more than ribbons of pulp.

The painting had been in its early stages, but sadness crawled through her. Such a fucking waste.

With controlled precision, he set the knife on the table holding his supplies. He was always controlled, a harsh contrast to the passion his hands meted out.

This is weird.

Uh-huh.

He is weird.

Yup.

You're obsessed with a weirdo.

That was…accurate. Depressingly accurate.

Her weirdo—her hot weirdo—stood staring at the wreckage of his work for a long moment. Then he pivoted, pacing away from the easel to head toward the en suite bathroom. He lifted his shirt, giving her a glimpse of his back before he kicked the door shut behind him.

Rana scooted until she could rest against the mound of pillows on her bed, deflated at both the destruction and the short amount of time she'd gotten to spend with him. She opened the curry and dipped the thick bread into it, uncaring that both were cold. Every day for lunch she scarfed down a salad or whatever veggies she could grab from the restaurant's kitchen. The heavy, rich food she brought home with her was her primary sinful indulgence.

Lord knew, she had so few sins left to her name lately.

You did this to yourself.

She swallowed her mouthful of meat and bread and dove in for another bite, barely giving her taste buds a chance to savor the flavors from the first. She had officially entered her twelfth consecutive month of celibacy last week. Did that earn her something? A chip or a gold watch? A diamond-encrusted chastity belt?

Oh, there was nothing *wrong* with celibacy as a concept. Rana hadn't even minded it much for the majority of those twelve months, so consumed was she with her family's expansion plans for the restaurant and her newfound zeal to get her personal life in order. Then Hottie McNeighborPants had moved in. He might as well have stood on his lawn, wiggling his penis about and reminding her of all the things she adored about sex.

She sniffled in self-pity and ate another delicious bite. The problem was, she adored all the things about sex. Maybe more than she adored chocolate, and there were times of the month she would cut a bitch for chocolate.

Sex was magnificent. The weight of a man's body on hers, the smell, the sweat, the pressure of a nice hard cock between her legs...

Right when she'd been so certain she'd kicked her habit, he'd dragged her needs out into the light. Now she craved him frightfully, the way a person on a carb-free diet might crave a huge muffin. She needed that muffin. She wanted to make love to that muffin. She wanted to engage in acts of questionable legality with that muffin.

No. No muffins for you.

At least not until she found someone she'd want to...nibble on...long-term.

She squinted. No, not nibble on. Bake? Knead?

Ugh. She'd never been good at metaphors. Someone she could have a serious relationship with, damn it. Her casual hook-ups had been fun, but at a certain point last year she'd looked up and realized she wanted…more.

That didn't mean she liked everything about her self-imposed finding-herself-and-love stretch. Clearly. Look at her sad life. Without a regular source of muffins, she was reduced to creeping on a hermit with a perfect butt and beautiful face.

Even telling herself he was probably fucked up didn't help her. He had to be fucked up, right? The obsessive way he painted, the way he destroyed his own work. He might be an asshole, which meant her lust would die a quick death. She'd never fucked a jerk, and she wasn't about to start now.

But her brain couldn't be tricked. Since she knew nothing about him, her mind was free to conjure up all sorts of fantasies. He was hurting; he was tortured; he was passionate; he was generous; he was alone.

Well, she did know that last part was fact. She'd seen no evidence to indicate anyone shared the three-bedroom home that was the mirror image of hers. He was always alone, except for the people he painted.

She frowned at the remnants of her meal and stuffed a last bite into her mouth before closing the lid and placing the container of curry on the nightstand. Maybe she was mistaken about his loneliness, though. He might have a family or a girlfriend or a boyfriend, and she simply never saw them because they were in the witness protection program because they'd witnessed a hit on someone and had to testify…

Something moved in the corner of her eye. She glanced up at the window and promptly choked on the food in her mouth.

She gasped and groped for the water bottle she'd tossed on her bed, opening it and swigging a giant gulp, her eyes locked on this new development.

He wasn't naked on his lawn, wiggling his penis about. But he was naked. Fully, delightfully naked.

He held a towel in his hand and used it to finish blotting his wide chest before he tossed it into the bathroom.

Even knowing he leaves wet towels on the floor doesn't diminish his sex appeal.

Uh-oh. She was in such a pickle.

Rana finally managed to swallow her half-masticated bite and absentmindedly threw the water bottle on the bed. Was it capped? Who cared. Let it soak her bedspread.

Holy Mary. His brown skin was darker then hers, and it gleamed under the studio lights. He was the same color all over, which meant he either never left the house, or he sunbathed naked.

After having observed the hermit in his natural habitat for months, she was aware the former answer was more likely. But she was going to go ahead and save a mental image of him sunbathing nude for her happy-times bank.

She'd known his body must be tight, but seeing it stripped of the soft white shirts and worn denim he favored was… There were no words adequate to describe this heavenly sight.

No, you're *drooling.*

There didn't appear to be any spare fat on him. Though she ought to touch him to be sure. Maybe measure those huge biceps or run her nails over the shifting slabs of muscles that made up his chest and stomach. He didn't have much chest hair, but he was blessed with a lovely happy trail that deserved an hour or so of worship on its own.

His powerful legs bunched and released as he walked to the sheet-draped couch, giving her an excellent side view of his sculpted ass. She wanted to see more of that ass, but he sank down on the couch.

His thighs spread wide, and she instantly stopped mourning the lack of an ass view. She could console herself with his penis.

She swallowed, her mouth dry. Her breath was coming in small pants, and she was unable to look away from that delightful appendage. He was only semi-erect, which made his size all the more impressive. Long and thick, with a fat head, his cock rose from a base of curly black hair and rested against his thigh, curving slightly to the left. She wanted to wrap her hand around him.

This is wrong. He doesn't know you're seeing him like this.

It was one thing to watch him without his knowledge while he painted or drew. As weird as that was, she could reconcile it with her tattered conscience.

This, though…this crossed far too many boundaries.

She was going to shut her blinds. Her curtains too, to be safe. Right now. Because she was a decent, good, non-perverted human being who was not ruled by lust and drama and base desires. She was new-and-improved Rana.

New Rana was not impulsive. New Rana was thoughtful.

New Rana could not, however, conserve electricity, because she'd once again left her bathroom light on, the door open enough to let a bit of illumination spill into her bedroom.

Rana, came her mother's annoyed, aggravated voice in her brain. *Why do you always leave the light on? You are throwing money down the drain.*

The money was a secondary concern. It might be hard for him to see into a darkened room. But one that was lit, when he was directly facing her? Fuck, if she could see him, he could see her.

Calling herself ten times a moron, she swung her legs over the edge of the bed slowly, fearful of making sudden motions that might catch his attention. Yeah, if he discovered her peeking when he was drawing, she might be embarrassed, but they'd both be beyond mortified if he saw her eating his cock with her eyes.

Rana stood on none-too-steady legs and took one step toward the window. She had the best of intentions. Close the curtains, put away her leftovers, shower, crawl into bed, and forget she ever saw her gorgeous neighbor's dick. Responsibly adulting like a pro, that was New Rana's game.

Yes, she had the absolute best of intentions. Until his perfect hand smoothed over his six-pack abs.

Her legs weakened, and she slid to the floor, uncaring that the hardwood thumped against her tailbone.

His hand moved down his belly, over the dip of his groin, and fisted his penis. His cock hardened as he jacked it slowly a couple of times, the mushroom-shaped tip peeping over his locked fingers as he ran his palm up and down.

Her breath came out in a sharp cry as he brought his hand to his mouth and licked it before returning to stroke his cock, faster now.

So wrong. Stop. Stop.

She couldn't stop. Neither could he.

That could be you. That could be your hand fucking his cock.

She whimpered when his head fell back against the couch and he parted his lips as if he was moaning. His pulls became harder, longer, his thighs tensing, feet braced against his own hardwood floors.

She swallowed as well, her gaze locked on that thick, fat cock. Her hands were rough, a side effect from carrying trays and working in kitchens for over a dozen years. No amount of manicures could file her calluses off, but she used that roughness to her advantage. She knew how to bring a man to tears with her grip on his body. A year's celibacy couldn't destroy those skills.

She could make him scream.

The bright lights of his studio made his forehead gleam. Drops of pre-come wept from the tip of his cock. She licked her dry lips, imagining leaning over and capturing that essence on her tongue, swallowing it. She could work her mouth even better than her hands. Suck him shallow and slow until he was clutching her head. She would let him fuck her mouth a little, then take control. Take him deep. Have him writhing beneath her.

So many options. There were so many ways to get him there. And then. And then, and then, and then, she would take the pleasure she had denied herself for a year.

She clenched her thighs together. Her mystery artist would let her play with him until he was wild, his hips arching. Then he'd shove her to the floor, kick her legs apart, and ram himself inside her, filling the emptiness that was suddenly unbearable.

Though her fingers itched to slide inside her panties and spread her wetness over her clit, she refrained. No distractions. He was close, and she didn't want to miss a second.

His fist twisted with every upward stroke, his beautiful face strained with pleasure, thick eyebrows meeting over his nose in a grimace of need. A strand of silky dark hair had escaped his stubby ponytail and stuck against the sweat on his neck. She'd pull off that elastic tie. Let the strands of his hair mingle and merge with hers as he fucked her.

His hips arched up. His mouth opened on a silent cry. She leaned forward, her panties so wet she was embarrassed by her need.

And then…nothing. He stopped, his hand falling away from his cock.

Rana waited a beat. Then another one.

He dug his hands into his eye sockets. His cock rested against his belly, so hard it looked painful.

His chest rose and fell, and Rana didn't move, fearing he was crying. But when he drew his hands away and launched to his feet, there was no wetness on his face. Only more stoic impassivity, an impressive feat when he had that erection bouncing in front of him.

He stalked to the door of the converted master bedroom and disappeared, smacking the light switch on the way out, draping the room in darkness.

Rana's breath came in shallow pants. Her fingers curled on the top of her thighs. Desire and lust mixed with confusion and guilt. Why had he stopped? Was he unable to come? Or had he simply decided to finish somewhere else?

Curiosity swirled inside her, so powerful it scared her.

Curiosity was probably a good thing for most people, but not for someone whose impulsive nature often outpaced her common sense. If beautiful men were her weakness, her tendency to jump before she looked was her downfall.

She'd always had a problem with impulse control. At least, that was the official diagnosis of more than a few of her frustrated teachers. *I'm sorry, Mrs. Malik. Rana is such a bright girl, but if only she would learn to control her impulses...*

And her beleaguered mother would haul her out of the detention room, her face pinched and angry.

She was already primed to find this man fascinating. Add in "inefficient masturbator" to what she already knew about him, and she was dangerously close to reverting back to her old self.

You don't even know him.

She could. She could meet him.

Her overactive imagination spun into play, imagining all the ways she could endeavor to casually bump into him. She was pretty sure she was out of sugar. Would he find it odd if she knocked on his door right this second to request a cup? Everyone engaged in some late-night baking, right?

Like...muffins. Her mouth was watering for some muffins.

Rana stiffened. No. No. No. Oh God, that was classic Old Rana thinking. Not. Acceptable. It didn't matter what his deal was.

Not your business. Like spying on him during an intimate moment was not your fucking business.

She winced at the shaft of guilt. Grimly ignoring the gnawing ache in her belly, she came to her feet, trying to find some balance on her watery legs. His room was dark now, his destroyed canvas and the white couch nondescript lumps. If he'd seen her, is that what she would have looked like to him? A lump of swirling need and desire?

She bit her lower lip hard, hard enough to jolt her back to the here and now, away from the Technicolor lustful fantasy in her head. She would forget this. Forget the image of his hand jerking his thick—

Rana inhaled and yanked the cord on her blinds, drawing them closed. She would forget this, she repeated, even if that meant she had to forget him. Cold turkey was the only way she'd ever quit anything.

Mechanically, she took her leftovers downstairs to the kitchen, ensured everything was tidied up, and came back upstairs to slip out of her uniform and into her hot bath. And if her hand eventually found its way to her pussy and she stroked herself to orgasm, she told herself that it wasn't a mysterious artist's paint-stained fingers tugging at her clit.

Sometimes New Rana was a very good liar.

CHAPTER 2

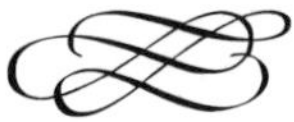

He'd lost his fucking mind.

Micah Hale stood outside his studio and gasped in an effort to get air into his starved lungs. The head of his cock brushed his belly, and he flinched, the sensation of skin on skin far too much for him to bear.

Finish it. Finish what you started.

All he had to do was wrap his hand around his dick. Stroke himself until he came, his semen spilling over his fist.

Micah ground his head against the wall, wishing he could crumble the plaster to dust. He clenched his right hand but didn't make a move toward his cock.

He'd stripped himself bare in that room and touched himself in front of the sexy voyeur he craved. He couldn't sink to a new level of pathetic and jerk off to completion in the empty hallway of his depressing, barely furnished home.

Those big eyes of hers hadn't looked away as he fucked his fist, not once. He'd studied her from under his lashes, but even if he hadn't, he would have known.

On some level, he'd registered her presence almost immediately upon moving in, a certain prickle of awareness that would come and go when he was at work. Then, one night a little over a month ago, the nagging sense of being watched had him glancing out the large picture window in the master bedroom he had converted.

She should have been invisible to him, only his reflection in the glass staring back at him. She would have been, but he'd dimmed his lights that night, and she'd chosen that moment to pick up her tablet. Her face was poorly illuminated in the backlight, but it was enough for him to catch a glimpse of the shadowy woman.

It was a coincidence, he told himself. She wasn't watching him, even if she was facing him.

When she'd looked up, he'd ducked his head. Casually, like he wasn't suspicious he had a spy, he'd cleaned off his brush, rested it on his table, and rose, walking slowly to his door. He'd killed the light and immediately plastered himself next to the door so he could peek through the crack.

Foolish and paranoid, that was the way he'd felt. Until a soft, warm glow lit her room, and she came up to the window, pressing her forehead to the glass. After a long minute, she lowered the blinds.

Micah ran his hand over the doorframe. His insomnia had kept him awake that night, as usual, but for the first time in a while, it was because he was thinking of someone other than himself. He'd finally fallen asleep, convinced his overactive imagination was playing tricks on him.

Until he caught her again the next evening, the outdoor light he'd purposefully left on shining into her room.

He'd pretended to appear fully engrossed in his project, sneaking a surreptitious glance whenever he could to find her playing with her phone, eating, lounging, but always,

always watching him.

Outrage had been his dominant emotion. *The trespassing sneak.*

His work was a private enterprise, especially now that he was so terrible at it. How long had she been watching him? Had she taken careful note of each of his failures, when he became so frustrated he acted like a stupid child, foolishly destroying his canvases?

Micah laughed now, but the sound was silent and without mirth. God, how filled with righteous indignation he'd been.

His anger and resentment had built that night as he slicked russet and ochre and ivory paint over the white background. How dare she watch him like he was an animal in a cage, or a circus freak put next door for her amusement. He would buy curtains. Hell, he would file a police report. He would, he would…

In the midst of his indignant fantasies, at maybe three or four a.m., he realized he'd been so distracted, he had actually completed a piece. A decent piece. The first painting, in fact, he hadn't been utterly repulsed by since he'd left England.

He'd stared at his new work for a good hour, inspecting it for flaws. His hypercritical eyes found a number of things he wasn't pleased with, but far less than any other work he'd managed to churn out in the past couple years.

After carefully putting away his tools, he'd killed the lights and dared to press his face against the window, seeking her out. She'd been barely perceptible in the shadows, asleep in her bed, buried under a pile of blankets. But still there.

He'd spent that night wrestling over his conflicting feelings. When he came downstairs the next morning, he did it convinced he had to confront her. It didn't matter that he'd been productive. She was crossing a line, a social and legal and moral one.

He'd jerked open his kitchen door when he heard her car start. And promptly lost every rational thought in his brain.

He hadn't seen her before, other than the brief glimpses he'd stolen over his shoulder. True, they lived next door to each other in the small, tidy subdivision filled with cookie-cutter houses, but he kept strange hours and barely left his home, except to get groceries or run the odd errand. Since he had nowhere to go and didn't care what his house looked like beyond basic cleanliness, his errands were fairly minimal. Like all of his neighbors, she wasn't home during the day to bump into the few times he did venture out.

That first glimpse…it was like he'd been living in a black-and-white television, and someone had given him an immediate upgrade to high-definition color. His annoyance had fizzled like a fire doused with cold water. He'd watched her long legs eat up the ground as she scurried from her idling car to her home and then back, a forgotten bag clutched in her hand. His kitchen door was on the side of his house, right under his master bedroom window. She didn't notice him standing there, poleaxed.

Her garden was teeming with a profusion of bright wildflowers and roses, and they created a colorful backdrop to frame her. Every step bounced with energy and vivaciousness, her waist-length black hair swinging as she moved. Her light golden-brown skin was smooth and silky and glowed with health. Her breasts jiggled as she sped up, and he imagined them overflowing his hands, her nipples peeking between his fingers as he licked them.

He never even made it over the threshold. Twin urges had slammed into him, freezing him in place. It had been so long since he had felt those needs, it took him a moment to comprehend them.

First, to trace her body and face with his fingers and tongue. Second, to capture every delectable inch of her on canvas.

He'd waited until she drove away before closing his door and returning to his morning protein shake, flummoxed and uncertain of what had just happened. Yes, she was beautiful. Gorgeous, even. But he'd seen stunning women before.

That didn't matter. His indignation had vanished. All that was left was need.

The next night he'd been working when he heard her car pull in. Barely ten minutes later, while making a show of mixing paint, he'd dared to sneak a look. There she sat, a shadowy figure.

Without another thought, he went back to work. And continued working for a month, always aware of her presence. It didn't happen every night. Some nights, he simply didn't have the energy to drag himself into this room and face his responsibilities. Other nights, she wasn't there, or her blinds were closed.

Micah scrubbed his hand over his face, exhaustion creeping over him. He pushed himself away from the wall and padded down the dark hall toward his bedroom.

He had always scoffed at the concept of a muse, but there was no denying that with her there, he'd managed to complete more pieces in the past month than he had in half a year. Decent pieces he wouldn't mind showing.

That he'd have to show, next week. He shuddered in distaste, the impending date a rapidly advancing monster he tried to avoid dwelling on.

Micah stumbled into the smallest bedroom in the house, which he'd claimed as his own. He didn't require much space. His furnishings were almost nonexistent—a full-sized frame, box spring, mattress, and a nightstand. There had been no need to spend more money. Hell, there was barely any need to have a bed. He could have slept his customary few hours a night anywhere, including the floor or the underutilized couch in his studio.

He sank onto the edge of his bed, the weight of exhaustion and unfulfilled lust riding him. Micah hesitated before running his hand down to his cock and daring to cradle it in his palm, hissing out a curse word when flesh met flesh. He was so hard it hurt, the skin stretched tight. His dick was flushed with pent-up need.

He stroked it once, shuddering at the sensation. It had been so long since he had sunk into a woman. How many fantasies had he spun about his voyeur over the past month? On her knees, in his studio, sucking on him while he painted. Lying on his couch nude, while he licked her until she screamed. Bent over his kitchen table as he thrust inside her.

He pulled away, self-denial the only punishment he could utilize against himself. *You don't get to come. Not after what you did in there.*

Shame tightened his stomach into a ball. God, what had possessed him to take himself in hand in front of her? He fell back on the bed, staring at the popcorn ceiling so he wouldn't look at his engorged cock.

Yes, she had been the first one to cross the line into the valley of inappropriate behavior. But she'd watched him *paint.* He was the one who had stripped down and bared his body to her. Guilt stabbed him again, a merciless pricking at his conscience.

When she'd risen from her bed, he'd assumed she'd storm off. Instead she'd fallen to her knees and stared at him. He couldn't see her face well, but her body language had screamed hunger.

Didn't matter that she could have stopped watching.

Before his life turned upside down, he would never have done such an outrageous, crude thing. Then again, lots of things had been different then.

As odd as it sounded, she'd brought a small kernel of hope back into his life. His work had improved, though it still lacked the passion it once contained. For a few weeks, he'd wondered if maybe he was getting better, back to normal, even if it was because of something as unconventional as a woman spying on him.

Stupid to hope. When he'd started his most recent painting yesterday, it had felt off from the first line. With each pencil stroke, he lost a minute amount of confidence while his frustration grew.

He wasn't crawling out of his slump or coming back victorious. Driven past the point of caring about who was watching, he'd destroyed the canvas in a flash of grim rage. A fuck-you to his audience. *I can't do this. Not even with your help.*

He'd regretted it almost immediately. Not the destruction of the canvas—the painting had been shit, and he didn't want to look at it anymore—but that she'd seen his bad behavior. He had taken a quick shower to wipe the distaste off him and had been about to put his clothes back on when the strange, overwhelming mix of reckless anger and helplessness had swept over his brain, mingling with the unsatisfied lust for a woman he didn't know at all but craved.

You want to look? Look what you do to me. Look at all my failures.

Stupid. Dumb. He punctuated each word with a thud of his head on the pillow. A part of him had actually hoped she would flee the room. Make it very clear his sexual interest was a one-sided thing brought on by his messed-up brain and lack of human interaction.

Another, secret part of him, the part that had once arrogantly taken pride in his body, had hoped seeing him unclothed would tempt her. Into what, he wasn't sure. Any one of his many fantasies?

He wanted her, needed her, though he didn't even know her.

You could get to know her. Walk outside, cross the driveway, knock on her door. Introduce yourself, like a normal human being.

For a moment, he imagined it, imagined being the man he'd once been. That man had adored women. Fat, skinny, large breasts, small breasts, white, black, Asian, pear-shaped, willowy—it didn't matter. He'd reveled in the beauty of every female body.

That man would have felt no hesitation about approaching and flirting with his lovely neighbor. Sex had come easily to him. Women had liked him, in bed and out.

He could do it. He could talk to her. Probably not with the ease and gentleness and charm he'd once possessed, but he could do it.

And then what? You flirt with her, like her, get into bed with her, and then…

Nothing. He had nothing to offer a woman beyond that.

He stared at the ceiling until his eyes blurred. Ah, that was the catch, wasn't it? What was stronger, his paralyzing fear of failure or his desire and curiosity for this woman?

He didn't know. He'd never know, unless push came to shove and she was standing right in front of him. Like that would ever happen.

Micah released a deep breath. He had to get his head on straight. The show was in a week. His agent and the gallery owner had assured him it would be small and exclusive, with minimal publicity. No fanfare about it being his first show in two years. He wasn't as well known in America as he was in England, so he hoped they were right.

Small steps were important. That had been the mantra his stern therapist back home had always yapped on about. Small steps toward healing. Small steps to get back to where he had once been.

The show didn't feel small, though, not to him. He needed to wrap his brain around it, not obsess over his neighbor. Maybe tomorrow, he would buy window coverings for his studio—

Immediately, he snorted, the thought laughable. Yeah, that wouldn't be happening. He hungered for her far too much. Not enough to face her, but enough that he wouldn't shut her out.

Micah rolled over and buried his face in the pillow, grimacing as he reached under him to adjust his cock. Unlike the studio, this room did have blinds. He never wanted to see the progress of the moon or the ascent of the sun in here. He was already acutely aware of how little he slept. The last thing he needed was to track it.

He screwed his eyes shut tighter, though he knew it would be a long, long time before he slept. One small blessing though: he could never really remember his dreams. Because there was no doubt his sexy voyeur maintained as much of a hold over his subconscious as she did his conscious mind.

CHAPTER 3

Five minutes into her first date with the successful lawyer her sister had set her up with, Rana had a fairly good idea there would not be a second date. Two hours later, as he slowly navigated her quiet residential street while pompously and seriously informing her about how much he disliked makeup on women because it made them look cheap, Rana was certain of it.

This means he is not shallow, she could hear her mother hissing in her ear. *He probably thinks you will be impressed.*

First problem was, she liked makeup. And was currently wearing it. In fact, she'd spent a solid twenty minutes primping and painting in front of the mirror before this guy had picked her up for their dinner date. Since she could do her face in a snap regularly, that meant she had actually put a lot of work into all of this.

The other problem was she didn't really give a flying fuck about men's opinions on her makeup. Or anything else she did to her body.

"...I just like the *natural* look."

Be quiet, her mother snarled. *Don't be nasty. Men don't*

like bitchy girls. They were pulling into her driveway right now. If she wanted—and oh God, she wanted—she never had to see him again.

"Women don't understand how much it turns men off to not know what a girl looks like under all that gross paint—"

"That's kind of a rude thing to say to my face." Oops.

But it shut him up. He stopped the car and killed the engine, giving her a baffled, wary look. He was handsome in a perfectly pressed, WASP-y sort of way. His hair was sandy colored and cut conservatively, his suit nicely displaying his lean body. He hadn't removed his tie, but he had loosened it the tiniest bit.

Wild man.

You don't want a wild man. Remember?

Yeah, well, she didn't want one who thought her face was disgusting either.

"Sorry, what?"

This isn't worth it. "It's rude to call me cheap and gross," she replied shortly. Being called cheap or even slutty was nothing new to her—hello, she'd been a rather friendly girl since she'd hit puberty—but most people had the grace to do it behind her back. Unwilling to sit in the car a second longer than necessary, she shoved her door open and stepped outside. Earlier, he'd made grand gestures of sweeping her doors wide for her. Sorry, bub. Chivalry wasn't just working door handles.

He scrambled out of the car to follow her. "I don't understand. Are...are you wearing makeup?"

She moved around the front of his vehicle and made a show of digging in her purse for her keys, the better to hide her expressive face. Otherwise he'd get treated to a whole lot of what the fuck.

He didn't even know? Well, that made it almost worse. No, she was not going to be able to be with a man who was stupid enough to think her lips were naturally a shade of Stoplight Red 911.

Weariness made her hands clumsy. God, she hated this. She'd been on so many first dates over the past year, she could no longer keep count. She was naturally extroverted, but this was getting…exhausting. She'd had some mild hope for this guy, since he worked with her sister Devi's boyfriend—well, one of her sisters' boyfriends—but he wasn't much better than the men she met through one of the six dating apps on her phone.

When could she give up this methodical search for Mr. Right? She'd never been so tired before, when dating had consisted of a series of casual hook-ups. Yet, she couldn't say she'd been totally happy then, she admitted with total honesty. At least, not for a while. Plus…

You're thirty-two, her mother muttered in her head, right on cue. *You do not have the luxury of waiting much longer to settle down.*

Thirty-two still didn't seem all that old to her. That was a hard thing to remember, though, when her mother called her up regularly to remind her her eggs were crumbling with every tick of the clock.

She gave the man—Charlie? Maybe?—a tight smile and walked up to her front door. "Thanks for dinner."

"I totally didn't realize you were wearing—"

"That's fine."

His long legs quickly ate up the ground until he stood

next to her. Another reason she'd had somewhat high hopes: he was taller than her. She wasn't opposed to shorter men, but since she hit six feet in the heels she wasn't willing to give up, she found a lot of shorter men were opposed to her.

Rana fitted her key into the lock and inhaled, pasting a smile on. The sooner she got rid of the man, the sooner she could get inside and get a glass of wine.

And drink it alone upstairs, in her lonely bedroom. With her blinds closed, like they had been for the past week. For reasons.

"I really am sorry." His voice was soft, his expression open and earnest. "I was babbling because I was so nervous. You're so insanely beautiful."

That was also supposed to be a compliment. She knew that, intellectually. She was supposed to want to be called beautiful. She'd always liked being called beautiful.

So why had it started to grate when anyone told her that lately?

His hand came to rest at her waist, and he leaned in, his face coming close to hers. He wasn't bad looking, and it had been so long. So she broke her own "no assholes" rule and permitted him to kiss her.

His lips were dry and firm. It was, in all respects, an unobjectionable first kiss, civilized and proper. He exerted neither too much nor too little pressure.

She could kiss this man and multitask, Rana thought. Damn, but if she went out with him again, she could be so efficient.

That wouldn't be fair to either of them. But a teeny part of her wished she was slightly more impressed. Because then she could end this never-ending search for the perfect partner and stop thinking about unattainable men and get on with the rest of her life.

A door slammed, and she jerked back, the relief she felt upon their lips separating telling her more than anything else that she couldn't see this man again. He wasn't right for her. She needed…

She followed Charlie's quick, annoyed sideways glance, and all of the oxygen sucked out of her lungs.

She needed.

There, in the gathering dusk of the evening, on the other side of her tidy hedge, stood the object of all her fevered fantasies. She blinked, certain she was imagining things. In her pursuit of avoiding thinking about the man for so many days, maybe she'd gone temporarily insane.

She could be forgiven for her brain short-circuiting. His hair was slicked back more severely than usual, caught in a tight, small bun at his nape. He wore a black jacket and pants and a crisp white shirt. With no tie, the collar was open to reveal his tanned throat. Gosh, raindrops on roses and whiskers on kittens and a beautiful man in a perfectly tailored suit: these were a few of Rana's favorite things.

Correction: A beautiful hermit artist neighbor in a tailored suit. Yes. That was her most favorite thing. Ugh, it was almost disgusting how nice he cleaned up. Why, she had half a mind to rip that suit off him.

The hottie wasn't looking her way. Of course not. When did he ever? He had no idea she existed, or that she'd seen him at his most intimate moments, or that it had taken herculean strength of will over the past week to keep her blinds shut in an effort to quit him.

He stepped off his front stoop, his head bent as he adjusted the cuff of his shirt. As he moved, the black fabric stretched over his wide shoulders as if the elegant trappings of civilization could barely contain him.

"Rana?"

"Huh?" She focused again on the man in front of her. Charlie. Right. Charlie was who she had to be concerned with. Charlie, and men like him, not her built, hung, temperamental, gorgeous-specimen-of-a-man neighbor.

"I had such a great time."

Or at least that's what she thought he said. Her hearing didn't work well when all her blood diverted to her private parts. "Yeah. Thanks."

"I'd love to see you again…"

Wah wah wah. Out of the corner of her eye, she watched the man in black walk to the silver SUV she'd never seen move from his driveway. The lights flashed once, and he climbed in, his pants tightening over his muscular leg.

"I'll call you?"

Charlie. Yes. No, wait, she didn't want him to call her. But by the time she snapped back to attention, he was already squeezing her waist gently and murmuring goodbye. She gave him a weak smile and waved as he got back into his car.

She glanced at the other driveway and froze, because she wasn't the only one watching Charlie. Her neighbor's eyes were trained on the other man. From the short distance, he looked like he was…glaring?

No, she was imagining that. Charlie backed out of the driveway, and her artist's eyes skated to her, as if he sensed her watching him. His face was grim and tight. Unwelcoming.

For a second, they stared at each other. It couldn't have been more than a second. That was enough time for her adrenaline to spike, blood rushing through her ears.

He broke eye contact, started his car, and reversed, driving far more slowly than Charlie had.

Oh no. Oh no, oh no, oh no.

Fight or flight. Or, more accurately, *fuck or flight.*

Terror and excitement zipped up Rana's spine. *I choose...fuck.*

The urge rose inside her, so big and thrilling she knew it would swallow her whole. An urge so crazy, she berated herself ten times as she yanked her keys out of her front door and zipped down her walkway to her car as fast as her three-inch heels could carry her, her breath coming in soft pants. She hadn't had a drink over dinner with Charlie because she hadn't wanted to prolong the agony of the evening, so she couldn't blame her bad decision-making skills on alcohol.

Catching up with her neighbor wasn't hard. He had stopped at the sign at the end of their street.

Just because you can, doesn't mean you should.

Right. Rana wiped her sweaty palms on her dress and gripped the wheel tighter.

You're stalking him.

Yes. He made a left turn, and she followed.

After countless episodes of creepy voyeuristic activity.

Yes. She rolled to a stop at a red light, irrationally annoyed when a tiny smart car came between them.

This is not part of the plan. You're supposed to be ignoring him, remember???!!!!

Uh. Yeah. About that…

He drove methodically, keeping under the posted speed limit, a courtesy she appreciated as the woman creeping on him. When he finally stopped in a busy, ritzy area of town, she carefully parallel parked a few spots away and waited.

He emerged from his car, his face even grimmer as he made his way to the building across the street. Rana was familiar with the area. The space they'd chosen for their new restaurant wasn't far from here.

Still, she had to squint to make out the swirling, elegant writing on the door. Davide's Gallery. Ah. A gallery. Made sense she was barely aware of its presence. Rana liked art, but splurging on it, for her, amounted to buying a painting not on sale at Home Goods.

Rana. What exactly are you doing here?

She had no idea. But instead of pulling her car out of the parking spot and heading home, chalking this up to a momentary blip of good sense, she shut off the engine and folded her hands over her stomach. Her fingers brushed against the silk of her dress.

Her mother was incredibly pleased with all of the changes Rana'd made in her life over the past year—cutting out the partying, searching for a suitable man. But unfortunately for her, Rana wasn't capable of changing her wardrobe, not even out of her newfound desires to settle down or please her mother. The red silk halter dress hit mid-thigh and practically guaranteed an aneurysm from any straight male in the vicinity. The top made the most of her firm breasts, and the skirt perfectly highlighted her long legs. Rana was suddenly glad she had picked one of her favorite outfits for her date tonight.

She hadn't known there was a possibility her masturbating hermit hottie painter neighbor would see her in it, but then, she hadn't thought him leaving his house was a possibility either.

Her hand reached for the door handle and then drew back. A year ago, she wouldn't have thought anything about marching in there, breasts blazing, fully confident in her ability to grab, seduce, and walk away from any man.

But then, she wasn't the woman she had been. Self-doubt assailed her. Maybe she didn't want to meet him. Maybe this was a bad idea. He could be terrible, or have a high-pitched voice, or an annoying laugh. He might be a dickhead with an Asian fetish, which was basically what she considered the scum of the earth. He could be—Rana's lips turned down—terrible in bed.

Whoa, whoa. Listen to yourself. You have him in bed already. What are you doing?

She breathed in and out, struggling to calm herself. Five minutes went by, then ten, then fifteen. When she hit the twenty-minute mark and her heart continued to thunder wildly in her ears, she gave up.

What was she doing? She had no idea. No plan. No hope that this man would fit the suitability test she'd devised.

There were so many things she didn't know anymore. Except she wanted to walk into that gallery behind her artist.

So badly. God. She stared at her fingers. Her hands were shaking with eagerness to meet that man without layers of glass between them.

What's stopping you?

Her mother wasn't here. Her family wasn't here. She rolled her lips inward. There was no one she could hurt by indulging this urge.

The logic was overly simple, but it made her decision. Immediately, her pulse calmed, and the anxiety buzzing in her brain dissipated. No thinking, no planning. Just do. Just this once. What was the worst that could happen?

She slid out of her small coupe. The mild breeze whipped her dress against her legs, the silk brushing her skin. The sun had started to set, and the lamps up and down the posh street had come to life, the clink of glasses and conversation spilling out from the bars and restaurants.

She tightened her fingers on her clutch as she came to the gallery entrance, drawing the tattered fabric of her self-confidence around her. The glass doors were heavy, resisting her touch.

Cool air conditioning kissed her skin, light harp music surrounding her. The gallery was larger than it appeared on the outside, and more crowded, filled with svelte, stylish people dressed in black and white, a low hum of conversation buzzing in the air. She twitched her skirt into place, refusing to feel garish or out of place.

Be cool. You're here now, so be cool.

She put one foot in front of another, her confidence growing as no one stopped her to demand what she was doing in the place. A waiter walked past her, and she snagged a glass of champagne from the man, flashing him a smile of thanks. She took a hearty sip and slipped her clutch under her arm.

Adopting an air of studied casualness, she glided along the perimeter of the room, attempting to hide her eagerness to see her target. Her eyes skipped over the tightly clumped crowds of people. There wasn't a single muscular male with silky black hair and artist's fingers amongst them.

Disappointment ran through her. Had she hallucinated? Were her stalking skills that subpar? Maybe he hadn't come in here—

She turned the corner and bumped into a woman exiting an alcove. "Sorry," she mumbled, and moved closer to the wall.

The woman ignored her, speaking to her escort and gesturing behind her. "I like this one. It's the best so far."

"A shame he isn't painting the way he used to..."

Out of instinct, Rana glanced in the direction the woman had indicated. And did a double take when the canvas in the small nook struck a chord of recognition.

She waited until the old man studying the painting wandered off, and then sidled closer. Of course she recognized this piece. She'd watched her neighbor paint it.

Rana tilted her head and released a shaky sigh. No, she didn't understand art. But this? This she understood.

He'd been her focus, when she'd watched him through her window, the paintings a peripheral interest. Plus, the distance had blunted the full impact of his artwork. This was so much better up close.

The nude couple stood face-to-face, the male's arm wrapped around the female, his hand splayed over her spine, the tip of his fingers brushing the lush swell of her ass. Her head was turned away from him while his was bent over hers. Her delicate hand rested against his pectoral.

A tiny, unobtrusive plaque had been placed on the wall. She leaned in close and read it. *Captivity. Micah Hale.*

Micah. Hale. She rolled the name around in her mind, her lips forming the words, tasting them. Perfect.

The other paintings, the ones tastefully arranged all over

the gallery, those were his too, all of them consisting of nude women and men. He wasn't a guest tonight. He was the star.

Her gaze was pulled back to the painting, and she wished she had any idea of art protocol. There was no price tag. Was she supposed to ask? Thanks to the restaurant's success, she could afford to splurge on occasion. Granted, usually that splurging was reserved for shoes and handbags, but she could make an exception tonight. She simply had to have this. She would fight that lady she'd bumped into for it. She'd fight anyone for it.

A shoe squeaked on the marble floor behind her, and she stiffened, a shiver of awareness running through her. She knew, even before she turned her head and glanced over her bare shoulder to meet a pair of stunning black eyes, thickly fringed by lashes. A detail she'd been too far away to notice before.

But she wasn't far away anymore. There was barely a foot between them. She could touch the man if she wanted to.

She wanted to.

Rana pivoted on her heel. As much as she coveted that painting, she coveted him more—he got all her attention right now. He took another step, his gaze unwavering. As she racked her brain for a clever, cool, sophisticated comment, he leaned in. Each word that fell from his scarred lips was like the stroke of a velvet-encased hand over her body, so stimulating it took her a second to process the content of his words.

"You came inside."

CHAPTER 4

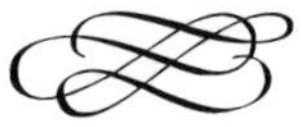

Rana was considered the most outgoing member of her family. Her youngest sister was naturally shy and preferred cooking to interacting. Her middle sister grew impatient when people didn't make as much sense as numbers.

Not Rana. She could converse with a stump, and probably make it smile. So it was a shame that the only word she could manage at that moment was, "What?"

His lips parted, and his black eyes narrowed in intense concentration on her face, skimming over her lips, cheekbones, eyes. He took his time answering her, but finally spoke. "You came inside."

He was...British. He was beautiful and jacked and talented and had the sexiest goddamn accent she'd ever heard in her life. *Um, excuse me, sir. Who the hell allowed you?*

Wait. Oh. Oh God.

Mortification raced through her as she processed the import of those simple words. He knew. Knew she had followed him. From his house. The house she lived next door to, which meant that she could never escape this humiliation, ever.

What was the worst that could happen? This, right here.

At least she had alcohol. She brought the glass to her lips and sucked down a hefty drink, wishing the champagne was a harder liquor.

Because I'm sure he'll be less alarmed if his stalker is drunk.

His eyes slid over her body, down her legs, and up again to her face. Even through her embarrassment, fire licked along her skin everywhere his gaze touched.

There were upsides to being so brown a blush was invisible. A trickle of sweat ran down the back of her neck, but at least she could rest easy in knowing she didn't look utterly discombobulated. "You know who..." She trailed off faintly, not eager to complete the sentence.

He shoved his hand into his pants pocket, the fine black of his jacket straining over his biceps. "I know who you are. You live next door to me."

While the silence stretched between them, her mind raced, thinking of ways to make her escape. She could dive through a window, but the glass would probably cut her up. She'd just had a dermabrasion session last week.

Alternatively, she could walk sedately past him, go home, steal a dead woman's identity, and flee the country. However, she'd miss her family an awful lot.

Mentally, she slapped herself. *You have game. Use it.* It was there. Buried deep beneath self-doubt and anxiety and a need to please others, but she had it.

Yes, this was embarrassing, but she could brazen this out, and then maybe she'd laugh about it tomorrow with her sisters. One more crazy stunt to add to her lifetime of crazy stunts. Gosh, that Rana sure is wacky, isn't she?

Especially when it comes to boys.

She tossed her head, cocking it. "Why, yes, I suppose we do live in the same neighborhood. What a coincidence we both ended up at the same place tonight." She lifted her shoulder. "It's not that big of a city, of course, but so weird."

Something flickered in his eyes. His face looked like it had been carved in granite. The scar bisecting his lip extended over his cheek, lending his already harsh masculinity a more violent edge. "A coincidence."

"Hmm."

"You tailed me here." His voice was rough, like a thousand pieces of glass, breaking over the clipped words.

She managed a breathy laugh, though what she really wanted to do was whimper. "Tailed you? I wouldn't know how to tail someone."

"I believe that," he murmured.

She lifted her chin at the dig. Like, okay, it was a dig at her stalking capabilities, but she was still mildly insulted. "I was at La Luna," she said coolly, referring to the nightclub down the street. "When I noticed something going on in here, and I thought I should come check it out."

His lashes shielded his thoughts. "Is that right."

"Yes." She licked her lips, trying to stem the urge to babble nervously. "I'm so glad I did. This show is wonderful." She wasn't supposed to know he was the artist. And it was wonderful.

"Hmm."

"This painting…" she gestured behind her, wincing when a drop of champagne spilled onto her wrist, "…for example. Isn't it stunning?"

He glanced past her at the painting. "This one?"

Desperate to play this for all it was worth, she turned to face the painting she'd hungered for so hard. Harder now that she had seen its creator up close. She lifted her glass and drained it completely, the small jolt of alcohol warming her. "Yes. It's great. Love it."

His shoe squeaked. Another step, though not close enough to touch her, but she could feel the heat rising off his body. The curve of the wall carved this small section away from the rest of the gallery, the shadows helping to hide them. "The gallery manager didn't like this piece. She thought it would be unmarketable. Plain. That's why it's hidden over here."

Distracted from her panic, a real frown pleated her brow. "She needs her eyes checked."

"She's considered one of the best in the business."

"Then the business is broken." This wasn't plain. The figures sang with vitality and life and passion. If Rana didn't know it would be the height of bad manners, she would trail her fingers over their bodies.

"I've created better."

She played dumb. "Oh, did you paint this?" She started to turn, but froze when a big finger brushed her bare shoulder. The touch was so light, she would have thought she imagined it, but there was no way she could imagine the tingle racing over her skin.

"What do you see?" His voice was luscious and deep, cool and commanding. She wanted to curl up with a smoky whiskey and have that voice say all sorts of erotic things to her.

"Need." Her answer was embarrassingly instantaneous.

She didn't just see the need, she felt it. It lifted off the canvas and sank into her veins.

He made an approving noise. Again, the lightest of butterfly touches whispered against her other shoulder.

She could demand he stop, but she loved it. Her body swayed backward, eager for more.

"And?"

Rana shifted. "Desire."

"And?"

She hesitated, twisting her empty champagne flute by the stem. Never had she thought about a piece of art so intently.

She wanted to please him. Maybe then he would give her another one of those light brushes of skin against skin.

She studied the way the man's head hovered over the woman's shoulder, his lips a breath away from kissing her. "Fear."

He paused for a second, as if he were caught off-guard. "Her fear."

She frowned. Her fear? No. The woman was pressing closer to the man, her hand on his chest hungry, not protesting. It was the man who was hesitating, his arm around the woman grasping, as if he feared she would vanish. "His fear."

There was silence for so long she wondered if she had scared him off. When he finally spoke, she released a sigh of relief. The relief vanished the second she processed his harsh, blunt words. "Do you see all of this now? Or did you see it when you watched me paint it?"

Oh God. Oh God, oh God, oh God. Where before she'd been hot, she grew suddenly, terribly cold, the blood draining from her face. Her fingers opened reflexively, the champagne flute tumbling.

With a speed and grace that was almost inhuman, his hand reached in front of her and plucked the glass out of mid-air. His front brushed against her backside, the fabric of his trousers scraping her bare legs. His arm crossed over her belly. To anyone watching, it would have seemed like a simple gesture, a man standing behind and putting his arm around a woman while they spoke in front of a painting.

There was nothing simple about the electricity that arced between them.

He withdrew his arm slowly. She heard the clink of glass on something as he set it down, and then his footsteps as he came to stand next to her. She continued to stare at the painting, her mind racing, struggling to come up with justification, lies, or apologies. Anything to get away from this mess.

Out of her peripheral vision, she caught his frown. A large palm cupped her hip, the heat of it making her jump, and he drew her close to his side. He was only a couple of inches taller than her, but his large frame made her feel tiny and surrounded. “Stop it,” he growled.

Her lips barely moved. “Stop what?”

“Stop being embarrassed.”

He might as well have asked grass to turn purple. Tears stung her eyes, blurring the painting. “How?”

“Just stop it.”

“I can’t. I’m mortified.”

“Are you smart?”

The seeming non sequitur distracted her from her crushing embarrassment. She side-eyed him. “I—What?”

He lifted his massive linebacker shoulders. “Are you smart? You don’t appear to be dim, but I don’t know you well enough to say.”

Did he mean, like…academically? Because no, then. She had barely graduated high school. Sitting still and learning had always been chores to Rana, much to her parents’ dismay. “I’m not stupid,” she finally wheezed, unclear on where the strange man was going with this.

His lips tightened, the scar turning white. “Then what do you make of the fact I know you followed me here tonight? And I know you’ve been watching me? And I’m not angry about either of those things?”

She froze.

Plot twist.

In a snap, the fog of humiliation lifted, the buzz around them returning to normal decibel levels. His hand remained on her waist, burning a brand on her skin through the thin fabric. She breathed in deep, eager to get air to her deprived brain cells.

“You let me,” she whispered. “You let me follow you.”

“I never drive under the speed limit.”

“You let me watch you.”

“I wanted you to watch me.”

“How long have you known?”

He looked away, but his fingers clenched, bringing her in closer to his side. They touched from hip to thigh. She tingled in every spot their bodies met. “Since the beginning, I think.”

Bewildered, she shook her head. “You weren’t mad? Why didn’t you…stop me?”

A muscle ticked in his jaw. “I don’t know.”

"You don't know?"

The recessed lighting brought out subtle red highlights in his dark hair. "I don't know a lot of things."

"I crossed a boundary. I'm not proud of…" She touched her finger to his. It twitched against her hip, sending fire racing through her. "I'm sorry."

He shifted. "This isn't something you do, then. Normally."

"No." Horrified, she leaned back. He twisted, keeping his arm where it was so they were face-to-face. "I've never done anything like this before in my life. Spying on someone. Following them places. And let me tell you, I've done some questionable shit. I can't apologize enough."

Impatience flashed in his eyes. "I told you. I wanted you to watch me."

"That doesn't make it okay." She swayed closer, daring to rest her palm on his chest. His muscles jumped under her. "It was wrong. Especially…" A thought occurred to her, and she watched him carefully as she asked the question. "Did you know I was there last Friday?"

Her heart pounded as she waited for him to answer. *Please let him say yes.* Otherwise, there was so much apologizing she'd be doing.

"Yes."

She closed her eyes. The answer she'd wanted, yet it opened up a whole new host of questions. "The entire time?"

"Yes."

Her eyes popped open. "You knew I was there when you—"

"Yes."

She shook her head, her earrings swinging. "I don't understand why you'd be okay with it at all, but why did you want me to see you doing *that*?"

At his silence, she opened her eyes. They were so close and tucked away, she could pretend the rest of the world didn't exist. She would say that his gaze was controlled and enigmatic, but that was a smokescreen. She could feel the hum of volatile emotion under his calm facade. "Why did you stay?"

She dipped her head, her guilt and shame impossible to ignore, even if he was offering her absolution. "It was like I couldn't stop myself." *From the moment I saw you, I've been unable to control my old, impulsive self.*

If someone had told her a day or two ago she'd be baring her soul to a man she barely knew in the middle of a semi-crowded gallery, she would have laughed.

"You haven't watched me since then."

"I felt guilty. For liking it." She glanced up at him from under her lashes. "This isn't normal. It's wrong, what I did."

"Yes. My stripping naked in front of you. Touching myself. That was wrong as well." His hand hovered over hers before finally covering it. "Maybe we bring out something...wrong in each other."

Her breath caught as she replayed his X-rated performance in her brain, the way his big hand had cupped his cock, the long, slow pulls as he fucked himself. He'd been performing, she could see that now, with his legs spread wide and his clenching abs. Performing for her benefit. "It felt good. Not wrong." The words slipped out, not entirely consciously.

His full lips curved—not a smirk, not quite a smile. It

was the kind of smirky smile that once might have gotten all of her aggressive instincts humming, the kind that urged her to offer him a drink. Off her body.

"I wasn't going to ever speak with you," he murmured. "Even when I saw you standing here, I told myself to walk away."

"Why didn't you?"

An indefinable expression flitted over his face. "I couldn't. I had to talk to you." He tightened his fingers over hers, his voice dropping an octave. "Touch you."

Not indefinable. She recognized that expression, because it was the same expression she saw in the mirror. *Starved.*

She was so hungry. Not hungry for a man, but hungry for him. A man as strange and wild and imperfect as she used to be.

Used to be? As you are.

Fuck her resolutions. Fuck going back to her dry, boring, sex-less bed. One little slip didn't hurt, did it? One little slip, and then she'd get back on the wagon. Like a smoker sneaking one tiny cigarette.

He was her cigarette, this man who created beautiful art and then smashed it to ribbons, who had a body that would make a Greek god weep, who brought himself to the brink of orgasm and denied himself.

Her eyes narrowed. One taste. That was all she needed.

She licked her lips, gratified when he stared at her mouth. She flexed her hand on his chest, letting him feel her long fingernails through his suit. She flicked open the button on his jacket, sliding her hand inside to rest on his stomach, only his shirt separating them. "Do you want to touch me more?"

He turned statue stiff.

A throat cleared behind them, followed by a censorious, "Micah? If you could come with me, I'd like to introduce you to—"

His eyes didn't leave her face. "Not now," he bit off, far too loud and harsh.

There was a humph, and they were left alone again, though Rana was suddenly, acutely aware they weren't really alone. And that she hadn't spoken very softly when she announced her desire for the guest of honor of this party tonight.

Smooth move, playa.

"Where can I touch you?" Unlike her, his voice was low. Thank God one of them could be discreet.

She took a step closer, their bodies brushing against each other. "Anywhere. Everywhere." The sexy words felt foreign and unusual to her, but at the same time, delightfully familiar.

Finally. Relief coursed through her. Finally she could speak plainly, not shove down her deepest desires. With the tip of her nail, she traced the exposed skin of his throat. His Adam's apple bobbed the instant their flesh made contact.

Fascinated by the rigid control he was exerting over his body, Rana dragged her finger lower, until it caught on his shirt.

She smiled up at him. "Boxers or briefs?"

"Does that matter?"

"Aren't you curious about my panties?" She leaned forward and pressed a closed-mouth kiss on his throat, the heat of his skin burning her. "Thong or boy?" Another kiss. "Bikini or G-string?" She let him feel the barest hint of her teeth as she nipped him. "Red or black?"

"No."

Rana pouted. "Why not?"

The hard hand that wrapped around her nape startled her, but no more than his face looming close to hers. "They won't be on you long enough for me to notice."

Oh. Good answer. Her knees weakened.

"You want me to fuck you. Is that right?" His whisper was rough and filled with wild promise.

Talk about speaking plainly. "Yes."

"Say it. I want this to be clear."

"I want you to fuck me."

His skin was stretched tight over his cheekbones. "I'm not looking for anything permanent."

More relief. If there was a pang of bittersweet sorrow mixed in with that relief, she ignored it. Her reply was immediate. "Neither am I." This was her allotted slip-up. It wasn't about bringing this man home to her mama. Especially since her mama had been displeased when Rana had dated a teacher last month because…well, because he hadn't been a doctor. Now that her oldest daughter was ready to settle down, basically only a son-in-law with a medical degree would do.

A long-haired artist who barely left his house? That she'd met because he caught her peeping in his windows? Rana didn't always see eye-to-eye with her mother, but she wasn't eager to give the woman a heart attack.

No, this particular muffin was just for her, someone wrong to tide her over until she found someone right. "One night. That's all I want." All she could have. "Nothing more."

Laser-sharp, his eyes bored into her. When she'd been fantasizing about him, she'd wondered what his personality was like. This...this blunt directness seemed right.

"That man you were with. Is he your boyfriend?"

It took her a second to understand who he was talking about. God, Charlie. The man had left her less than an hour ago, and he'd basically been wiped from her memory. She gave a short laugh. "No."

"Are you sure?"

"It was a first date. Yeah, I'm sure."

"Are you seeing anyone else?"

"No." Her smile was crooked. "I'm free as a bird." She paused. "What about you?"

"No."

She barely had time to release her sigh of relief before he lowered his head, his lips a hairsbreadth from her ear. "What's your name?"

She had to stifle her wince. Propositioning a man before they exchanged names. Definitely a first, even with her checkered past. "Rana."

"Rana." He pronounced it properly, Ray-na. His tongue rolled over the syllables. "I'm Micah."

"I know." She tipped her head toward the plaque under the painting. "It's right there."

"I have to stay here for another hour and a half."

Nooooo. She tried not to keen the word, but it was a struggle. An hour and a half? That was ages away.

He continued speaking. "If you want me to come over when I get home, leave your curtains open and your door unlocked. And be naked. I won't be patient." He stepped away, his lips twisting. "If you've changed your mind—well,

I won't bother you again. But I'll expect the same courtesy."

"I won't change my mind." How could she? This was all she could have dreamed of. And more. A night of pure physical lust with the man who had ensnared her mind and body since the first minute she'd seen him.

Tomorrow might be strange or complicated, but she'd worry about tomorrow then. Giddiness made her want to laugh and dance. Poor man had no idea what was about to hit him. But he'd thank her in the end. They always did.

He gave her a long, thorough look, as if her clothes were as good as gone already. "Naked," he repeated, before turning on his heel and brushing past a middle-aged couple who cast him covert, curious looks. Looks they transferred to her when he was gone.

She supplied them with a wobbly smile and tilted her head at the painting behind her. "This one's mine."

CHAPTER 5

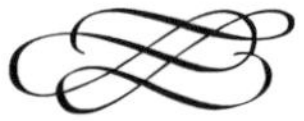

She'd left her blinds open.

Micah stood in the darkness of his studio, staring into her darkened bedroom.

Those blinds had been shut since he'd spun out of control last week. He'd assumed she'd been disgusted by his vulgar display. God knew, he'd been consumed with plenty of self-hatred for scaring her off.

I felt guilty. For liking it.

She'd uttered those words, and elation had coursed through him.

From the moment he'd made the exhilarating connection that she was following him—which was roughly ten seconds after she started following him, she was truly terrible at reconnaissance—he'd wrestled with what he would do if a face-to-face confrontation came to a head. He'd never spent a more agonizing half hour than the time she'd made him wait before walking into the gallery.

Then he'd spotted her, standing in front of his painting, the one he had actually liked but the gallery manager had been less than enthused about, and the decision had been remarkably easy. He couldn't not talk to her. Not when she was right there.

He'd thought her beautiful before, but tonight, she'd launched herself into super-model territory. While she'd studied his painting, emotions flitting over her lively face, he'd searched her for some imperfection, but there was nothing about her he didn't like.

Rana. Now that he knew it, he couldn't stop repeating her name in his head.

She'd smiled at him, and he'd lost whatever shred of sanity he'd retained, forgetting he was no longer the type of man who would boldly demand a woman go home and wait for him naked.

Are you smart?

Micah winced. Conversation had never been his strength, given his solitary nature, but he'd become a barbarian during his self-imposed exile of the past two years. She deserved better than his fumbled attempts to charm her.

Luckily, she was quick. And brash. And she took initiative.

He liked that. Because lately, he couldn't do a single fucking thing without becoming paralyzed with indecision.

Like right now. The instant she had left him, he'd reverted back to the broken man he had become, filled with doubt and second thoughts.

He grimaced, staring at her house like it held all the answers to the universe. Or, at the very least, the answer that would tell him what to do now.

What was there to be indecisive about? If he didn't go, he would only spend the rest of the night agonizing over his failures—the way he'd had to pretend not to see people's curious glances or hear their whispers over the past few hours. Or how he'd had to not take offense when the gallery manager told him they'd sold some paintings.

Some? She'd been pleased by that, and he'd wanted to throw a champagne glass at the wall. There had been a time when people had fought over his work, when every show had sold out.

Why had he given in to his agent's nagging?

Because eventually your money will run out, and you need some sort of career.

Correct. He'd be damned if, on top of everything else, he had to ask his parents for financial help.

Yes, there was nothing productive he would do at home. Anyway, didn't being with Rana trump basically every other option open to him?

He slipped his hand over the front placket of his pants. As much as he missed fucking, a large part of him simply wanted to surround himself with her, have those soft thighs and gently rounded arms around him for a night. Was that so much to ask?

Small steps.

Was she in her living room, waiting for him? Was she, as he'd demanded, naked?

There was only one way to find out.

Bare feet padding on the hardwood floor, he walked out of his studio and down the stairs to his front door. He didn't bother to put on shoes.

The full moon lit his way. The cold, wet grass tickled his feet, and the small rocks in her driveway pricked them, but he didn't much care. Her home was dark, and if it weren't for her car in the driveway, he'd think she wasn't home.

When he looked closer, though, he noticed the glow of a dim light peeking out from under the brocade curtains shielding the large bay window at the front of the house.

He paused at the door, his hand hovering over the doorknob. He had told her to leave it unlocked. Had she?

Micah stopped before he could touch the polished brass. The doorknob wasn't his. The house wasn't his, though it was identical in build. He barely knew the woman inside, for all the strange connection he'd felt with her from the second he'd caught her watching him.

They'd both intruded on each other enough. He made a fist, knocking lightly.

Before his hand could fall twice, the door opened, and there she stood.

It took him a second to realize he'd forgotten to exhale, and he let his breath out in a rush. The overhead light in her foyer was soft and caressed her face, the shadows making her eyes pools of mysterious black. Her cheekbones appeared more pronounced, her lips a deeper, more vibrant shade of scarlet.

She had changed her makeup for him, or maybe touched it up. She hadn't needed to, but he couldn't deny he was flattered. It was another sign she truly wanted him.

He shifted, aware of his bare feet. Would it have killed him to put his shoes on? Or maybe shower first?

Rana wasn't wearing shoes, though. Her feet were delicately arched, slender and elegant. She'd donned a lavender silk robe that ended above her knees, leaving her long silky legs bare. She wasn't exposing any more skin than she had in the gallery, but he had seen enough women in robes—

both models and in his personal life—to know when a woman was naked underneath one.

His body tightened. Had he ever felt like this, even before his accident? Like he wanted to lay a woman down on the floor and feast on her body for hours?

Her lips curled up, and she spoke, breaking their silence. "You said to leave the door open. I thought you would come right in."

He looked at the door. "I didn't want to... It seemed presumptuous," he said finally, aware how silly that sounded, when she'd been not-so-secretly watching him for weeks. When he had already bared his body to her.

That was the problem, though. He'd wanted a clear, non-equivocal sign he was welcome, that this was freely given on both sides. He didn't want any shame or guilt tainting tonight.

"I wouldn't have minded." While he warmed at her simple statement, she opened the door wider and stepped aside, giving him the physical invitation he'd needed.

Feeling rather brave, he stepped over the threshold. He wasn't here to examine her decorating, but he appreciated the warm colors and soft lighting. She closed the door behind him with a snick.

He dipped his head and started to turn. "Rana..."

Upon pain of death, he wouldn't have been able to tell someone what he'd been about to say. She was stroking the knot in the tie of her robe, and how was a man supposed to have rational thoughts when that was happening?

"Yes?" A finger tucked inside the knot, tugging at it. His vision narrowed, until he couldn't see anything else but that tie. The one barrier left between him and her skin.

Small steps.

He cleared his throat. Having her unclothed would be nice. Having her inflamed with lust would be better. "Are you naked under there?"

"That's what you asked of me," she purred. She freed the knot and paused a beat before letting the two sides fall away, the lapels opening to reveal a sliver of tawny skin, the inner curve of her breasts, the toned expanse of her belly, a flash of dark pubic hair.

Drama. He didn't know what she did for a living, but this woman was born to be an actress or model. She knew how to work a captive audience.

She shrugged the robe open, letting it slither over her shoulders and down her arms, until it caught on the curve of her elbows for a brief moment. His heart stopped, then started again as he viewed her body surrounded by a frame of frothy light purple.

Proportionally, her breasts were a little too big for her slender body, firm and ripe and heavy on the bottom, the nipples large and dark brown. He'd always been a breast man. If someone, right this moment, offered him the choice between ten million American dollars and a minute where he could bury his face in those tits, licking and sucking on her nipples until she screamed out loud with pleasure? The minute would win.

The robe fell to pool around her elegant feet, and his eyes followed the path it had taken, skimming over her toned legs, lingering over the neatly trimmed bush between her thighs.

His voice sounded like a raspy stranger's when he finally spoke. "Are you wet?"

Rana leaned back so her shoulders rested against the door, displaying her body in an arch, and smiled. A siren's smile. She was exceptional at playing to the audience. "Why don't you come over here and take a look?"

If he did, he wouldn't stop at a look. He'd have his pants around his ankles and his cock fucking inside her before either of them could say two words. "Show me."

She quirked an eyebrow at him, but her red-tipped nails stroked down over her chest and her belly, heading to the juncture between her thighs. She raked over the curls there, and then her fingers were gliding over the sweet flesh he was dying to touch.

Men did not grow weak in the knees, but there was no other reason for him to sink to the floor. Though he immediately saw the benefit in this position. "Come here."

He was grateful to note he wasn't the only one with unsteady legs. She came to a stop in front of him, his head level with her pussy. Her hand still cradled it, giving him tiny peeks of dark hair and pink flesh between her fingers. He looked up her body, admiring the way her breasts rose and fell, her nipples hard. "Open up for me."

Two of her fingers slid over her vulva, separating the puffy lips. He wanted to run his tongue all over that soft flesh, suck her down. Examine her and absorb her, taste every drop of her slick, swollen body.

It had been so long since he had had his mouth on a woman, and he didn't think he'd ever wanted a woman like her.

"I want to see," he said, his voice so guttural he barely recognized it, "how wet you are inside. Don't move."

Without further warning, he buried his face in her pussy, lapping her first before spearing his tongue inside her. Her muscular channel contracted around him, sucking him deeper.

She gasped and stumbled back a step, separating their bodies.

That wouldn't do.

He reacted like an animal that had been denied his favorite treat. Clutching the cheek of her ass with one hand, he dragged her toward him. "I said don't move."

"S-sorry."

Knocking her hand aside, he spread her pussy open for his mouth. "Let me…" he muttered, aware he sounded like a lunatic, but unable to temper the desperation. "Just stand still, Rana, and let me fuck you a little. I need it."

She might have said something. He didn't know, couldn't think past the fact that her legs were parting, her hand on his head urging him closer. Somewhere in his brain, part of him stood apart from this and watched in shock. He'd always been a demanding lover, but this was…absurd.

He'd stop if she told him to, but if she was willing? God, if she was willing, he'd push her wherever she would let him. Straight to hell, even, though he'd make sure they both enjoyed the ride.

She tasted sweet and salty, better and richer than any woman he had ever had. Her ass was round and high, thick handfuls for him to grip and use to hold her tight to his mouth. He squeezed her buttocks again and again, rocking her against him, alternating between fucking her with his tongue, and tugging and rubbing her clit.

The scar bisecting his upper lip made his touch rough,

he knew that. At first, he tried to be mindful of it. But once he realized she was grasping his hair tighter each time he inadvertently scraped her, he threw careful kisses out the window. The next time he drew her clit between his lips to suck it, he made sure to roll his lips in and press down, compressing the nub. Instantly, her grasping hands turned to claws.

She ripped a few strands of his hair when she pulled out the tie keeping it back, but he didn't care, because then her fingers were sliding through the strands and using them to guide him where she needed him.

His cock was throbbing, his pants a painful restraint. The only thing he wanted more than getting inside her was having her come on him. Words were spilling from her lips, a rush of *pleasegodyesfuckmedon'tstop*, every single syllable making him feel like a god. How had he gone two years without this?

It took him a second to realize she was saying his name over and over, her hands pushing him away rather than toward her. He jerked his head up, aware her juices covered his face.

"Do you need me to stop? Please. Don't..." He tried to cut himself off. Begging. He never begged. Even when he had been lying on the ground in a pool of his own blood, he hadn't begged.

He would beg this woman. "I need—"

She shook her head, long black hair flying, and he realized her eyes were glazed over with as much lust as he was feeling. A fine layer of sweat covered her body, and her breasts moved fast with the power of her breaths. "Micah...can't come like this. Standing."

Relief crashed through him. Thank God. Was that the only problem? She couldn't come on her feet? Fine.

He pulled her down to straddle his lap and then spilled her back, grateful she'd placed a rug on the tile floor. The better to cushion her.

He grasped her legs at her knees and wrenched her open, laying her pretty pink pussy bare for him. It was his. She was his.

Only for tonight.

He swatted away the nagging thought like he would a fly. Not now. This wasn't the time.

This position worked. He liked her like this. He had more room to maneuver now. He pressed her thighs wider, planting her feet on the floor to give him more access. "Better?" he asked.

"Yes." Her eyes fell to half-mast. "Now get back to work."

He attempted to match the teasing humor she employed so effortlessly. "Demanding." He liked it. Liked someone taking the choice and the thought out of things for him. His cock jumped, but he could wait. He'd waited all this time.

For her.

She didn't respond, but she did shift restlessly under him. God, how long had he been lost in her pussy, eating her out, before she'd told him what she needed? The last thing he'd do was deny her pleasure. "Shh. I know. You need to come." He could do that much. Women's bodies, he understood.

She nodded and made a pitiable mewling sound, her hips arching. His hands pinned her down and limited her movement.

He stroked her inner thigh. She was so damn perfectly formed.

A vision flashed in his mind, of her spread out on the couch in his studio, bathed in sunlight. He could paint her like that.

No. Don't bring work into this. It's enough you're breaking your long celibacy here. One milestone at a time. "What gets you off quickest? Show me."

Her lashes fluttered, and he wondered if perhaps he was pushing her too hard. Maybe she was too shy to—

Nope.

There was nothing shy about the long fingers that cupped her pussy, nothing remotely bashful of the thumb that rubbed her clit in tight, focused circles.

He drank in her actions, memorizing every move of her body and fingers, before lowering his head. "Keep that up," he said quietly, and sank his tongue inside her again. She gave a small shriek, her thumb's motions becoming tighter and harder on her clit.

Once he was certain he had her rhythm down, he pushed her hand aside and took over, closing his eyes so he could properly savor the feel of her round clit beneath his thumb and the sweetness of the pussy he was fucking with his tongue.

He knew when she was coming, her hands clutching at his head and her muscular channel contracting around his tongue. She was going to tear his hair out and he didn't care.

Exultant satisfaction coursed through him when she fell back limp, and he gave her pussy one last lingering lick.

Yes. He could at least manage this.

CHAPTER 6

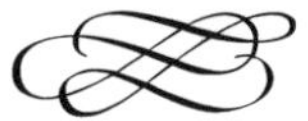

Rana stared at the ceiling of her foyer and contemplated every facet of her destruction.

It wasn't that she'd never had a good lover before. She'd had some fine lovers in the past. Unfortunately, none of them had ever made her feel like she was having a religious experience when they went down on her.

Maybe it was because it had been a while? Or the desperate enthusiasm with which he approached eating her out? Or the scar that rasped over her intimate flesh, giving her the perfect bite of roughness?

She blew out a puff of air. Whatever the fuck it was, this could be a real problem. She had anticipated great sex. She hadn't anticipated having her soul ripped out and stomped on.

Don't be melodramatic. It was an orgasm. A powerful one. A very, very, powerful one. But an orgasm. No big deal.

Hell, she hadn't even seen his body yet. Maybe the best was yet to come.

Pun intended.

She raised herself up on her elbows, aware she was

splayed in an undignified, naked heap on her foyer floor. As comfortable as she was with her body, she suffered a momentary pang of self-consciousness, and she moved to close her legs, but Micah was in the way. She met his eyes and inwardly reeled at the hot darkness within.

If she wasn't so spent, she would have made grabby hands at him, but it was all she could do to curl her fingers. A tingle ran through her.

She'd always been greedy. Another flaw.

He ran his thumb over his lip, not taking his eyes off her. The dim light of the foyer gleamed over the wetness on his face. Her wetness.

She managed to bring herself to a seated position. His eyes dipped over her breasts and stomach, lingering over her pussy. "You're still dressed," she pointed out, feeling foolish at the obvious statement.

His Adam's apple bobbed. "I am."

So greedy.

She held out her hand, relieved it wasn't shaking. If it had reflected the wobbliness of her emotions, it would have been. "We should fix that."

He stared at her hand. The moment stretched between them for so long, Rana wondered if maybe she had misread the painful desire strumming through his body.

Mentally, she snorted. Like she could have mistaken his excitement to fuck her with his mouth. The man had been all in to go downtown.

Finally, he slipped his hand in hers and helped her get to her feet, his eyes hooded. She ran her fingers down his chest, over the buttons of his shirt. "You're good at that."

"What?"

"Going down on a woman."

His thick, angled eyebrows lowered. "It's a personal favorite."

She had to bite back her sigh of longing. Why was she not tying this man up and keeping him in her bedroom for the indefinite future again?

Oh right, blah blah, happily ever after, blah blah, turning a new leaf, blah blah, meeting Mr. Right.

But he likes eating pussy! He's good at eating pussy. Are you aware of how often those two magical qualities overlap? He's like a leprechaun riding a unicorn.

Rana gave a mental groan. Nope, sorry. She would not be getting distracted by a mystical mouth. Time to think about something else.

She raised her hand and grasped a lock of his hair between her thumb and forefinger. She'd yanked that motherfucking elastic out of his hair like she was personally offended by it, and she hoped she hadn't hurt him.

Why hadn't she found long hair attractive before this? It was thick, and coarser then she'd imagined, but shiny. The almost-black mass fell to his shoulders, the ends blunt and rough, like it'd been a while since he'd had a good haircut. "I like your hair."

He shrugged and grasped a handful of her hair. The slight tug on her scalp made her want to purr. "Yours is prettier."

"Mmm." His mouth drew her attention. He smelled like some woodsy cologne and man and her. "Question."

"Yes."

"Your scar…"

She was so attuned to his body, she could feel the instant non-sexual tension invaded his muscles. In the same split-second, she changed her mind, shelving the question she was going to ask. The question he was apparently dreading. Hell, it was none of her business where he'd gotten the damn thing.

She could control *some* impulses. Especially when she might hurt a man who'd shown her nothing but generosity until now.

"Yes?" he bit out, when she didn't speak.

She cupped his head, her fingers subtly massaging his scalp until he relaxed. Then she closed the distance between them...and licked the scar, from where it started on his lip, following the silvery line across his cheek. The moan he gave was strangled, his body going stiff and hard against her. "I've...I've been wanting to do this, is all." Not a lie. She took a step back and swallowed, tasting herself.

Sweet Mary, she was going to have fun tonight.

His chest was working hard, his face set in rigid lines of pained arousal. Poor baby. She hooked her finger in the vee of his shirt and tugged. He was too large for her to move, but he swayed toward her by an infinitesimal degree. "Why don't we go to my bedroom, and we can see what other favorite things we can discover?"

Though she was entirely naked, and she was certain he liked looking at her body, his eyes didn't leave hers. "Lead the way."

She walked ahead of him and mounted the stairs, only a little self-conscious that her bare butt was in his face. They were halfway to the second-floor landing when he gave a rough groan. Large hands wrapped around her hips and halted her.

She shivered when his lips brushed the curve of her ass, only to jump at the nip he gave her. Rana glanced over her shoulder at the dark head below her. "You keep that up and this is going to end right here."

His finger traced the crease of her buttocks. "I have no desire to end this." The finger insinuated between her cheeks, gently testing her.

"My bedroom?" She meant it as a statement, but it came out as a squeaky question.

He stroked his hand over her ass, over the spot he had bitten. "Hurry."

Yes, hurry. The sooner she got him inside her, the sooner she could bang him out of her system and forget him.

She ignored the part of her that laughed in amusement over the thought of her ever being able to forget him.

He'd told her to leave her blinds open, so she'd done just that, eager to eliminate any ambiguity over her welcome. Moonlight streamed in to her bedroom. He didn't look around at all, his entire focus on her.

She didn't want to miss a single detail. "Can you hit the light switch by the door?"

He didn't move right away, but then he shook his head. "I like it like this," he said quietly.

Ooookay. "But I want to look at you. Especially once you're naked."

He took a step toward her. "You've already seen me."

From many, many feet away, while she struggled with a paralyzing sense of shame and guilt.

Another step. She backed up. Not because she wanted to get away, but because it would get her nearer to the bed behind her. "Not up close."

His gaze dragged over her body, making her sizzle. "There's enough light."

"I want more." She wasn't arguing for argument's sake. If this was a one-shot deal, she wanted enough memories to store away. That way she could take them out and cuddle them when she was in her lonely bed.

"I'll be on top of you and inside you. You'll be able to see the important things."

Was he shy? Did he think she wouldn't like his—?

All coherent thought fled from her brain then, because his hands went to his belt.

Forget the light. She could squint. They had more important things to do.

The buckle clinked as he undid it and pulled the belt free of its loops. It hit the oak floors with a thud. She held her breath as he unbuttoned and unzipped his fly, the widening vee revealing the bulge of his cock beneath dark cotton fabric.

He treated his pants with the same disregard as his belt, kicking them aside. He unbuttoned his shirt, but didn't strip it off right away. The crisp bright white framed his ridged abs and powerful chest. His thighs were like tree trunks, muscle upon muscle, bunching and releasing as he came closer.

Unable to resist his rippled stomach, she traced a finger over the washboard, dipping it into his navel. His belly contracted, the bulge in his underwear growing. She dragged her hand down, until it caught on the wide waistband. "Boxer briefs," she remarked, amazed her voice was so steady.

His lips quirked up at the corners. He was solemn, this

one, not given to wide grins and jokes. That was okay. This was no joking matter. "You approve."

"Very much so." Her thighs were wet, her clit hard, her stomach in knots like she hadn't just had a powerful orgasm on the tile floor of her foyer. Her fingers flirted with the reveal, easing the waistband of his underwear down, then up again. "Do you play sports?"

His stomach tightened as she traced the back of her fingers over his stomach. "Rugby. Or I used to. Now I run and lift."

Rugby. She knew less than a thimbleful about rugby, except that it entailed large men ramming into each other. If it resulted in a body like this, she was on board with the sport, though.

She sank down on the bed so her face was level with his groin. She used both hands to ease down his boxer briefs, her mouth salivating as each hard inch of his cock was revealed, until he was free of the cotton completely. He wasn't enormously long, but his cock was proportional to the rest of his body. Thick enough to fill her to bursting. She'd be stuffed.

As she watched, a drop of moisture appeared on that mushroom tip. If he'd let her, she'd tie him up somewhere and lick his cock all day. "We might be well suited for each other," she said absentmindedly.

A fine thread of tension seized him, and she realized what she'd said and how it might be construed. Oops. Nothing permanent. Schooling her face into a teasing smile, she glanced up at him. "I mean I like giving blowjobs as much as you seem to like giving head." Suiting action to thought, she wrapped her fist around his cock, lowering her lips to hover over the tip. A sizzle of heat ran through her when she realized she could barely get her hand around him.

He was going to feel so fucking good between her legs.

Before she could lick off the drop of semen tempting her, he placed his hand over hers, stilling her. "I want something else right now. I think you do too."

Oh, dilemma. That ridiculously thick cock in her mouth or her pussy?

Her vagina clenched. Well, that answered that.

"Lay back."

He didn't have to tell her twice. She scooted back on the bed and lay down. He stripped off his underwear and prowled up her body until he knelt between her spread and bent legs, his cock inches away from her.

He was still wearing his shirt, but she didn't care. He could be wearing a rubber chicken suit and she'd let him between her legs.

Rubber.

Rana blinked. She lifted her leg and slapped her foot against his chest, halting him when he would have moved closer. His chest vibrated with a growl. A big palm slipped over her calf, fingers moving in a subtly massaging move that slicked over her muscles, turning her legs into jelly.

"Let me," he said roughly. "Let me fuck you. Please."

She could feel her willpower weakening at the desperate tone in his voice. Hell, she could feel it weakening at the mere thought of his sexy penis.

Yet, there were some things Rana did not compromise on. Even when she had a man with a dick like a fertility god's mere inches away from where she needed him most. "Condom."

He froze so fast, she thought he might have turned to stone. "You don't have one?"

No. No. No. No. "You didn't bring one?"

His chest rose and fell. "I don't have any at home."

Her eyes burned. Was she crying? No, not yet. She might, though. In pure frustration. She nudged his shoulder with her toes, maybe harder than necessary. "Then you stop at the pharmacy and you get some." Rana heard her voice rising, and she breathed in deeply. Hell, she could yell at herself too. She could have made a pit stop on the way home as well. She had merely assumed…

He raked his hands through his hair. She'd had so many fantasies of that hair draping around her as he fucked her.

Thwarted because of a condom? Ugh. The orgasm she'd had downstairs suddenly seemed like the tiny tip of the iceberg of what she could get from this guy. She wanted more, damn it.

He stared down at her, eyes burning, surveying her spread body. She wanted to drag him onto her and damn the consequences, and he seemed to have the same idea. He shifted, the wet head of his cock brushing her thigh.

"Are you sure you don't have something at home?" she asked, in mad desperation.

He shook his head. "I haven't had a need for it…" His hand smoothed over her thigh, touching the spot his cock had. Her muscle clenched when she realized he was massaging his pre-come into her skin.

Oh Jesus. In a desperate bid to control both of them, she extended her leg, pushing him back. His eyes were hot when they met hers. "I'm clean. Are you on anything?"

What she'd give to say yes. "No." She had stopped taking the pill a year ago. It played havoc with her emotions, and she didn't need it for anything other than birth control. It had seemed like a pointless exercise in monthly tears and seesawing feelings.

That stymied him, but not for long. "I won't come inside you."

She raised an eyebrow at that. "Yeah. Next you're going to say you'll just put in the tip."

He frowned. "I'd never be able to put in just the tip. If my cock so much as brushed against your muff right now, I'd be balls-deep before you could scream."

Her leg weakened, and he took advantage of it, running his hand over her leg to the crease of her groin, his calloused fingers playing with the sensitive skin there. "Or," he said, in that steady, deep, posh voice, "I can tongue-fuck you again. All night."

She struggled to find her breath. "You really do like that, don't you."

"Always." His eyes gleamed. "Especially with you. It's like your pussy was waiting for my mouth. No one's ever tightened up on my tongue like that."

The rush of wetness between her thighs would have been embarrassing, but when his fingers slicked over her entrance, he made such a guttural, appreciative sound of pleasure, she couldn't be mortified.

His thumb found her clit, and he pressed, rotating exactly as she had shown him when she was lying on the floor downstairs. Quick study, this one.

"How many orgasms do you think you can have before you pass out?" he murmured. "That's how many times I want to make you come."

Oh, God, he was a *prince* among men. A leprechaun riding a unicorn holding a fairy. "What about you?" she managed.

His face was cloaked in shadows. "I'm going to enjoy myself. Trust me."

Her eyes rolled back in her head when he slid two fingers inside her, and she arched her back, almost ready to agree to his proposal, even if she'd rather he replace those fingers with his cock. Argh. Responsibility wasn't her thing, but she'd learned early how important it was to protect herself. Since she'd been celibate, she'd gotten lazy. Otherwise, she'd always kept a stash of condoms in her nightstand. Or in the cute purses she used to carry when she went out on the town, though she hadn't had a reason to use those in a while, since she no longer went out…

Her eyes widened. Jackpot.

She reared up, dislodging Micah's hand. "Get up. Get up, get up, get up."

He pulled back immediately. "Sorry. Do you want me to leave, or…?"

"Leave?" She snorted as she awkwardly rolled out from under him. "No, you aren't going anywhere, except inside of me." Uncaring that she was naked and all her parts were jiggling, she darted to her closet and hit the switch to turn on the single bulb. It wasn't a huge closet, but it held her extensive wardrobe well enough.

"But—"

"Shh." She dug farther into her closet, shoving aside her haphazardly hung clothes and all her shoes, finally finding what she was looking for way in the back, in a heap of silk and satin and leather. She came out with her hands full of purses and threw them on her bed.

Micah still knelt in the middle of her king-sized mattress. He looked from her to the pile of purses. "I am not entirely certain what is happening."

She gave him a mischievous smile, her humor restored now that she had a line on a way to get his dick inside her. "Don't worry. This isn't some sort of fetish. I mean, I might have a fetish for purses, but it's not a sexual fetish." She grabbed the gold Kate Spade clutch first and dug inside. A lipstick she'd thought she'd lost and a casino card. She hesitated and tossed the lipstick on the floor. She'd want that later.

Next came the teal Coach wristlet. Nothing but some crumpled receipts. "Come on," she muttered, and grabbed the sequined black crossbody she'd discovered in a discount bin at a department store. As soon as she opened it, her fingers brushed over foil, and she almost wept in joy.

Thank God for her inherent sloppiness. She'd never clean out her handbags again.

She yanked out both condoms and checked them in the faint light from the closet. She pumped her fist. "Got 'em. And look at that, unexpire—"

"Rana."

She glanced up, and her crowing died a quick death.

While she'd been searching her bags, Micah had been removing his shirt. He faced her, his face set in intense lines, his cock so ready for her it curved upward toward his belly. The muscles in his biceps bunched as he clenched the comforter. He held the other hand out to her, palm up. His gaze dipped over her body, lingering between her legs, before rising to meet hers. "Give me."

Her hand shook as she dropped the condoms into his palm, their fingers brushing against each other. He threw one on the mattress and ripped the other one open.

He held the ring out to her. "Put it on me."

She clambered back on the bed, accepting the rubber from him. This wasn't her first rodeo, but she felt clumsy and uncertain as she grasped his cock with one hand. The snug latex seemed overly tight, hard to smooth over the fat tip of his cock. He moaned, and she looked up at him from under her lashes. "Does it hurt?"

"Yes," he gritted out. "But not because of the condom."

She finally managed to get the thing on him, and he wasted no time, pushing her to her back and creating a space for himself between her spread legs.

He placed his hand on her knee, his thumb stroking. "This will be rough. I won't be able to help it."

She wasn't sure if that was supposed to be a warning or a promise. Either way… "I don't mind." What an understatement. She craved it rough. Wild. She wanted him to fuck her like he'd die if he didn't.

He angled her hips, and eased inside. They both gasped; hers, a long shuddery sigh, and his, a sharp inhale of breath. He felt excessively thick. A pang of doubt assailed her as he pressed forward another inch, struggling to move even that much. Maybe she was too small and tender for this beast of a man.

"Fuck," he said between set teeth. "So tight."

Well, yeah. Because he was huge.

"So wet. Are you always this wet?"

She was wet, and the reminder of how much she wanted him made her relax. It was all for him, a result of the foreplay that had started months ago when she first spotted him. She ran her hand over his chest and around his neck, drawing him down so his lips hovered over hers. They hadn't kissed, she realized. He'd licked her pussy like a starving man, but she hadn't felt his tongue in her mouth. "If I said yes?"

His lashes fell, and he drew away, creating an inch of space between their mouths. She hated that inch. "I'd say I don't know how I'll ever stop fucking you."

Ohhhh. They were sex words, designed to arouse. She knew that. Yet she couldn't stop the small flutter in her heart. *No, this is only for you. No, don't leave me.*

He exhaled, the dusting of hair on his chest rasping her nipples, and he slowly pulled out, pushing forward again. It was easier this time, and she softened more, until his hips were pumping, working between her spread thighs, pistoning back and forth, driving rational thought from her head. He alternated his thrusts between deep and shallow, as if he couldn't decide what to give her.

The friction tightened the ball of lust between her legs, her toes curling. She wrapped her arms and legs around him, clinging as his thrusts picked up a steady rhythm.

Yes, she had missed this, the driving force, the knot of tension aching to explode.

What she didn't understand was how, since this was the first and only time they had been together, she could possibly feel like she had missed *him.*

He moaned and dropped his head to her neck. The sound was helpless, lost. Responding to the distress in him, she moved her hands from his shoulders to his back, coasting them down his sweat-slick skin.

He froze, a split-second she was only aware of because she was so concentrated on every move he was making. A heartbeat later, he exploded with a flurry of motion.

He grasped and manacled her wrists above her head in one of his hands, and used the other one to clutch her thigh and shove her leg farther to the side, deepening his thrusts. She came with a shriek, all of her muscles contracting and releasing. She didn't bother to muffle her cries. Damn it, she wasn't going to censor a single moment of tonight.

The sharp exhale of his breath came in puffs against her temple as she floated back to reality.

Micah didn't give her a second to recover before he rolled over onto his back, taking her with him. He was still inside her, hard as iron. She scrambled for purchase at his shoulders, but they were slick with sweat, and her motor skills were still weak. "Wait," she managed. "I need to…"

"Come," he breathed, and thrust upward, hard. She gasped as the banked fire smoldered, instantly brought back to life by his body. "You get even tighter when you come. It's the most delicious thing I've ever felt. Give it to me again." He arched up, this time slower. Did he just intuitively *know* she needed the sensual tug and drag of flesh now instead of the rapid-fire fucking she'd wanted earlier?

"But you didn't come," she tried to protest. It was a weak protest. Like she'd actually stop him. Magical amazing unicorn leprechaun man. *Sigh.*

"We have two condoms. I intend to use them well."

Rana's next words were lost when he rose and drew her nipple into his mouth, sucking lazily while his lower body fucked into her in easy, short strokes. She closed her eyes and arched her back. Really. Who was she to argue with this man?

CHAPTER 7

Micah didn't want to stop. He had to, though.

Rana's dazed eyes had disappeared under a flutter of eyelashes. Her breathing was slow and regular, signaling a deeper sleep than the light dozing he had allowed her during the past several hours. How many orgasms had he given her now? Five? Six? He'd lost count.

If he had more condoms, he would keep at her until neither of them could walk.

He closed his eyes, practicing the meditation techniques they'd taught him after the incident. He'd originally learned the breathing exercises to recover from panic attacks, but they could surely work under circumstances like these, right? When his balls were drawn up tight, sexual frustration still clawing at his insides? Clear his mind, control his body.

In. Out. In. Out.

He winced. No, no. Bad choice of mental imagery.

One, two, three. One, two, three. One…

After several minutes of slow, measured breathing, he opened his eyes. His cock remained hard, but at least his mind was able to focus on something other than the demands of his body.

What time was it? His phone was in his pants pocket, but the sky was lightening, a paler shade of blue streaming in through the huge picture window. From the bed, he could see into his empty, sterile home. The studio was silent and still. The huge fabric-draped couch was a lump in the corner.

He'd bought the cheap couch at a discount store, more out of habit than anything else. His art had previously almost always focused on live models. His old studio had had couches and chairs and stools and all sorts of props.

He turned his head away, suddenly hating his studio, his couch, his house. He didn't want to go back in there.

They'd kicked the blankets off the king-sized bed, but for the first time in a long time, he felt warm and comfortable. Part of the reason was because Rana seemed to have an affinity for a soothing, whimsical color palette in his favorite colors. The main reason, however, had nothing to do with the rich furnishings or blue and green decor, and everything to do with the woman lying next to him.

If at any time during the night she'd indicated she was done with him, he would have backed off. On the contrary, each time he stroked her body, she stunned him with her enthusiastic response. He felt a little more like a god every time she contracted around his cock, her climaxes making her vagina squeeze him so tight he thought he'd die.

The best sex of his life.

He couldn't lie and say he only thought that because he hadn't had it in so long. His memory was as good as ever. Something about this woman was simply different.

He shifted. She snuffled and rolled over, her body following the dip in the mattress made by his weight. He'd thought this was a big bed for a single woman, but her long body liked the space. She settled on her side, one leg bent, her breasts plumped. Her hand rested near her mouth, the fingers curled in. Her hair fell over her face, concealing most of it. He could spy her sleep-flushed cheeks and rosy lips through the strands.

It was cheesy to stare at her face or stroke her hair while she was sleeping, but he had to touch the soft mass one last time. If he was a different man, one who had the luxury of entangling his life with a woman, he would spend the whole day petting her. She looked…sweet when she was sleeping. Less sex kitten, without her short dress and high heels. More kitten.

He liked her either way.

He wound her hair tighter around his finger and let it go, allowing it to fall back into place before smoothing it back. The light in the room had changed to a hazy blue-gray that signaled morning.

The clock's struck, Cinderella. Time to return to your hovel.

His head spun as he sat up. Probably because all the blood in his body was still in his dick. A cold shower, he promised himself. The second he got home, he was going to blast himself with freezing water.

You'll be washing her away.

He clenched his jaw against the vague melancholy that thought brought.

He gathered his clothes as quietly as he could and dressed in his rumpled suit, not bothering to button his shirt. It was early enough no neighbors would be outside to witness his creeping back to his own house. Not that he cared what the neighbors thought. He didn't know any of them. He bet Rana did, though. She probably checked up on the elderly ones, made them laugh with her irreverent sense of humor.

He couldn't resist looking at her again. She hadn't moved. Her ass gleamed in the shadowy dawn, the plush place between her legs obscured.

He padded over to the bed and grabbed the comforter and pillows from the floor where they'd kicked them off. He couldn't do much about the sheets, but he could make sure she was comfortable for however long she chose to sleep. He drew the blanket over her and clumsily tucked it around her shoulders. She stirred when he lifted her head slightly to push an embroidered pillow under it, her lashes fluttering open. Mascara had smudged beneath her eyes, the delicate skin looking bruised. "Whaa—?"

"Shhh," he whispered, hoping she would fall back asleep and let him tend to her.

Her eyes were blurry and uncomprehending as she stared at him, but she gave a sleepy smile that shot straight to his battered soul.

His ears still rung with her sobs and cries and moans. They would play in his mind on a never-ending loop for the indefinite future. It would have been nice if he could have gone at her with a little more finesse, less like a starving man facing a buffet of flesh, but he'd always been an earthy lover, and combined with his long celibacy…well, he was glad he'd managed to restrain himself as much as he had.

She graced him with another sweet smile, and he almost covered her lips with his and mounted her again. The only thing that stopped him was the fact that she would most assuredly be sore when she woke up. Well, that and the growing light filling the room.

So, instead, he stroked her hair with a touch that was dangerously possessive. She sniffed, and her eyes fell shut.

He straightened and made his way to the door. Halfway there, his bare feet fell on something silky and soft. He crouched and picked up the pile of Rana's purses, the small feminine bags far too frilly and inconsequential in his hands. Carefully, he placed them on top of her dresser, his fingers lingering on an emerald-green purse. The color would look good on her. He could visualize her spread out on a green silk sheet, her body kissed by moonlight.

He wanted to see her naked form bathed in every light imaginable. The hazy blue of this predawn, the warmth of the sun, the pale gold of the moon, the bright fluorescent of his studio…

No. No. Not his studio. Frowning, he shook his head, as if to dispel the image from his mind. He wouldn't be painting her. He hadn't had a live model since…

Since.

One night. That's all I want.

His lips turned down, and he placed the purse on the dresser with the others. He walked out and closed her bedroom door quietly behind him. He had agreed to her terms. Had said he wasn't looking for anything permanent either. It wasn't a lie. As much as he craved physical intimacy, as much as he wanted nothing more than to return to her bed, he knew he couldn't have more. It wouldn't be fair to her, not when she was a sweet, clever, generous woman, and he was…

Well. Whatever he was.

CHAPTER 8

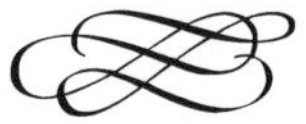

Rana glanced at her watch and walked quickly to the kitchen to tell Devi she was leaving. She only had about fourteen minutes to spare before her date.

Since she was on a time crunch, it was natural that there would be some sort of crisis going on. She heard Devi swearing before she spotted her in the large, gleaming kitchen. Her youngest sister was soft, round, sweet, and most definitely not given to the foul language coming out of her mouth, which meant someone, somewhere, had fucked up.

Moonwalk away.

Too late. Devi popped up from behind a counter, her eyes widening as she caught sight of Rana. "Oh thank God. Grab an apron."

"Problem?" she asked. She didn't have time for a problem, not really, but there didn't seem to be anyone else around. Four other people were in the kitchen—sous-chefs, a prep cook and a dishwasher—but they were industriously avoiding drama by busying themselves at various tasks.

Devi placed her hands on her rounded hips and glared

at Rana. She looked so much like their mother, Rana automatically started racking her brain for any possible infractions she might have committed. “Leena was just here.”

Oh, well, that sort of explained things. Their middle sister could be abrasive even when she wasn’t trying, and Devi’s personal life over the past year had definitely driven a wedge between the two of them. “Ah.”

“Apparently, the Miramontes firm upped their order for their party tonight. In an hour.”

“Hmmm.”

“*In one hour.*” Devi flung her arms out. “I have a full dinner service. I don’t have time to make oodles more food on a whim.”

“Yeah.” Rana nodded, hiding a smile. “What did they ask you to add?”

“Everything needs to be increased.” She frowned. “Also, they want a platter of pigs in a blanket. Pigs in a blanket!”

There it was. Devi didn’t play the temperamental chef card often, but when she did, it was hella funny. Rana dutifully played along. “Those assholes.”

“Leena said they wanted food for people who didn’t eat Indian, and that’s fine.” Devi turned back to the counter and started hacking into a potato. “I can do any kind of dish they want. Puff pastries. Seared scallops. Chicken kebabs… But pigs in a blanket? Really? If Marcus didn’t work at this firm, I’d tell them to go stuff their pigs in a blanket up their asses…”

Rana cleared her throat to hide her laughter. Even if one of Devi’s boyfriends didn’t work there, she couldn’t imagine her sweet sister saying such a thing to anyone’s face. “You should absolutely do that."

Devi swiped her arm over her forehead. "Why haven't you put on an apron yet? I need a hand."

Rana immediately shook her head. "I can't. I..."

"Rana, this is important, and we're short-staffed."

"I know. That's why I'm here at all. Tonight's my night off, remember?" she said mildly. They were flexible on their rotating nights off, so Rana hadn't much minded coming in, but she'd made it clear to Leena she'd have to leave when the dinner rush slowed.

"Please?"

Ah, she was such an easy mark when her baby sister used those puppy eyes. She sighed, fished her phone out of her pocket, and sent a quick text. *I'm so sorry, I had a work emergency come up. I won't be able to make it tonight. Rain check?*

The response came a heartbeat later. *No problem. I didn't know waitresses had emergencies! Haha.*

It was supposed to be funny. She was sure this guy meant it to be funny, and not a dig about how she was a waitress and he was a...what was he again? A sales rep of some sort. Maybe.

She hadn't asked too many questions. He'd been able to hold up his end of an email exchange, he used "you" instead of "u", and he was employed, all of which put him in the top 85th percentile of men on online dating sites. She texted back, more slowly, *Haha. Thanks for understanding,* and placed the phone in her pocket. "What do you need me to do? The pigs in a blanket?"

"Oh, God, no. Anyone can churn those out." Devi winced and raised her voice, calling down the line. "I mean, anyone who's as good as you are, Saranna."

Rana rolled her eyes. Always empathetic, their Devi.

Saranna raised her head from where she was rolling out dough. "Huh? Oh, thanks."

Devi turned back to her. "The puran poli. No one can make it like we can."

This was true. Devi was the one who'd inherited the passion for cooking, but Rana had spent her fair share of time at their mother's elbow, learning how to make the sweet.

All three of the Malik sisters had, actually. They'd basically been raised here, playing quietly in the back office or the kitchen while their parents worked. The minute they'd been old enough, they'd helped wherever they could.

Handy, since their father had passed away when Rana was nineteen. She'd been able to seamlessly step in and help their mother run the place. Then Leena had graduated from college and Devi from cooking school, and the three of them had taken over. Over the years, they had naturally carved the business into thirds. Devi got the kitchens, Leena got the back-end operations, and Rana got the front. The best part, really, the front end. It was the part everyone got to see.

Rana finished tying on the apron she'd fetched. "Are all the ingredients out?"

"Yeah. I made the dough, so put the paste together and start cooking."

Rana walked over to the counter. The chana daal had already been cooked in the pressure cooker until it was soft, and had been drained and dried. Not bothering to measure, she added jaggary, cardamom, saffron, and nutmeg to the paste and started to mash it.

"Who were you texting? I didn't make you postpone a date, did I?"

She shrugged. "No big deal."

"Oh no." Devi froze. "I did, didn't I? Why didn't you say something?"

"Because I told you, it's no big deal."

"Aw. I feel bad enough Charlie didn't work out. I didn't mean to stand in the way of possible true love."

True love? She thought of the mild-mannered sales rep. At best, she could say he was *not objectionable.* That might change after the waitress crack. She wasn't sure yet. "It's not true love."

"You don't know that."

No, she did. He seemed like a nice guy. Good-looking, fit. He'd posted a picture of him cuddling a puppy. She liked puppies.

But he wasn't, say, a beautiful, long-haired artist who could make her body weep with pleasure.

Not that she was thinking about Micah at all. Nope. She'd barely thought of him in the past week, since she'd woken up all alone in her bed, her body aching in places she didn't know it could ache. Micah who?

Wow, you're so convincing.

Rana exhaled. Taking him to her bed had been a tactical error. Hard enough not to think about him when he was the stranger who lived next door. It became impossible when she was certain she could still smell him on her sheets after washing them twice.

"You haven't met him face-to-face yet," Devi argued. "It could be magical."

"Yeah, well. He's not going anywhere." Should she have been more excited about the guy? More dismayed they couldn't get together tonight? If it wasn't for Micah, she might have been. Rana tried to manufacture some enthusiasm. "He can be my date tomorrow. Or next week."

"You're really sticking strong to this date-a-week thing, huh?"

"Until one of them works out? Yes." She had considered taking this week off, but then decided to keep it business as usual, treating her night with Micah as nothing more than a twelve-hour detour from her ultimate goal. She wouldn't forget the best sex of her life, but she wasn't about to start pining after the man. They'd agreed on the parameters of this deal, and she wasn't a welsher.

So there was no reason to change up her normal schedule. Since she'd decided a year ago to tackle her love life with the grim determination of a general, she'd scheduled one date a week. One date, with a completely appropriate and eligible man she would not be ashamed to bring home to Mama.

"Did Mama pick tonight's guy?"

Speaking of which. "That's not something we joke about." Judging the paste to be the proper consistency, she began to scoop it out, rolling it into smooth balls and setting them aside.

Upon learning her eldest daughter was giving up her promiscuous ways to search for Mr. Right, their mother had practically fallen to her knees in joy and attempted to "help" despite Rana's gentle rebuffs.

Rana shuddered. Mama's help wasn't always…helpful. Not when it came to this.

Devi chuckled, the way only a desi girl who had two unmarried older sisters and a serious relationship of her own could—with utter freedom and confidence that their mother hadn't yet painted a matrimonial bull's-eye on her. "It was a legit question."

"Uh-huh. Like I'd go out with anyone she picked." She adopted an accent that was uncannily similar to their mother's. "Rana, you need to act quickly on this boy. A lawyer with such light skin?"

Devi mimicked her. "He is tall too. You need someone tall, because you have so much height."

"No, you cannot email him. Call him. He will not last long."

Devi nodded sagely, dropping the accent. "Everyone knows men are like Groupons."

Rana snorted out a relieved laugh. "Thank God I can bitch about her to you. Leena always takes her side."

"You've been really good at not snapping at either of them." Devi shot her a quick smile. "I'm proud of you. It's been so peaceful lately."

Rana and her mother didn't have the most amicable history—the older woman had never approved of anything Rana did. Rana, in turn, had spent most of her life pretending she didn't care if she was tweaking her mom with her clothes, her men, her partying.

Of course she'd cared. Now that she'd discovered what it was like not to live with constant dismissal and chiding, Rana didn't know if she could go back to how it had been before. Not perpetually disappointing your only living parent was weirdly pleasant.

All she'd had to do was bury herself.

She flinched away from that thought. Silly, but it felt vaguely treasonous. To what, she wasn't sure. The Republic of Her Mama?

No, she wasn't burying herself. How overdramatic. She was improving herself. She'd thoughtlessly damaged some important relationships over the years. Clawing her way back, earning everyone's trust and respect would take some time and pain, but it was okay if it was her pain.

Plus, it was working, if Devi had noticed. Rana placed the sweet mixture on top of the dough and folded the edges around to cover it completely. "I'm trying."

"Well, I bet your guy is right around the corner," Devi said emphatically.

Or next door. "I'm sure," she managed.

"And he'll be kind and funny and generous."

Or rough and silent and really good at giving head. "Yeah, right."

"And you'll fall madly in love." Devi gave a gusty sigh. She'd always been the most romantic of the sisters.

Rana'd fallen madly into something, all right. "Mm-hmm. Yup. Love."

"And..."

"How are your lover boys anyway?" Desperation prompted the low question. Every word Devi spoke was only making her think of Micah more. Wasn't it enough her entire house reminded her of the man? She needed her workplace to be her solace.

At the silence, Rana looked up to find Devi's gaze far away, a small smile playing about her mouth. "That good, huh?"

Devi modestly dropped her eyes. "That good."

A rush of warmth distracted her and brought the slight sting of tears to Rana's eyes. Her youngest sister was her baby. She'd sheltered her, pampered her…and hurt her.

Once upon a time, Devi had dated a cheating worm of a man, Tarek. The asshole was sweet as pie around Devi, but the minute her back was turned, he'd hit on anything in a skirt. Rana had tried to tell herself not to interfere, but her sister had seemed to be falling for his line of bullshit.

She should have trusted in Devi, but she'd been blinded by her desperate worry for her sister. She'd thought there hadn't been any other expedient option but for her to make the dude's assholic tendencies crystal clear…by engineering a setup with herself cast as the other woman.

Rana swallowed, the bitter taste of regret tainting her mouth. She'd found out later that Devi had been well aware of everything and planning to break things off with the guy. Of course she had. Because even when Rana tried to be helpful and noble, she managed to fuck things up.

Devi had forgiven her of course, and assured her countless times she didn't blame Rana. But that terrible scene would haunt Rana for a long time. It was possibly the most heinous thing she'd ever done. Impulsive, dramatic Old Rana. The instant she'd looked up from Devi's ex's arms, she'd known that her plan had been butt stupid.

After that disastrous relationship had imploded, Devi had closed herself off from companionship, a choice that had spilled more guilt onto Rana's conscience.

You made up for it. She'd had no choice but to fix things. Rana's plan had been to enable a hot poly one-night stand for her sister with the tall dark wolves who came in and made googly eyes at their chef every Tuesday.

To everyone's surprise—meaning her and Leena, since Devi and the Callahans managed to keep their relationship fairly discreet—the fantasy threesome had become permanent for Devi. Devi had never looked happier and more content, and it was obvious to anyone with half a brain how much the two men adored her sister.

Even if it hadn't worked out exactly as she had planned, Rana still counted it as a checkmark in her favor. Granted, the relationship was unconventional and their mother would probably murder Devi—and Rana, when she found out who had introduced the three of them—if she ever found out, but other than that small chance of homicide, it was practically perfect.

If there was a sting of jealousy mixed in with her happiness for her sister...well, Rana would do her best not to acknowledge that any time soon.

Rana pressed too hard on the rolling pin, and the dough split under the pressure, revealing the sugary filling inside. "Damn it. I messed it up."

"Redo it."

She pulled off another chunk of dough and started the process again. "You should have gotten Leena to help. I don't have the patience for this."

"I know you can do it."

Rana bent her head. Saint Devi. Filled with confidence for other people, even her screw-up of a sister. They were silent for a while, the sounds of the kitchen surrounding both of them. The other occupants in the room murmured to each other in low tones while Devi started the oil sizzling on the griddle.

Finally, Rana managed to roll out a perfect poli. "Griddle hot?"

"Yup."

Rana transferred the poli to the ungreased pan, watching carefully as the dough turned a pretty yellow brown. She could feel the rush of words on the tip of her tongue, and she tried to control them, but they burst free. "Do you think…?"

"What?" Devi asked when Rana trailed off.

Do you think there's something wrong with me? Because I had the best sex of my life last week with this weird hermit guy who lives less than a hundred feet from me. We agreed it would be a one-night thing, but I can't stop thinking about him, and I'm scared Old Rana's going to grab a hold of me and I'll march over to his door and demand more. Did I mention that we met because I was spying on him? Yeah, I could have been arrested for that shit. It was pervy as hell.

How do you think Mama would feel about all of this? Like, would she disown me right away, or wait ten minutes?

Rana cleared her throat. "Do you know your neighbors?" she finished lamely.

Devi shrugged. "Of course. Why?"

She flipped the poli, heating it for a moment before moving it off the stove onto a waiting plate. The circular sweet was perfect, no cracks or blemishes revealing the secret deliciousness hidden inside. "New guy moved in."

"Oh. You should take him some baked goods. That's how I made friends with all my neighbors. Bake cookies."

Or some muffins.

No, no, no. She'd gotten her fucking muffin, her single cigarette. She was finished. Rana pulled off another chunk of dough and began the laborious process of turning it into a perfect poli. “I’ll think about it.”

Devi stirred the curry in one of the pots on the stove, the steam making the small hairs around her face curl. “It’s important to be neighborly.”

Rana smiled, though it felt like a shadow of her usual grin. “Right. Neighborly.”

CHAPTER 9

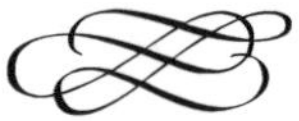

Micah stared at the phone on the couch next to him. He had both a landline and a cell phone, though he barely used either. His parents had insisted on them as a condition of his moving here, and though he was thirty-five and well past the age where he should care what his parents thought about anything, he understood his situation was peculiar.

His family had been through enough because of him, and it caused them a great deal of heartache that he now lived an ocean away. He couldn't deny them this small measure of comfort.

Which was why he was sitting here on the couch in his studio, staring at his phone. Though his mother called any time she grew anxious over him—which was quite a bit—his father only called him Thursdays, after he'd eaten dinner. Micah suspected the scheduled call was an effort to counterbalance his mother's more erratic behavior.

Right on time, the phone buzzed. He snatched it up, and Papa's face filled the screen. "Micah," his father boomed. The booming was normal. The man didn't know how to speak at a quieter volume.

The older man's broad face crinkled, his smile beaming through the video. Micah gave a tight smile, the now-familiar mix of love, shame, and frustration running through him. "Hello, Papa."

"Angie," his father said over his shoulder. "I told you he was fine. Come see."

His mother's worried face appeared over her husband's shoulder. Ah, more guilt. Before his injuries, his mum's face had never had so much as a wrinkle on it. Now there were lines around her lips and mouth. They were always creased when she looked at him. "Stop yelling, David. Hello, my love."

"Mum."

"You didn't call me back yesterday," she chided.

"I know. I apologize. It slipped my mind." He was speaking formally, sitting up straighter. *Look normal. Be normal.*

His mum tsked. "I would have called the police if you hadn't picked up today."

"Please don't do that," he said mildly. She'd called the police twice in the past year when he ignored her calls in London.

He'd tried to be understanding, but he couldn't deny that had been tiring. A benefit of moving here was that his family didn't have his local emergency numbers memorized. Yet.

"Then you need to keep in touch," she said sternly.

"Angie, don't lecture the boy," his father practically shouted. He leaned in closer. "How are you doing, son?"

"Well, thank you." *Be normal.*

"You look pale." His mother frowned at him.

"I don't get pale."

"You're lighter than you were when you lived here. It's called the sunshine state, isn't it? Not because it rains all the time, surely. If you were leaving your house, you wouldn't look like that."

The woman should have been a detective, not a nurse. "I leave my house."

She harrumphed. "Your hair is getting longer."

How she could tell, he wasn't sure. Before the call, he'd ensured his hair was tightly restrained, solely because his mother was mildly obsessed with its length.

There was a barber not far from the flat where Micah had grown up. He'd visited the old man once a month since he was fourteen until about two weeks before the incident. He'd used to wear his hair shorn close to his skull, hating the hassle of how thick and fast it grew.

He didn't wear it long now out of fashion, but because the idea of someone standing behind him with a sharp object made him want to throw up. He couldn't use an electric razor on himself, because the noise unnerved him. So, long hair it was, for the indefinite future. At least that way he could tie it back and forget it for a while.

"Boy looks like a warrior. The ladies like long hair," his father piped up, saving Micah from a reply. Papa winked at her and patted his now-short hair. "Remember how beautiful my hair was when you first saw me? Made you fall in love at first sight."

"Who says I fell in love with you at first sight?" his mother groused, but she covered her husband's hand with her own, darker brown over light.

Micah dropped his eyes, a pang in his chest. His parents were poster children for a happy marriage, the best role models he could have had. He'd always been blithe about the fact that someday he would have a relationship like theirs. Now, though…

He studiously avoided looking out his window. He knew Rana's blinds would be shut, as they had been for the past week. A couple of times, he had thought he heard her car in the driveway, and he'd had to bitterly argue with himself not to go out and drool all over her like an overeager puppy.

One night only, Cinderella. Now you're done.

They weren't soul mates like his parents were. Silly to imagine her sitting next to him with her hand on his leg.

"If you came home, I could trim your hair for you," his mother said.

His shoulders tensed. She'd cut his hair once, because he'd hoped he'd at least be able to tolerate and trust the woman who had birthed him. He hadn't had a panic attack, but he'd still had to drug himself for the experience. It was far easier to hack it off himself when it grew to an unmanageable length. "I'm not taking an international flight for a haircut, Mum."

His father cleared his throat. "We miss you."

The weight of his guilt pressed down on him. "I know. But I—This place is starting to grow on me."

His mother's lips tightened, and he didn't miss Papa bolstering her by wrapping his arm around her waist. "The weather's nicer, eh?" his father joked, but there was a deep sadness in his eyes.

"Yeah." That was the excuse he'd given: he needed to

get away before the chill of England worked its way through his bones.

It wasn't all a lie. He'd always preferred warm climates. Florida had been the warmest place farthest away from everyone who knew him.

"If you want nicer weather, why don't you go to Oahu? It's paradise," his mother asked, a trace of desperation in her voice.

He was shaking his head before she stopped speaking. This was an old argument. "No. I don't want to go to Hawaii." Both sides of his family were huge, but the maternal branch had some sense of typical British reserve—not much, but some. His father's people, on the other hand, were so loud and boisterous, Micah could barely think when he was around them.

They would take care of him, of course. Of that he had no doubt. He could imagine his closest cousin Noah throwing a beefy arm around his neck and dragging him—on his paternal side, Micah was considered small—into his favorite bar. *This is my cousin. Don't make fun of his accent, he's got an English mother. Micah, come meet this girl.*

His aunts would shove food in front of him and demand he eat every bite, and he'd spend long, lazy days basking in the sun, with toddlers running around and over him while every adult and contemporary smothered him with pampering. He'd want for nothing.

Except uninterrupted time to himself.

Micah shuddered. He deeply loved every member of his extended clan. But he couldn't imagine being the center of attention amongst a giant group of people who were aware of what had happened to him and genuinely cared for him.

They would watch him the way his parents and former friends watched him. With worry and wariness that racked him with guilt and inadequacy.

His father pursed his lips, but his mother sighed. "How's therapy?"

He didn't hesitate with his standard response. "Great." He wasn't lying. The two appointments he'd kept since he'd moved had been unobjectionable.

It wasn't that he didn't like the American doctor. Dr. Kim had a gentle manner about him. Micah's old psychologist had been one of the best in London, but his reserved and clinical attitude had made Micah dread visiting him. Kim, with his messy hair and worn office, was a vast improvement.

That didn't mean he wanted to go.

Micah controlled his instinctive grimace. He'd never been the most verbose of men. He had always just done things, accomplished things. Before he became stuck in place.

He hated talking, the way it made him hyper-aware of his *problems*. The problem was his whole life. He knew that. He didn't need to hear himself lay it all out for some stranger every week.

Because his family and friends had been so focused on him, he'd had no choice in London. There was no one here, though, to push and prod him into "opening up."

"You never told us how the show went," his mum said.

"I'm sure you know," he said. "You do have a Google alert set up on me. I'm not big news here, but it made the art section of at least one paper."

His mother cast his father an annoyed look, but Papa

shrugged. "I didn't tell him about the Google alert. You know your sister has a soft spot for the boy."

"The alert didn't tell me how it went for you," she said, exasperated.

A vague pang of guilt had him shifting, as if his career was a woman he was cheating on. He had barely thought about the disaster of the show. If his night with Rana hadn't happened, he would have spent the last week obsessing over his professional failures. He parroted the manager of the gallery. "Not bad. Sold about half of the paintings." Closer to forty percent, actually.

He didn't expect his parents to be any happier with that number than he was. But his mother's brave, determinedly cheerful smile had him looking away, rubbing at the ache in his chest, grateful they could only see him above the neck. "Well, that's wonderful."

"Good job, son," Papa trumpeted. "Half is better than zero, eh."

All was better than half. The words remained unsaid between them.

"It's the venue," his mother said. "The size of the city. Why, if you had been in London, you would have sold out in ten minutes."

He tightened his jaw until it ached. He doubted he would have sold any more paintings even if he had been in London. Because his work wasn't as good as it used to be. The few sales had certainly been born of pity or curiosity.

"It's an important step you took, putting yourself out there like that," his father said. "We're so proud of you. Look how far you've come in two years."

Ah, yes. His old psychologist wasn't the only one who

liked to talk about taking steps.

Micah tried to banish the disloyal thought. His parents tried. They were so encouraging. He knew he was imagining the subtle thread of impatience they watched him with.

It's been two years, Micah, he pictured them thinking. *Why aren't you better? It's been two years, Micah. You need to be over this by now.*

They'd never think those things, of course. Those were the thoughts in his brain. Perfectionism was his curse. Was it any wonder it was killing him that he couldn't be perfect in this?

He shifted. "How's the family? Aunt Karen?"

His mother's face softened. "Very good. You know, I saw Paige the other day…"

"She's well, then," he broke in. He wanted Paige Wilson to be doing okay, but he wasn't eager to chat about her. He bore his former model no ill will, though it had been her boyfriend who had landed him in critical care.

Still, it was…difficult to speak of her. Or with her. Micah didn't often have flashbacks anymore, but sometimes the dark thoughts came and didn't leave, rendering him unable to function. When that happened, all he could do was replay the parts of that afternoon he could remember, his brain occasionally filling in the blanks with more nightmarish scenarios.

Better to avoid Paige as much as possible than risk her triggering one of those episodes.

"She's doing fine." His mother smiled. "Such a sweet girl. I gave her your new number."

So that was who had called him a couple days ago. He only picked up family members' calls. If there was a default voicemail set up on the phone, he still hadn't bothered to check it. "Fine. I'll call her sometime," he lied.

"I think that would be nice, Micah. Your friends do miss you."

I know that. The flash of anger dismayed him, as it always did. He'd always been passionate, yes, but never angry. Since he got out of the hospital, he'd had to constantly battle his surging temper. He clenched his hand into a fist and counted to ten slowly in his head, aware his parents were watching him. He refused to take his temper out on the people who loved him. Better to rip into a canvas than rip into his parents. He'd learned something good from all those therapy sessions.

When he had his emotions under control, he spoke. "Yeah. I know. I want…"

I want everything to return to the way it was. I want that normal back.

Sex had never been hard for him. Work had never been difficult for him. Family had never been something he rebelled against.

Why couldn't something just be perfect? Why did everything have to be a goddamn issue now?

Focus on the present, what's going on right now. It was all well and good for his therapists to say that, yeah? They weren't a gigantic seething mess right now.

He shook his head. "Never mind."

"So walk us around your new place," his father said, changing the subject with his usual lack of grace.

"Uh, maybe some other time," he hedged. No need for his parents to see how barren his lifestyle was. It would only worry them. He quickly asked about his cousin, who had recently been detained by police on a car-theft charge. That sent his mother on a long rant about her ne'er-do-well brother's family.

At the thirty-minute mark exactly—God bless his father and his schedule—they all gave each other strained, worried, loving smiles and hung up.

He tossed the phone on the couch, cradled his head in his hands and breathed out a slow sigh. He was so tired of talking to people who only looked at him and saw something *wrong.*

Rana hadn't.

In a burst of motion, he came to his feet and strode over to his window, gripping the sill.

She hadn't thought he was messed up. She might have been lying about liking his painting—he was skeptical when so many others were panning his work—but she hadn't been able to hide the way her body responded to his. She hadn't been thinking he was broken when she clenched her legs around his head.

He ran his tongue over his upper lip and the scar there, remembering how she had licked it. Even now, he could swear he still tasted her.

Long ago, he had liked his women sweet, had liked chasing them and watching them blush. Rana was…intrusive. Bold. Aggressive. Crossing boundaries. Following him. Propositioning him. Leaving her curtains open for him.

Cute. He leaned against the window, remembering her triumphant face when she had found the condoms in her purse. She was cute and funny, and she made him want to smile when little else did.

It'd been a one-time thing. He had told her he wasn't

looking for anything more. She'd agreed.

He glanced back at the couch. Studiously avoiding thinking about her wasn't working. So for a brief second he allowed himself to indulge, imagining Rana spread out on his couch while he sketched her.

Mistake.

The images wouldn't stop coming once they'd started. Rana, modeling for him. Rana, tumbled on his lonely mattress. Rana, sitting in his kitchen, eating cereal with him.

On her back, bent over his table, on her knees.

God, how he wanted her again.

No one else would do. He wanted *her*.

The night he'd spent in her arms had been like a balm to his soul, the most physical intimacy he'd experienced in forever. He had no idea how long he'd been waiting for it.

He needed that intimacy again. How could it be over?

He straightened. Perhaps it didn't have to be. Perhaps he could simply…see her again. They'd agreed on nothing permanent, but talking didn't mean permanence. He'd happily steal another few minutes in her company.

He needed to see her. Right now, right this minute. She didn't make him feel like the man he used to be, but she sure as hell made him feel something.

As his father had said, half was better than none. Something was better than nothing.

CHAPTER 10

"Rana?"

Using the office's small mirror, Rana finished putting on her lipstick. "Yes, Jyoti?"

"Um. There's, um…"

Rana mentally sighed. The restaurant's newest hire was a sweetheart and somehow vaguely related to their family, but she was timid as hell. Though Rana tried to rein herself in at work, the other servers were mostly young, and they didn't mind her occasional F-bomb or her more outrageous skirt lengths. Jyoti made big eyes at her and stammered.

Rana pressed her lips together and examined the effect of the bright red lipstick. She looked fresh and young, and the poppy went well with her skin. Her date tonight ought to be impressed.

Briefly, Charlie's words about makeup slid through her head, but she shook them off. She could change a lot of things about herself, but asking her to go without her favorite colors brightening her face? That was inhumane.

"Um, Rana?"

Giving herself one last check in the mirror, Rana heaved

a barely perceptible sigh and turned. "Jyoti, if there's something you need tonight, Leena is going to—" She cut herself off. She'd only turned on the banker's lamp sitting on Leena's desk in order to get ready, but the light from the hallway was more than enough for her to see the hulking man standing behind Jyoti.

His long hair was clubbed back, as usual, his snug white T-shirt and faded jeans displaying the powerful body she'd had on top of her. Under her. Between her legs.

The body she hadn't gotten nearly enough of.

How had he found her? Why was he here? "Whaaaat is happening?" she whispered.

"Rana? I—I'm so sorry, I told him to wait out front." Jyoti cast the man a terrified glance.

"I followed her back here. It's not her fault," the mountain man rumbled.

Shaking herself out of her stupor, she cast Micah an irritated glance. Like she'd blame the girl for his presence? "We only beat our staff on Wednesdays." Gentling her tone, she directed her words at the waitress. "It's okay, Jyoti. Thanks for your help. You can go back to your tables now."

The girl gave him one last startled look and then scooted away, her black braid swinging.

"Timid," Micah remarked, and stepped inside.

He was so damn big, it was like he sucked up all of the air inside the small office, making it feel so much tinier than it was. "Please," she managed. "Look at you. Of course you scare her."

His face tightened, and he raised his hand to touch the scar on his lip and cheek.

Oh, that cruel, cruel bastard. Like she needed to recall

what that scar tissue had felt like when he'd pressed it against her clit.

Rana crossed her arms over her chest. She was wearing a thin silk top, and her demi bra wouldn't hide her perked-up nipples for shit. *Come on, body. Don't betray me now.*

"It's a good thing she didn't see me when the scar was fresh, then," Micah said coolly, and she blinked at him, realizing he wasn't merely fingering his lips to trigger memories of the most exquisite cunnilingus she had ever received.

She shook her head, annoyed. "Um, it's not the scar. You're like eighteen feet tall, if you didn't notice, and built like a linebacker." She frowned. "A linebacker is a football player. Football is, of course, our version of rugby."

The corner of his mouth curled in a subtle sneer. "I am well aware of what a linebacker is and understand what you mean when you refer to football, thank you. But your American football players would cry if they ever had to play rugby." His face softened, and he stopped a couple feet away from her. "You're looking well."

Needing some sort of stabilizing force, Rana stepped over to the desk and leaned against it, all the while keeping her arms crossed over her chest. She didn't trust her damn nipples not to wave at the man. "Thanks. Ah. What are you doing here?"

A shrug. He avoided her eyes, glancing around the small office. "I wanted to see you. You weren't home. I assumed you were at work."

She pushed aside her excitement and immediate response to the first part of his statement. *OMG I've been wanting to see you too! Take off your pants.*

Focus. "How did you know where I work?"

"I…" Was that a flush? "I Googled you."

Not a crime, out and out. Hell, she Googled all sorts of people, including every single date she went out with. Except… "You don't know my last name."

He shifted. "I went to your mailbox and looked at your mail."

Her mouth dropped open. "What? You…you can't do that! That's a crime. You committed a federal offense."

"I'm ignorant of some American laws, but I believe that I would have had to tamper with your mail in order for it to be a crime."

She narrowed her eyes, standing up straighter, filled with righteous indignation. "Regardless. You can't just, like, look at my mail, Google my name, and then come to my workplace. That crosses so many boundaries—"

"You spied on me for weeks."

Fuck. That took the wind out of her sails. *Months. More like months.* Um, maybe he didn't know the extent of her spying. Oops. She opened her mouth. Closed it again. "Well. That's. That's…different."

"How?" His eyes glinted. "Still a crossing of boundaries, I'd say."

She gritted her teeth. "Because I wasn't stalking you. I was…"

"What?"

"I don't know," she admitted, more softly. "Okay, fine. But no more tit for tat, okay? I already apologized for that."

He exhaled a long, slow sigh. "I didn't bring that up to… Fuck me." He ran his hand over his hair, the motion making the muscle in his biceps jump.

She bet the sales rep she was going out with tonight didn't have biceps like that. Sad face.

"I didn't Google you to get back at you for something you did. I did it because I wanted to see you, and I didn't want to wait until you were home."

Surely it was the light in the office that made it seem like he was flushing.

Ahh, no. It wasn't the light. God damn, but he was so stinkin' cute.

She tried to school her face so she wasn't simply staring at him in glee. "Why did you want to see me so urgently?"

He opened his mouth, but she raised her finger, the click of high heels distracting her. The restrooms were down this hall, and while the restaurant was currently slow, she didn't want to be disturbed by anyone, not when this new turn of events was so utterly fascinating. She crossed over to the door and shut it, then turned around, holding the doorknob in her hand. Not because she wanted an escape route—she felt no fear with this man—but she needed something to keep her tethered to reality. "Sorry. Now, what was so urgent?"

He rubbed his fingers together. They were stained black under the nails. Charcoal, or maybe pen. She imagined him not taking the time to scrub his nails thoroughly before hunting her down.

Heart. Melting.

His lashes shielded his dark eyes. "It was silly now. I see that. I should have waited."

"Nope." She pressed her shoulders against the door when he took a step toward her, as if he was going to leave. If he wanted to get through the exit, he would have to ram through her. "You broke a federal law and came all the way down here. You don't get to leave without telling me why."

He walked toward her until his chest was a few inches from hers. She wanted to breathe harder so her nipples could brush against him.

Damn. She'd had sex with this man? Go her.

"Why aren't *you* scared of me?"

She blinked at the question coming out of left field. "Um, I'm not scared of any man."

He shifted closer. This time her nipples did brush his chest. Her breath hitched in her throat.

"No?"

"N-nope." She cleared her throat. "Men are easy. Simple creatures. Uncomplicated."

His lashes fell to half-mast. "Uncomplicated."

"Yup." The back of his hand brushed over her belly, and she tightened her abdominal muscles.

"Hmm." Another stroke of his hand. "Is this what you wear as hostess here?"

If there had been a hint of condemnation in his tone, she would have verbally smacked him, but she heard only interest. She glanced down at the tight dark jeans and bright purple tank top. "No. I have a date."

She looked up in time to catch a flicker of…huh. Was that anger tightening his expression? He stepped away immediately, putting a few feet of distance between them. "You said you weren't with that man."

It was hard to remember the face of any other man when this guy was in front of her. "Charlie? I'm not. This is someone else."

His nostrils flared. "You're certainly popular."

"I am indeed," she said lightly, though annoyance and disappointment stirred. Ugh. Save her from men who couldn't handle a girl seeing more than one man in her lifetime.

She'd hoped he was different, though God knew why. It wasn't like she nurtured hopes that they could have some sort of relationship. "Do you want to see my little black book? It's pretty thick."

His lips twisted. "How long have you been with tonight's man?"

She rested her hands on her hips, growing displeased with his moody tone. "I don't think that's any of your business."

"I asked you if you were involved with anyone before we slept together. That was important to me."

"And I told you I wasn't," she snapped. "I wasn't lying. So put two and two together, genius."

The silence in the room was heavy with tension, but she could see the instant he realized what she was saying. His shoulders relaxed. "You weren't with this man then. This is another first date."

"Ding, ding, ding."

His throat worked as he swallowed. "I…apologize. I was out of line. It's none of my business who you see now."

"Damn right."

"I have some…issues related to getting involved with women who are already in relationships."

"Well, don't take your issues out on me."

He winced. "Yes. Apologies."

Rana pursed her lips. She could make him squirm some more, but he did sound remorseful. She'd let it go, she supposed. For now. "Fine. Are you going to tell me about what brings you here?"

He stared down at the floor and exhaled, as if he were facing a very difficult task, before looking up again. "I can't stop thinking about you."

Her jaded, skeptical, cynical heart fluttered. It fucking fluttered. She stopped herself shy of placing her hand over it and sighing.

Other men had told her the same thing, but never had the words held such a ring of sincerity and truth. "Oh."

He stuffed his hands in the pockets of his well-worn jeans. "Oh?"

"Well, give me a minute." Her words were calm, but her mind had started to churn. What did he mean, he couldn't stop thinking about her? He couldn't stop thinking about the sex?

Neither can I. Can we have it again, pretty please?

"I...may have thought about you during the last week," she admitted.

"Your blinds have been closed."

Because she'd had to keep them closed. The man still hadn't bought window coverings, and she wasn't about to risk seeing him and then crawling over on her belly and begging for more orgasms. She had her pride. Kind of.

She gave a jerky shrug. "I didn't think it was appropriate. I might have been tempted to watch you."

"I like it when you watch me."

Her breath hitched, and she grew more breathless when he loomed closer and slowly drew his arm around her middle, as if he were afraid she would break or bolt. He turned, walking her backwards until she was pressed against the desk and he was pressed against her. "I can't function, Rana. All I can see is you."

There went her heart, fluttering a second time. "I—You want to sleep with me again?"

"Yes."

She nodded, feeling like one of those silly bobblehead dolls. "I thought you weren't looking for a relationship."

His eyes cooled. "I'm not."

Silly to feel disappointed. So this was nothing more than a need to scratch an itch that hadn't gone away. One night hadn't been enough, but maybe another night would be. "Oh."

"I thought you weren't, either."

She wasn't. *You're not.*

She had to think, damn it. What would New Rana do?

She wouldn't be in this situation in the first place, moron, because she wouldn't have gotten into her car and followed her hot neighbor and then tumbled into bed with him.

Look at him, standing in her family restaurant's office, with his scruffy clothes and long hair and giant shoulders and tree-trunk thighs and that ass she hadn't even gotten to explore, not really—

How many times do I have to tell you to focus, idiot?

He wasn't the type of man she could bring home to her mama. And that was the only kind of man she could have now. So she couldn't have him.

But if this was simply an affair, an extension of their one night together, what would it hurt? No one would find out. She could make it into like...a week-long binge instead of a secret nibble. Maybe a couple-weeks-long binge.

She was still wrestling with herself when he rested his

hands on either side of her hips. "If you don't want to sleep with me, at least model for me."

She reared back. "What?"

"Model for me. I have to get you out of my system one way or another."

She thought of that couch in his studio, the one she'd never seen a man or woman on. Then she thought about his paintings. "Um. Do you always do nudes?"

His lashes shielded his eyes and his thoughts from her. "Generally, yes."

"So what you mean is you'll get me naked one way or another," she half-joked, but he didn't smile. No surprise. Did he ever smile?

"I don't need to hire models to look at naked women," he said with so much arrogance she was tempted to punch him in the shoulder, but she couldn't, because he was dead right, the jerk. He could fondle her boobs now, if he wanted to, and she would only be able to make excited squeaks. "I do actually want you to model for me." He squinted, and suddenly that dark gaze was very far away, locked on something only he could see.

She was…flattered. Utterly and totally flattered. Hell, she had a good body and a decent face. This wasn't the first man who had told her she should be a model. But she had seen the caliber of his work, and she knew he was the real deal.

This was art. The ultimate selfie. She'd be immortalized.

A thrill ran up her spine.

Oh, God. She'd been called shallow and vain before, and maybe she was those things, because the thought of him preserving her likeness on canvas sounded so fucking cool.

No, New Rana spoke up, concerned and oh so proper. That fun-killing whore. *You mustn't do this. Mama will murder you.* Her family could find out. Hell, if he had another show in the community, the whole town could find out. That would be terrible for business. Her family had done well for themselves, but their livelihood depended on this place.

She swallowed, hating that she couldn't just accept everything he had handed her and to hell with everyone else. Why did she have to think?

"I would work around your schedule," he continued, blissfully unaware of how close she was to accepting his offer. Offers. Whatever. "I would prefer some of it to be during the day, so I can see you in daylight, but I would also not mind evening and nighttime sits." He leaned in closer, his body brushing against hers. His arms were so damn big on either side of her. "I'm a professional. I'd be happy to give you references to past models."

Was that code? Did he mean he wouldn't leap on her upon viewing her naked body? As if she would want him to stay professional, if she did model for him. How was she supposed to sit with him nude, day after day, and not eventually climb him like a tree? Impossible, truly.

At her continued silence, his lips twisted. "You don't believe me. I'm not always such an animal as I was that night. It had been…a while, for me."

Oooh. "How long?"

He closed his eyes for a brief second. "A very long—"

The door opened without warning, and they both jumped, Micah taking a few steps away from her.

Leena raised an eyebrow at both of them, but the indulgent resignation in her face made Rana want to punch something. Okay, so maybe this wasn't the first time she'd been caught with a guy in this office, but it hadn't happened in a while, now had it?

"Excuse me. I didn't mean to interrupt." Leena stepped back, like she was going to leave. She was dressed in an elegant pantsuit, which meant her sister had probably come from overseeing a catering event or networking.

"That's fine." Micah inclined his head to Rana, avoiding her eyes. "I was just leaving."

"You don't have to go," she blurted out, even though she wasn't sure what she would say if he did stay. *Yes, we can have sex? Yes, I'll be your model? Yes, stand still and let me lick you please?*

"It's fine." He nodded stiffly to them both and walked toward the door.

"I'll come over—" She stopped. She couldn't cancel on her date tonight, not when she'd already done it once, and not when the man was probably on his way to the bar. Even if she had a sneaking suspicion she wouldn't be able to concentrate on the kindly sales rep for shit.

Plus, maybe it would be good to have the night to think about all of this. Since she was *trying* not to be impulsive and all.

Thinking was the worst.

His step faltered. He cast a quick glance at her over a broad shoulder.

"Tomorrow?" she finished lamely.

His eyes shuttered, and he gave the barest dip of his head to acknowledge her.

Leena stepped aside to let him pass and continued

watching him as he walked down the hall.

Rana folded her arms over her chest, this time to hide her puckered nipples from Leena. What the hell had she been thinking, wearing this bra and this shirt? Never again around Micah. These headlights were totally going to be the death of her.

Not that Leena would notice. She was leaning out the door.

"Do you want my phone? You can take a picture." Catty, perhaps, but she didn't particularly care for the way her younger sister was straining her neck to catch a glimpse of her man.

Your man?

Shut up.

Leena snapped out of her trance and came inside the office, shutting the door behind her. Her eyes were big. "Oh my God. It took me a minute, but I just realized who that is."

"You know him?"

Leena didn't answer right away, but fanned her face. "Uh, yeah."

"Right." Rana cocked her hip. "How do you know him?"

"I keep up on the news."

Rana tucked her chin to her chest. Figured Leena would know about the local art scene. *Why can't you be more polished like Leena? Men like a woman who's cultured, not common.*

Rana shoved her mother's voice aside. "Oh."

"I heard he had a show. I would have gone, but we had that gig across town."

Rana tried not to scowl. What if Leena had gone to the show instead of Rana? Her little sister was beautiful, with her shiny, angled bob, her delicate features, and her ruthlessly maintained body. Combined with her sharp intelligence and innate classiness, she was probably a better match than Rana for any man.

Leena has a serious boyfriend. You need to stop.

It would help if Leena would quit looking so damn dreamy eyed. "I should have said something to him. Maybe gotten him to doodle on a napkin. Did he eat here? Oh my God. Maybe he did doodle on a napkin. What table was he at?"

Rana raised an eyebrow. "Hold up. We have linens, not napkins, and he didn't eat here."

Leena pursed her lips. "He…came to see you? Oh, wait. Wow. Was he tonight's date?"

"What? No." Even to her ears, her laugh sounded forced.

"Phew." Leena shook her head. "I mean, he's hot and all, but he's probably not what you're looking for."

Right. Because there were men you fucked and men you fell in love with and married, and the two could never be the same. How many times had she heard that over the years? *Rana, you're not dating the right type of man.*

"What was Micah Hale doing here then?"

Rana shrugged. "He's my neighbor. He wanted to talk to me about some stuff. Related to…our houses."

"He's your neighbor? Huh." Leena moved around the desk and dropped into the chair. It was huge and leather, one of the few pieces of furniture in the entire restaurant that remained from when their father had been running the show.

"Why's that surprising?"

Leena cast her a dry look. "He's probably rich. He could afford something more luxurious."

Based on the price of the painting Rana had bought last week, she'd figured Micah did okay for himself. Rich, though? There was nothing about him that screamed rich. "Maybe he doesn't need anything more luxurious." Their houses were large for single individuals. She'd tried a condo, but found she hated shared walls. Rana needed space, for herself and all her clutter.

Leena made a disbelieving sound. She was the most frugal of all of them, but that didn't mean she didn't have champagne tastes. "I guess so. He's unlikely to get recognized in your neighborhood, at least."

She tried to imagine her elderly neighbors knowing about a British artist who painted naked people. "I think you're overestimating how many people know anything about art."

Leena stared at her. "Rana…I don't know who he is because he's an artist."

"So how did you recognize him?"

"Wait, do you seriously not know?" Her sister shook her head. "It was all over the news a couple years ago. I think he was famous enough for even our media to care, though it happened in England."

Rana didn't watch the news. Well, entertainment news, yes, and she kept up on the big headlines, but she wasn't a twenty-four-hour news junkie like Leena.

A strange sense of dread crept over Rana. She knew she wouldn't like what Leena was going to say, but she couldn't help asking, "What? What happened?"

"I don't remember exactly." Leena wrinkled her nose. "Just that some guy tried to murder him."

CHAPTER 11

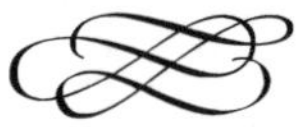

Rana had never been nervous about knocking on a door before.

She clenched her hand into a fist, apprehension making her stomach rock. *He's just a man. Not a dragon or a beast. You understand men. You adore men. Get this over with.*

She rapped lightly. It was early, the dew on the grass still wet, the sun not quite hot yet. She shifted from one sandaled foot to the other, waiting. She was about to raise her hand and knock again when a scuffling came from behind the door. The peephole darkened, and she raised her chin, doing her best to look calm and collected, though she was anything but.

The lock disengaged, and the door hinges squealed as he opened it. Then he was standing in the narrow opening, frowning at her.

It wasn't an angry frown. It was a perplexed frown.

She'd said she would come by this morning, hadn't she? She would have even come by the night before after she'd made it home from her date, but his house had been dark.

Turns out, she hadn't needed the night to think about

his proposal. She'd only needed a few minutes into her date with the perfectly kind and acceptable sales rep to realize she wouldn't be able to turn her attention to any other man until she dealt with the one occupying her brain.

So here she was. Ready to deal with him.

She pasted a smile on her face, hoping her makeup adequately covered the dark circles under her eyes. "Good morning."

He watched her warily. "Good…morning," he said more slowly.

"I brought you buns."

His eyes dropped to the plate of cinnamon buns she thrust toward him. She'd iced them when they were still warm, so the gooey part was melting over the sides of rolls, pooling on the plate. They weren't the prettiest things she'd ever made—Devi could whip up baked goods that looked like they belonged in magazines—but she knew they would taste like airy bites of heaven.

She'd considered making muffins as her own private joke, but that would have taken her too long.

"Buns." His hand made a movement, as if to take the plate from her.

She yanked it back, keeping her smile on her mouth. *Noooooo, sorry, sir.* He wasn't touching these buns 'til they got some things straight.

Double meaning intended. "Have you eaten yet? I thought we could have breakfast together."

"Together?" He glanced over his shoulder.

She frowned, a sickening feeling spreading through her stomach. Was he…not alone?

He didn't *look* like he was in the midst of an orgy. The

dark jeans he wore rode low on his hips, his blue T-shirt threadbare. His hair was clubbed back messily in his usual stubby ponytail.

Then again, perhaps this was how he looked in the midst of an orgy. If he strolled up to her like this, she couldn't guarantee she wouldn't orgy the fuck out of him.

"I've found that when people parrot words back at someone, it's because they're trying to hide something," she informed him, trying and failing to control the bite in her voice. "You can tell me to hit the road, if you're busy."

His thick brows drew together. "I am parroting, as you put it, because I'm surprised to see you."

"I told you I would be here today."

His shrug was jerky. "You went on that date last night."

Rana squinted at him. "I already canceled on the guy once. I couldn't cancel on him again for another dude. I'm not a flake."

"You didn't come home that late last night."

She raised her chin at his moody tone. Oh, she did not like that tone. Now she only wanted to orgy the fuck out of him a little. "What are you saying, that I should have come over the second I got home to answer your out-of-nowhere proposition? Okay, first of all, don't track my comings and goings. That's weird, and I thought we both decided not to do any more weird shit."

"I can't help hearing your vehicle," he said, snooty as can be.

"Try," she returned. "Secondly, what was I supposed to do, walk up to your house in the dark? Put your damn porch light on if you want someone to think you're home."

He frowned. "I don't quite know if I have a porch

light."

"Then don't bitch at me for not dropping everything and running over right away. Not when you were the one who changed all the rules to start with." She took a deep breath and lifted the plate. "Now do you want my buns or not?"

His nod was brief but quick enough that some of her ire was appeased.

Still, he was slow to step aside. She walked past him, her arm tingling where it brushed against his chest.

For a second, as she came inside, she wondered if she was in the wrong house. Surely, this bland, beige house did not belong to the passionate artist standing behind her, right?

Like her home, his had an open floor plan, so she could see into his dining area to the left and the living room to her right. The family room was tucked away, but she was certain it was probably as boring as this.

Sure, his studio was all white and sterile. She had figured that was an artist…thing, though, like he wanted the white background.

Where was the art? The interesting colors? The bold statement furniture?

The bare walls were a standard off-white that was common to rental properties. There was no furniture at all in the dining room, and the living room held only a beat-up brown couch and a small television, which looked like he might have picked up from someone on craigslist.

Now that she thought about it, she hadn't seen a moving truck pull up to the house with Micah's belongings. His car had one day simply appeared, and that was that.

He had moved from another country. It took time to furnish a home. Or maybe he liked living like a college frat guy? Or perhaps he was terrible with money, and he frittered away those big checks from his art on hookers and blow.

Because what did she know about him, really? Not much. Not nearly enough for her to be here.

Too bad she was too entranced to stop herself.

The door closed behind her. "Apologies." He spoke stiffly. "My place isn't fit for company."

He walked past her and scooped up the mail sitting in a huge stack on the third step. He hesitated, his head turning this way and that, looking for a place to put it.

Oh. Oh dear.

He was embarrassed. He hadn't been ill at ease at the thought of her walking in on his nonexistent orgy. He'd been worried she would judge his home.

Her heart tugged. She transferred the plate to one hand, barely conscious that she was using what Leena called her waitress hold, and cocked her hip. "Any of that mine?" She nodded at the stack of mail in his hand.

The corner of his mouth kicked up. Was...was that a smile? Had she, by chance, amused him?

It was close, but she was going to hang in there for the real deal.

He dropped the mail back on the stairs. His shirt rode up as he bent, revealing a strip of smooth brown skin. "I told you, I merely looked at your mail. I didn't touch it."

"That's what all the mail bandits say." She started toward the kitchen. "Shall we eat?"

"Right. Yes."

Since baking calmed her and she spent a decent amount of time in her kitchen, Rana had put some money into updating hers. Micah's landlord had…not. A yellowish fridge sat in the corner, next to an older model stove. The wooden table and pair of chairs looked similarly rundown. However, a shiny microwave sat on the chipped Formica table, new and out of place amongst the dated fixtures.

"I was intending to buy furnishings before I had guests."

The defensiveness in his voice made her heart twinge. "Babbleposh, Jeeves."

"Babble—?"

"It sounds like something you Brits would say."

"Someday, I'd love to hear what you imagine my people are like."

"Stiff. Formal. Everyone's a time traveler, a wizard, or works for MI6." She placed her plate on the table, pretending not to notice the legs wobbling a little at the weight.

"That's not quite right. Only some of us are wizards. The rest are Muggles."

Ack. She shot him a narrow look, inwardly delighted. "Okay, we're going to put a pin in this convo for right now, but later you and I are going to have a lengthy Harry Potter discussion."

She went to the counter. The first cupboard held a set of plates, and she grabbed two and brought them back to the table.

"I apologize for the mismatched plates."

Yeah, that formal part of her assessment was spot-on, huh? His accent had grown more clipped. "Stop worrying. Our underpants no-no areas have bumped, and you told me you'd like a repeat. I'm hardly a guest."

He was silent for a second. "Are you always so…?"

She arranged a bun on each plate carefully, as if the gooey lopsided treats needed to be plated properly. "So…what?" She sat down, and then kicked the other seat out from the table, looking up at him expectantly.

He came to sit slowly, lowering into the chair. The cheap wood protested as he settled his bulk in it, making her wonder if he had even purchased the few furnishings in this house for himself.

"Provocative?"

She liked the way his full lips shaped the word. Provocative. It was a better word than what other people had labeled her with at an early age. Like "outrageous" or "drama queen" or "attention whore". "Sometimes. But I'm never really trying to provoke anything." She grimaced. "Sorry. I'm usually just saying whatever's in my head."

"Don't apologize," he rumbled. "It's rather refreshing not to wonder what a person is thinking." He sounded as surprised by that admission as she was.

After a beat, she gave him a small smile. He might say it was refreshing, but everyone, including the people who loved her, eventually grew exasperated with her lack of filter. "Right." She picked up her cinnamon roll and pulled off the outer ring. "Well? Go ahead. Try my buns."

"Are you going to keep this play on words going for a while, or…"

"Yes. Because I'm emotionally twelve, and I giggle every time I say the word buns." She widened her eyes. "Guess what happens when I meet a man named Richard? Oh, man. So many dick jokes."

He looked down at his plate. "This was nice of you."

She peeled off the second layer of the roll, discarding it. "I'm not the chef in my family, but I am a good cook. Especially when it comes to baking."

"I believe you." But he made no move to pick up his roll, only watched her as she took a bite of hers.

She closed her eyes, letting the cinnamon and sugar melt over her tongue. Damn, but she had a sweet tooth. If her slowing metabolism would allow it, she'd eat nothing but dessert for every meal.

Her eyes popped open when Micah shifted across from her. She finished her roll in a couple of bites and snagged another one, unraveling this one as well.

"Why do you do that?"

"I only like the center." She ate the stripped roll in a few bites. "It's the best part. The part with the ooey-gooey cinnamon."

"Then why not make only centers?"

She cast him a chiding look. "That would be cheating. I like to work a little for my pleasures."

"Ah."

He still hadn't touched his roll.

"Are you…allergic to something? Gluten-free?"

He shook his head. "I don't care for sweets overly much."

She considered that, and then quickly swapped plates with him, giving him her leftovers. "There. I'll handle the sweetest part. You can eat the parts I don't like, how's that?"

His mouth kicked up. "I don't eat much in the mornings, also."

She surveyed his huge form skeptically. "In my experience, men who look like you are always hungry."

"Men who look like me?"

"Yeah. You know." She puffed up her cheeks and straightened, putting her arms out at her side to simulate his bigness. "Tall and jacked? All massive muscle? You must need like ten thousand calories a day."

His mouth edged up a little more. A few more jokes and maybe she would get a smile out of him. "I drink a lot of protein shakes."

"Ew." Rana wrinkled her nose. "Protein shakes? You're making me hurt." She nodded at the plate. "Try it."

He paused for a beat and then picked up one of the pieces she had shredded. He shoved it into his mouth with no reverence for the treat. His face changed as he chewed, his jaw slowing before he swallowed. "This is good."

"Don't sound so surprised. I'm fairly competent."

"I never said you weren't." His hand hovered over his plate. After a second's hesitation, he picked up another piece and ate it in a single bite.

"Better than a protein shake?"

"I don't usually think about what things taste like. But yes," he continued, before she could flinch from that sad remark. "This is better than a protein shake."

She touched the tips of her sticky fingers together and glanced at the empty counter. "Do you have any napki—?"

A big hand wrapped around her wrist and extended her arm over the table. His head dipped, and his lips closed over her thumb. Her abs clenched when he drew the finger inside his mouth, rasping his rough tongue over it.

He cleaned off each of her fingers, sucking her pinky for a second before releasing it. Her chest felt too tight. She could tug her hand away from his grip, but she wouldn't.

"I Googled you."

The words fell in the silence with the weight of an atomic bomb. His face shuttered, and he drew back, releasing her. "Did you, now." His voice was soft. "And what did you find?"

"I found your Wikipedia page. Read that. I know you were raised in London, and you have no siblings. You got your first big break when you were nineteen. You were considered a prodigy. By the time you hit thirty, you were pretty much famous and rich. It was a brief page."

"My mother considers it her life goal now to keep it brief and pleasant," he said. "Editing Wikipedia may be one of the few technologically savvy things she is capable of. What else did you see?"

She swallowed. "There were lots of gallery showings you did, plus some hits on people selling your art on the private market. For a lot, by the way. I mean, I thought your stuff at the gallery here was priced high, but that's nothing compared to the stuff on, like, auction sites."

"It's my early work." His voice was even flatter, if possible, his dark eyes piercing. "The paintings at the gallery were purposefully marked lower than anything I've done in ten years. The manager realized the resale potential is not there."

"Why not?"

He didn't answer her question, but asked one of his own. "What else?"

"News articles. Lots of news articles."

He closed his eyes briefly and then opened them again. "There it is."

She swallowed. "I didn't click on them," she murmured.

"Not the articles."

His chest lifted. "Why not?"

The headlines flashed in front of her eyes. *Artist Attacked in his Studio. Artist Left for Dead. Attempted Murder in the Docklands. Jealous Lover Attempts Murder, Takes Girlfriend Hostage.*

She gave a halfhearted shrug, unable to articulate all the ways she'd been disturbed by the thought of reading the gory details. It felt far more voyeuristic then watching him in his studio. "I don't know. Maybe 'cause we'd just talked about not crossing any more weird boundaries with each other?"

"Clicking on the articles would have crossed a line but Googling me didn't?"

She eyed him as if he had sprouted two heads. "Um, honey, Googling is normal. I feel bad for people who don't Google. It's healthy."

Another lip twitch.

Since she was being so honest, she continued. "I did read the headlines before I clicked away."

His face was like granite. "They were sensational, if I remember correctly."

"Yeah." She poked at the roll on her plate. "Sounds like you went through a rough time."

"It was years ago. I'm over it. So if you're only here because you feel sorry for me—"

"Would you kick me out if I was only here because I feel sorry for you?" she interrupted.

His jaw clenched, and she held her breath, gambling over the fact *she* probably wouldn't kick this man out of her life even if he did come to her out of pity.

This was all his fault. All of it. Rana might have pined over him a bit, but she'd been moving on. The memories of their night together would have faded eventually. Then this beautiful asshole had come waltzing back into her life, offering her the sweetest of things, the things she craved.

Lust. Excitement. Desire. Attention.

She could have them. Extend their affair. Get everything she needed from him. Because, God, she needed.

And then she would walk away. There was no other choice.

"No." He responded to her question quietly. "I would not kick you out. I don't think I could."

She closed her hands into fists to hide the trembling. "I don't feel sorry for you, by the way, so relax. I won't pry into what happened. If you want to tell me, that's fine. If you don't feel comfortable, that's fine too."

His eye twitched. "Good."

"I'll pose for you."

He jerked. She hadn't realized how tightly controlled he'd been, until he looked at her like this. Like he wanted to throw her down and bite into her the way she had those cinnamon buns.

Maybe she wasn't the only one with a craving.

He opened his mouth, but she raised her hand. "I have some conditions."

He subsided, his shoulders tensing imperceptibly, but he gave a nod.

"Like you said, it can't interfere with my job. We're rolling out a second location right now, and I've been doing a lot of the legwork. Plus, there's my regular shifts at the restaurant. I don't know how long this will take, but I'm not going to check out on my sisters."

His voice vibrated with intensity. "That's simple enough. We can work around your schedule. As for how long… I've had models for a few days to a few weeks. It depends on how quickly I'm able to work, and that varies."

"Okay. Let's say a few weeks, to be on the safe side." *And because I want as long with you as possible,* she thought guiltily. "You'll pay me for my time. This is going to be as professional as we can make it. I want you to treat me like a real model."

To that, he nodded immediately. "I didn't imagine anything else."

"I'll leave the actual compensation to you." She raised an eyebrow. "But I've seen what you sell your paintings for, so don't cheap out."

His head dipped. "Understood."

"I will, however, need you to agree that you can't use my face. You can paint me from the neck down. Or hide my face some other way. I can't be easily recognizable."

At that, he balked. "I love your face."

Her heart hitched. *Dummy. I love your face is different from I love you, as you well know. And you don't want his love.* "Be that as it may, my family won't be cool with seeing nudes of me, even if it is art. So I want to remain anonymous."

"This is a hard line?"

The phrase brought to mind sex, of course, but she knew he didn't intend it that way. She crossed her arms over her chest. "A very hard line."

His lips compressed. "Fine. But…I often spend part of my early time with a model sketching various parts of them so I can become familiar with their face and body, and I will do that with you."

Oh, okay, yeah, you can totally get comfortable with my face and body. "That's fine. I don't want my face ever put in public, is all."

He gave a short nod. "Very well."

"Okay." She took a deep breath. This was the tricky part. "Now. The sex."

He looked away from her, intently studying the window. Though the place wasn't decorated, it was cleaner than her own. Maybe because he didn't use the kitchen for anything other than mixing protein shakes.

"What about it?"

She pushed her plate out of the way. "I want to have sex with you. Again and again and again."

He had turned back to her, his eyes darkening while she spoke, his hands gripping the edge of the table. Talk about craving. He looked like he was ready to leap over the thing and tackle her.

She would be okay with that.

"You're the first man I've been with in a year."

He frowned at her confession.

"Not because I don't like sex. I love it. But as my mother keeps reminding me, I'm getting too old for hook-ups."

At that, he frowned harder. "How old are you?"

"Thirty-two."

"You're three years younger than me."

Her mouth twisted. "And if I were a dude, no one would ever hassle me about my age and my reproductive organs. But there you have it. I'm not a dude. Wouldn't want to be one, really. Penises seem like a lot of work."

"They have their moments."

"Where was I?"

"You're decrepit," he said dryly.

"Right. Putting aside my age, I feel like it's time for me to settle down. I want to find love. Maybe get married." She smiled wryly at the flash of panic in his eyes. "That doesn't mean I want to have your babies. I'm just saying where my head's at."

"But you still want to..."

"Have sex with you. Yes. And that's my final condition." Rana took a deep breath. "You can't fall in love with me."

CHAPTER 12

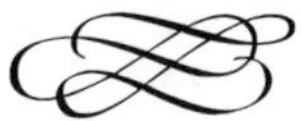

"More importantly, I can't fall in love with you either." Rana tucked her hair behind her ear. "Don't get me wrong. It's not like I fall in love easily. I've had flings. But like I said, my head's not in the same place it used to be in. We both walk, no hard feelings, if that becomes a danger, okay?" Rana stared at Micah expectantly, her face open and honest. In her white tank top and yellow skirt, she looked like a fresh daisy plopped into a barren field.

Was he supposed to be annoyed at her implication that he was Mr. Right Now while she searched for Mr. Right? He wasn't. He would take whatever she gave him, a dog satisfied with scraps.

There was a slight risk he might fall in love with her. A risk because she seemed rather loveable. Slight because he couldn't even love his family properly anymore. What made him think he could love anyone else?

The reverse, however, was unlikely to happen. Maybe if she'd met him a few years ago, she might have fallen for him. There was no danger of that with the man he was today.

If she did foolishly show any signs of love, he'd end things, no matter how he felt. She deserved far better than him.

"I have two conditions as well," he said, his voice unexpectedly hoarse.

She motioned for him to continue.

"You don't date anyone while we're together."

"Obviously."

Her immediate agreement soothed him. Micah swallowed, this issue having occurred to him last night, while he lay alone and sleepless in his bed. "And I don't want you to stare at my back."

Her eyes dipped to his lips. To the scar that bisected the upper lip and then traveled over his cheek. He couldn't hide that one, but it didn't bother him as much. The cut had been deep, but not as deep as the wounds on his back and side.

"Is it scarred? From the attack?"

Micah inwardly flinched, though he kept his face impassive. Most people tended to call it the incident or the accident—like it was something unpleasant he had simply bumbled into, not something that had been thrust upon him.

The attack.

He could correct Rana, but he didn't want to. Something about the jarring roughness of the word felt good, like a dash of cold water on his overheated face. "Yes."

"That's why you wouldn't let me turn the light on that night? Why you took your shirt off last?"

It was also why, even when he'd paraded in front of her

nude in his studio, he'd been careful to keep his scars out of her line of vision. "Yes."

She rose from her chair. He had to fight his embarrassment when it made a loud creaking noise. He clearly hadn't been thinking when he'd propositioned her so clumsily yesterday, or he would have realized that she would have to come over to his place in order for him to paint her.

Right now, his home looked like a poor bachelor resided in it. Or a serial killer with few ties to the outside world. If his family knew he'd allowed a guest to see he lived like this, they would be horrified en masse.

Rana was too kind to remark on it, though he had caught her quick once-over of the place. She was kind, in general.

She walked around the table, nudging the leg of his chair. She couldn't have actually moved it—he was far too large for that—but he obliged her, shoving the seat out. Her hand fluttered to rest on his shoulder, and she straddled his lap, her skirt sliding up her round thighs.

"Are you self-conscious?" she asked, continuing their conversation like his cock wasn't hardening against the notch of her thighs.

"No." It wasn't self-consciousness. The plastic surgeon had managed to minimize his scarring, and he had enough nicks and cuts on his body that he didn't much care about a couple of extra silvery scars. They were reminders, was all.

He didn't want anything from his past intrusively ruining the time he spent in her arms.

True to her word not to pry, she accepted his condition with a simple nod. Her hand dragged up his shoulder, her nails scraping his neck. "Since we're still in talks, I do have one more term to add."

Micah couldn't resist touching Rana. How could he? She was warm and soft on his lap, her long legs spread on either side of his hips. He wanted to tip her back on the table. Wreck her with his lust. Imprint himself on her body until she couldn't smell or feel anything but him.

"What's that?" he asked. Her lips were slicked bright pink today, a color he was desperate to see around his cock.

"I want you to kiss me," she whispered almost shyly. "You haven't done that yet."

He froze, struck by her words. Hell. He hadn't kissed this woman? He'd been inside her body, ridden her to exhaustion, and he hadn't kissed her?

What the hell was wrong with him?

He ran his hands up her sides, over the fragile stem of her neck, until they buried in her hair. She had left it loose today, and it spilled over her back, a waterfall of dark brown softness. "I accept that condition," he murmured against her lips, and took her mouth.

She tasted as sweet as that cinnamon roll she had cajoled him into eating. She moaned, and the small noise made him crazier to get inside her.

He swept his tongue into her mouth, and it tangled with hers. She was aggressive, but he didn't expect anything else. He liked the way she took no prisoners. Loved the way she held nothing back. He didn't have to wonder what she was thinking or feeling, not when she made it so damn obvious all the time.

He cradled her head and coasted his other hand down her body to her breast. Her nipple was stiff through the soft cotton tank top she wore. He handled her roughly, swallowing her gasp.

She ripped her mouth free and arched so her breast plumped against his hand. "Harder," she commanded.

He obeyed, squeezing again, before shoving her top up and yanking her bra down, admiring her breasts in the morning sun. Compared to the rest of her body, her skin was paler here.

He bent his head and licked around a dark areola, savoring her muffled cry. "You taste so good," he said roughly. "Sweeter than those rolls. I would eat you every day for breakfast." He ran his hand over her pussy and squeezed, pulling another muffled cry from her. "Right here, right? That's where you need it."

Her eyes blazed down at him, dark pools of neediness. "Yes. I need it."

He moved to tilt her back, but she stopped him by cupping his cock. "But you need it more, I think."

He barely moved, frozen in place by her hand. "I want to take care of you first."

"Mm-mmm," she purred. "You are far, far behind me on the orgasm spreadsheet, sir."

She had a certain funny way of phrasing things that made him want to smile, though he barely remembered how. "We only had two condoms that night. I thought it silly for us both to suffer."

"Let's not get carried away. You were hardly suffering," she said archly. "But please tell me you have one today."

He winced. She caught it and glared at him. "Are you kidding me?"

"Yes."

She blinked at him, and then gave him a blinding smile.

"Where?"

He shifted her weight until he could reach inside his jeans pocket to pull out the foil wrapper.

"You've been carrying it in your pocket?"

"I was hopeful," he said defensively. "Did you want to go on a treasure hunt for the damnable things again?"

She rolled her eyes and expertly ripped the foil open. "Fair enough."

They fought to open his pants, and then her sure hands were smoothing the latex over him.

He filled his hands with her ass and rubbed her pussy lips over him, making his cock slick. She gasped.

"You want this?" he asked. Acknowledging her nod with a squeeze of her cheeks, he pressed against her opening, holding his breath as she came down on him hard.

She was so fucking beautiful: tank top twisted above her breasts, skirt hiked up to her waist, panties merely shoved aside to make room for his thick cock ramming into her tiny channel.

Her fingers attacked the elastic that kept his hair tied, throwing it to the floor and grasping greedy handfuls of the strands. He filed away the information that she liked his hair loose when they were fucking.

At least his inability to get it cut could please someone.

He stroked her buttocks. "I love your ass," he growled. "It's mine, isn't it?"

Her lashes lowered. "For now."

His brain acknowledged the fairness and honesty of her words, but that wasn't the body part in charge now. He groaned and hauled her up until the tip of his cock was barely resting inside her. She whimpered and struggled to take him, but he was stronger than her, and she didn't have a chance.

"But it's mine for now, isn't it?" he said coldly.

Her nails scraped over his shoulders, sharp enough for him to feel through the fabric of his T-shirt. It was a reprimand and a spur. "Yes."

"Good." He shoved her back down and used his grip to fuck her like he wanted. Like he needed.

When he got her in his studio, he would strip her down. Learn all of her body's secrets. Make her immortal on paper.

He shuddered. And after each session was done, he would bury himself between these warm, willing thighs.

For now. She was his for now. It would have to be enough.

He could tell she was close when she trembled and clenched up on him. He didn't stop, giving her exactly what she needed.

Her head tipped back, and she let out a low moan. "Yes, yes, yes," she chanted as she came.

"I need you," he whispered, and clutched her close, burying his head between her breasts. "God, I need you. Please… Let me. Don't stop."

"No, I won't." Her hips moved more lazily now that she had gotten her orgasm. He raised his head and pushed her back so her body arched, long and lean.

She looked down and smiled, satisfied. "Look at us."

He obeyed, watching his cock pushing in and out of her. She was pink and puffy, her juices making him shiny and wet. He pressed his thumb against her clit and stroked her.

She squirmed. "Do what you need to do."

"I don't want to hurt you."

She draped her hands over his shoulders and came in for a kiss. "You couldn't."

Their lips and tongues tangled. She smiled when he pulled away, withdrawing from her. He grasped her by the hips and rose from his seat, placing her on her feet. She was so lithe, her muscles small but powerful. He spun her around and placed his hand on her back, forcing her to bend over the table.

Micah gave her a second to curl her fingers around the edge of the cheap table he had inherited from the previous tenant before he entered her hard. Her squeal made him pause. "Okay?"

"Yes," she gasped, and that was all he needed. He fucked her harder, harder than he would have dared if she hadn't told him to do so. He wanted to run himself through her. The cheap table squeaked on the floor and skidded forward to ram into the wall. He didn't care if he dented the damn thing. He couldn't help himself.

He closed his eyes and came, feeling like the top of his head might blast off.

He was panting when he rested his forehead on her shoulder, his sweaty chest layering over her back. Instantly doubt assailed him. What had he done? What would she think of him? He shouldn't have been so rough…

She shifted, and he realized she was struggling to get up. He lurched away from her immediately. "Apologies."

"For what?" She straightened away from the table. He had to grasp her arm when she staggered a step. She gave him a cocky smile and fixed her top.

He had to look away from that smile. It was far too

pretty for his piece of mind. He turned his back, dealt with the condom and adjusted his clothes, his mind racing as fast as his heart.

He couldn't just stand there like a beast though, so he faced her again. Whatever words were in his head vanished when she stood on her tiptoes and kissed his cheek. "I'm going to be late for work. I'll be home around nine. Did you want to start the modeling sessions tonight?"

He curled his fingers so he wouldn't touch the warm spot on his face that held the imprint of her lips. "Tonight is fine," he confirmed, because she was looking at him expectantly. His tongue felt thick and clumsy. Was he supposed to be able to talk?

"Great," she chirped. She gave him another chaste kiss on the other cheek. Like a baby duckling, he followed her to the door.

"Wait," he blurted out.

She cast an inquiring glance over her shoulder.

"I..." He fumbled in his pocket for his phone, thankful it hadn't fallen out when he'd been ramming into her willing body. For the first time since he had grudgingly purchased the mobile, he was happy to have the damn thing. "You need my number. In case."

"I left my cell in my house. Call me so I have it." She rattled her number off, and he quickly dialed it. He let it ring until her voicemail picked up, before hanging up.

Now he had exactly three numbers stored in this phone. His parents, who he would love to avoid, his therapist, who he avoided...and Rana. Who he couldn't begin to fathom avoiding.

He stood there, staring like a lovesick fool as she sashayed across the driveways to her house. She gave him a cheery wave before disappearing inside. Probably to shower before she went to work.

He wished she wouldn't. He imagined her walking around the large restaurant he had been in, the scent of his body on her. It was...barbarically exciting. He wanted to mark her, like the basest of animals, and keep every single other man out of her vicinity.

He caught himself, and he flinched. Jesus, who was this man he'd turned into? With more force than necessary, he shut the door and went to the stairs.

He was about to disappear into his studio to prepare it for her arrival, when he realized his home smelled different.

Fresh. Clean.

Cinnamony.

There was a time when he'd had quite the sweet tooth. After the incident—the attack—his mother had often brought him his favorite cakes and tarts in an effort to jumpstart his appetite, but he hadn't been able to choke them down. Taking pleasure in food had seemed...wrong.

For the first few months he'd barely eaten at all, his muscles wasting away, until his frightened parents had demanded he speak with his doctor, which had led to a nutritionist and a carefully constructed menu. He learned all about calories and fat and complex carbohydrates and exactly how many of each he needed to maintain his frame. Rana was right—he did require a large caloric intake. That was why he supplemented the small amount of food he was able to choke down every day with multiple shakes. Even if he didn't feel like eating—which was most of the time—he could drink his calories and not freak out his family. Win-

win.

He wandered into the kitchen and righted the chairs and table. She'd left the remainder of rolls—about a half dozen of them—for him.

Micah picked up a roll and brought it to his nose. The scent of cinnamon and dough and sugar and butter wafted to his nostrils, triggering a gnawing ache in his belly he'd thought long buried.

Very gingerly, he unraveled the roll as Rana had done, and took a bite out of the center. The burst of flavors on his tongue made him moan, the sound startling him.

He finished the entire roll in two bites, as if someone were going to come and take it away. He eyed the plate of remaining buns before scooping them up in his arm and heading for the stairs.

He could manage a couple more. He did have a whole day to kill before Rana showed up again, after all, and there were only so many ways he could fill the hours. Somehow, he didn't think obsessing over tonight would be the healthiest use of his time.

CHAPTER 13

Rana stood in front of her closet, tapping a foot. Every few months, she went through a closet cleanup, where she vowed to be tidy. She'd sort all her clothes, toss the ones she didn't need, and arrange everything on her hangers in color-coordinated groups.

Rana poked the pile of clothes on the floor. Sadly, she hadn't had one of those days in a while.

Not that she blamed her inability to find an outfit on her utter lack of organization. She simply didn't know what to wear. She'd Googled "What to wear as a nude model," but the majority of the answers had been "nothing." Haha. Well played, Internet jokesters.

Well, she wouldn't be in the clothes for long, right? She would pick something she could get out of easily. Striding out of the closet, she went to her drawer and pulled out a soft pair of yoga pants and a matching fitted T-shirt, her usual workout wear. She stepped into them, skimming them over her hips and trying not to shiver over her underwear-less status. *It's for ease,* she reminded herself sternly. *Not sexiness.*

But it was pretty damn sexy.

She jogged downstairs and slipped flip-flops on before striding out. Rana slowed as she approached Micah's house. Before she could knock, the door swung open and Micah was glowering down at her. Heaven help her, but she'd never found glaring quite so hot before.

"It's past nine," he said. "I thought you changed your mind."

She raised an eyebrow and stepped past him into the foyer. "I had to shower and change and brush my teeth."

"You didn't have to do any of those things," he countered.

"Okay. Next time I'll smell like onions during the entire evening, and we can see how you like it." She hesitated, wondering if he'd grown tired waiting for her. "Is it too late?"

"No," he responded quickly. "It's fine. Let's get started."

She swallowed as she mounted the stairs behind him, a few nerves creeping in to mix with the excitement in her stomach. What was going to happen? Would he want her to strip right away? Would she have to contort her body into weird positions? What if he started working and realized he didn't like her body? That would be awkward.

They entered his studio, and he went to the couch and picked up something flimsy. He held it out to her. "You can change in the bathroom and put this on."

She grasped the insubstantial silk robe. "You're right, I didn't have to take the time to get dressed. I should have come over in my robe," she joked.

A muscle in his jaw twitched. "You'll do nothing of the sort. Someone could see you. You'll always change here."

She rolled her eyes. "I'm joking."

He placed his hands on his hips, and then linked them behind his back. "Yes. Right." Micah gestured to the bathroom. "I'll set up while you..."

"Right." She went to the bathroom and shut the door, feeling mildly silly. He had already seen her naked. She could have changed in front of him, right?

Or maybe this was part of the model experience. She had demanded professionalism, after all.

She stripped down and folded her pants and shirt, showing more care for the workout clothes than they deserved. She shook the black silk robe out and put her arms in it. Something scratched her neck, and she reached back to find a tag there. The robe was new.

She yanked the tag off and tossed it in the wastebasket before tying the belt. The robe probably came to mid-thigh on shorter women. It barely covered her butt. She gave the hem a tug as she walked out of the bathroom.

He'd dimmed the lights and was crouched in front of the sofa, fiddling with a small space heater. He glanced up and gave her a quick once-over, his gaze burning a hole through the robe. Then he looked back at the space heater, as if it were incredibly difficult to operate. "I turned the lights away from the couch so you wouldn't get overly hot, but then I thought you may get cold...you can tell me how you feel," he said, though she hadn't asked for an explanation.

She nodded. "Okay."

"Do you want something to eat? Drink?" He rose to his full height and tucked his hands in his back pockets. "I would offer you some of your rolls, but I ate them all."

Delight burned some of her nerves away, though why she was so happy he had eaten her food, she had no idea. "All of them?"

"Yeah. Sorry. Your plate's over there."

"Don't be sorry. And, no. I ate dinner. I'm okay."

"Great. Okay." He cocked his head toward the couch. "Can you…?"

"Yup." This was it. Showtime.

She unknotted her robe but couldn't seem to shrug the silk off her shoulders. The two sides hung in front of her.

Get naked. Now. This is what you wanted.

She'd done this before. Stood in front of him, untied her robe, dropped it. She'd done it when she barely knew the first thing about him. It shouldn't be hard now.

"Rana."

She looked up to find him studying her, his face as soft as she'd ever seen it. He backed away and sat on a stool a few feet from the sofa. Probably so he wouldn't seem so big and intimidating. "You don't have to do this," he said quietly.

"I wanted to."

"I know."

"You've seen me naked. I don't know why I'm nervous."

Micah cocked his head. He didn't look gruff and cranky anymore, but understanding and patient. Like he'd flipped some switch and settled into a persona she'd never seen before. Was this the professional, experienced artist Micah? "Because it's a different sort of trust that's required here."

"You've been inside my body. I trust you."

He placed his hands on his knees. "You're letting me inside your soul now."

She waited a beat before letting out a peal of laughter. When she was able to speak, she asked, "You're joking with that shit, right?"

His lips curled. Ah! It wasn't quite a smile, but it was definitely amusement. "I thought you'd like that."

Still smiling, she snorted. "Good one."

"In all seriousness, though, I understand it's not quite the same thing. You might sleep with someone and not let them take nude photos of you, correct? Different levels of trust."

"I suppose. But this is…art."

"A naked photo captured on a camera phone can be art. In any case, both are a form of recreating your likeness when you're at your most vulnerable." He hitched a shoulder. "Perhaps not quite seeing into your soul. But there is intimacy. I understand if you don't feel ready yet. I understand if you never feel ready. If you like, I can paint you as you are, clad in a robe. Or a sheet. Or dressed. Or I can not paint you at all."

She ran a hand down the lapel of her robe. "No one's ever had to coax me to strip. When I lost my virginity, I was the one tearing off the dude's clothes."

"I'm not coaxing you. I'm telling you you have a choice." He cocked his head. "I will still sleep with you, if you're worried about that."

"Ha." She shifted her weight from one foot to the other. "You won't really paint me clothed. You only paint nudes."

"I grew famous for painting nudes," he corrected. "I have painted all sorts of people."

"Oh?"

"When I started art school, I didn't even have plans to

paint, not really. I was going to be a sculptor."

"But you discovered you liked painting more?"

His gaze was far away. "I discovered I enjoyed the thing that made me money. Success meant I was good at it, yeah? I liked being good at things." He refocused on her. "But success isn't an issue here. Anything I make with your body as a model—clothed or unclothed—will sell like nothing I've made in a long time."

No pressure, though. "How do you know that?"

His eyes glittered. "You inspire me."

Her breath hitched. The words should have been as cheesy as his joke about seeing inside her soul, but they weren't. Because he sounded…honest. And puzzled. And frustrated. Like he didn't want her to inspire him, but he had no choice in the matter.

Her decision was made.

She drew the robe open and let it slip off her shoulders, giving it a little kick so it lay away from the sofa.

He didn't say anything, but he surveyed her, starting at her feet and moving slowly upward. She shivered, goose bumps coasting along her skin as he looked his fill.

Her heart thundered, beating double time when he finally met her gaze. There was heat in his eyes, yes, but it was banked and simmering in the background, behind excitement and wonder.

"Are you sure?" he asked, his voice quiet.

"Yes," she answered, with no hesitation.

"You can stop me at anytime."

This was sort of like losing one's virginity, she thought. She was damn glad Micah was the one who was popping her cherry.

He nodded to the couch. "Sit down. However you feel comfortable. Curl up your legs, leave them straight, whatever you want."

She sat down on the far right, the cool cotton of the sheet rubbing against her ass. Everything felt heightened. It was like sensory overload.

"Are you cold? Hot?"

"No. I'm fine." Since he'd told her to be comfortable, she leaned against the arm of the sofa and curled her legs under her. Her usual TV-watching pose. "Is this okay?"

"Perfect." He picked up a huge pad of thin paper and a stub of charcoal from the paint-spattered table next to him, and rested the pad on his thigh. "These first few times we meet, I'll just be sketching. I'll tell you when to move and occasionally give you directions. We'll run through a number of positions. Mostly so I can get accustomed to your body."

"How long will our session be tonight?"

"Until you get tired." He eyed her sternly. "So you mustn't be shy about telling me when you're tired."

"What about when you get tired?"

"I don't get tired," he said absently. He stared at her, critically examining her breasts and belly, his charcoal hovering above the paper.

Her skin prickled, in a good way. "Paint me like one of your French girls, Micah."

He smirked, but his eyes were on her stomach. "I've never had a French model. Only English ones." He paused. "One other American."

She picked up on the odd note in his voice. "You slept with her. The American."

His gaze flew to her face. "Do you have a radar for sex?"

"Something like that."

"I was a twenty-year-old-virgin. She was a twenty-five-year-old not-a-virgin who inexplicably liked my inability to speak to her without stuttering."

"Aw. You were a bit of a late bloomer, Micah."

"Very much so."

"So you do sleep with your models."

He shook his head. "She was the first. You're the second."

"Must be us Americans. You can't resist our charm."

His fingers were moving over the paper, fast and sharp. He was barely looking at what he drew, though. His eyes were on her, probing and a little unfocused.

He was in his zone. It was sexy. "Yes. Perhaps it's my American side dominating," he said absently.

She propped her chin in her hand. "Your American side?"

"I have dual citizenship. I was born in Hawaii."

Surprise. "I didn't know that."

"No reason for you to know." The words were matter-of-fact.

"Is it bothering you when I talk?"

"If talking makes you more comfortable, go ahead."

"Can I ask you questions?"

His fingers stuttered, but otherwise he gave no outward sign of discomfort at the question. "Depends on the question."

Oh man, did she have a ton of questions. She settled on continuing their conversation. "Are you Hawaiian, then?"

"Yes. Half."

"What's the other half?" she asked, and then made a face when she heard herself. "Sorry, you can tell me to shut up if you don't want to talk about your ethnicity. I only ask because when I first saw you, I thought you might have some Indian in you. Just wondering if I need to welcome you into the brotherhood."

His lips curved. His charcoal didn't stop, his eyes traveling down to her legs. "There's a brotherhood?"

"Oh yes. The Order of the Samosa. We have a handshake and everything."

Oh, oh, oh! There it was. A smile. So quick and fleeting Rana would have missed it if she hadn't been staring at him, but the flash of white teeth and the crinkles at his eyes made her heart swell.

Damn. Had she thought he was sexy before? Nope. It was nothing compared to him smiling.

"You have a good eye, but I don't know if I would qualify for the order. I'm..." He narrowed his eyes and ripped off the sketch he had been working on, tossing it onto the floor next to him. "Can you shift a hair to the left? Put your hands in front of you if you can. I'm shite at drawing hands."

She obeyed, arranging into a different position. His charcoal flew again. She wished she could see the sketch he had done of her, but the paper had landed face down.

"You were saying?" she prompted.

"I'm one-eighth Indian. My father is Hawaiian. My mother is Jamaican. But, racially, she's a little of everything. I believe her grandfather was Indian." He shrugged. "Might be a Chinese grandparent or two in there as well."

She flexed her foot. "Now I feel boring."

"Nothing boring about the Order of the Samosa."

She chuckled. When she stopped, she noted him watching her mouth, his pencil arrested, a perplexed expression on his face.

He ripped off another sheet. When she stirred, he shook his head. "No, you can stay where you are for now."

She made a minute adjustment so her leg wouldn't fall asleep. "So, you have a Jamaican mother and a Hawaiian father, and you grew up in England instead of some tropical paradise?"

His eyes warmed the slightest degree. For such a solitary, reserved man, it was practically a declaration of adoration. "My mother is English. Born and raised. She met my father when she was on holiday from uni." He dipped his head. "Papa was working at his friend's restaurant. A tourist trap, it was, where they did hula and ate fire. Story is he looked up from the show, saw my mother, and that was it. They got married a month later. I was born in ten months."

Rana wasn't the romantic in her family, but her heart was pretty damn close to melting. "Aww. That's so cute."

He didn't disagree with her. "I would have been raised in Hawaii. But my mother missed her life and her family, and my father has never been capable of denying her anything. We moved to England for good when I was under a year old."

"They sound like a sweet couple."

His face softened even more. "They are very devoted to each other. And to me."

"No other siblings?"

He ripped off his sketch. "No. I'm it."

"Only child."

"Yes," he replied dryly. "It's exactly as wonderful and lonely and sad and whatever else the stereotypes are. Straighten your legs?"

She straightened them, surprised to find her legs asleep. Good thing he was moving her around, or she might actually be in pain at the end of this.

He caught her wince. "Do you need a break?"

"No. Pins and needles in my legs is all."

He leaned over, grabbed a cloth from the table and wiped his charcoal-dusted hands off before he rose and took the couple of steps to the couch. Unexpectedly, he put his hands on her legs and massaged them softly, until the discomfort was gone.

"You fondle all your models like this, Micah?"

His dark eyes met hers. "No. Only you." He lowered his head and pressed a kiss on her hip, rising with a self-satisfied smirk when he heard her indrawn breath. "I would fondle you some more, but you wanted this to be professional."

She narrowed her eyes on him. "Yeah, yeah. Keep drawing, sir."

CHAPTER 14

Rana glanced up at the two enthralled men in front of her. "I hope everything is to your liking."

The blond cleared his throat, his eyes fixed on her breasts. "Everything looks great."

With one last pat on the back of the loveseat, she straightened away from the sofa nestled in the corner of the restaurant. She'd pestered her sisters into ordering the plush couches last month, and the after-work crowd tended to love them. "There you go. Best seat in the house."

"I doubt that." The dark-haired man leered at her.

Normally, she might have smiled, but these two were barely welcome as it was. She gave a nod. "Your waiter will be with you shortly."

"Rana, you won't be waiting on us?"

So you can have too many martinis and make veiled innuendos you think I'm too stupid to understand? In a perfect world, Rana could have banished the assholes from her restaurant after the first and only time they'd decided to ogle her ass and act like obnoxious, sexist fifties ad executives instead of progressive, intelligent humans. Sadly, diplomacy and customer satisfaction had been drummed into her head from an early age.

Still, the front end was her domain, damn it, and its people were her responsibility. So far, at least, these two behaved around the other waitstaff. If they didn't, she would ensure they never came back.

"Sorry, boys, not tonight. Enjoy your dinner."

Rana walked away, leaving the men nudging and grinning. Rana could feel their gazes on her ass. Out of their sight, she rolled her eyes. Jerk wads.

She surveyed the restaurant, mentally checking off every employee's position in her head as well as each customer's general well-being. As she skirted through the tables, she smiled and greeted the table of blue-haired crones who came in every Friday for dinner, righted a toddler's sippy cup, and signaled a waitress to refill drinks.

As she put some distance between her and the problem customers, her mood perked up. More than one person had commented on her happiness today. How could she hide it? It was basically impossible.

She'd avoided her sisters, fearful they would somehow take one look at her smirking face and know she was bringing shame on their family by posing naked for a world-renowned artist. And having sex with him, sex with so many lovely orgasms. Without a single thought to putting a ring on it! My, she was naughty.

The modeling part was surprisingly tiring work. Last night, their second session together, Micah had her standing in different poses for almost two hours before she'd called uncle, tired from the strain of not moving. Lying-down poses were much easier. She didn't have to think quite so much, and could simply enjoy the pleasure of being naked while he admired her.

To his credit, he had spent a good half hour massaging her muscles and fingering her clit before sending her home on weak legs, so she couldn't complain that he didn't take care of her. And she got to do it all again tonight. Hallelu-iah.

"There you are."

Oh, shit. Rana hid the instant flash of guilt, and turned to face her sister. Leena was frowning at her. Bah. What had she done now? Other than the whole naked-modeling thing.

"Hey there, you," Rana said, with such forced cheerfulness she was surprised Leena didn't immediately challenge her on it. "What are you doing here? Thought you were grabbing a bite with Rahul." Look at that, she managed to say the guy's name without hissing like a cat. Leena's long-time boyfriend wasn't overtly awful, but Rana disliked him intensely. When Leena was with him it was like she became someone else, all of her personality sucked away.

Gosh, though, he was a doctor, so their mother had been in love with him since the moment Leena had brought him home almost four years ago. Enough that she'd turned a blind eye to the two of them living together. It was understood they'd be married as soon as he finished his residency. As far as their mother was concerned, living in sin could be forgiven if one ended up with a doctor son-in-law.

Leena froze for a beat, but then recovered. "No. I've been looking for you. Did you tell the contractors to wait a week to paint?"

"I—Oh! Oh, yes." They would have expanded to this second location a long time ago, but for their mother's worry it would be a bad risk. Mama wasn't in charge any longer, but all three of them found it difficult not to defer to her. "I did. Because we didn't talk about what the color scheme will be."

Leena made an impatient noise. "It'll be the same as here, obviously."

"No, see it doesn't have to be." Rana reached into her back pocket and pulled out her phone, bringing up the picture that had triggered her imagination. "Ta-da!"

Leena eyed the soft blue dress. "I don't like the cut."

"Not the cut. The color. That's the color that should go on our wall."

Leena gave a frustrated sigh. "Rana. Please call the contractors tomorrow and tell them to slap some red on one of the walls so we can see what it looks like, okay?"

Rana wilted a bit. "I think..."

"We don't have time to get held up on tiny decisions like this."

Paint colors weren't a tiny decision. They would influence the whole feel of the restaurant.

"But..." Rana was about to say as much when she caught sight of Jyoti out of the corner of her eye, scrambling away, her face flushed and long braid swinging. Odd. The girl did get flustered, but that didn't look like simple bashfulness. "Hang on. We can continue this conversation later."

"We're not continuing it. I told you, we're on a tight schedule."

Ugh. If Rana had time to get her mad on properly, she would, but she didn't right now. She gave her sister an irritated wave and followed Jyoti.

"Hey, girl," she said when she caught up to the younger woman at the hostess stand. "What's up?"

Jyoti cast her a terrified glance. Her eyes were red with unshed tears. "Nothing."

"Something's wrong." Rana leaned against the counter. "Spill."

Jyoti clasped her hands together. "Those two men at table eleven made some lewd remarks when I delivered their food, is all."

The ad execs. Rana clenched her hand into a fist. "Lewd, eh?"

"One said I—" Jyoti bit her trembling lip. "I can't repeat it. I'm sorry. They didn't touch me or anything. It's okay. I overreact sometimes."

"Aw, no, darlin'. No such thing as an overreaction when a dickhead's dicking." She would have moderated her language for Jyoti, but she was furious. The girl didn't seem to mind, a sign of how upset she was.

Jyoti nodded once. "Do you…? Could you maybe assign Ken to finish waiting on them? He could have my tip and everything," she tacked on, referring to one of the busboys.

"Don't worry about it," Rana soothed, and moved over to the register. She quickly tapped in some information and waited for the check to print. "You'll be getting your tip. But you don't have to see them. They're leaving."

"Oh." Dismay made her face fall. "You can't mean you're going to kick them out. I didn't want to cause any trouble."

Rana smiled at her, making sure not to direct her anger at the girl. Jyoti was painfully young, and it seemed like she wasn't used to people sticking up for her. Not her fault. She did, however, have to get used to Rana sticking up for her.

These were her people.

She wanted to kick herself. She should have booted the assholes out the second she got a bad feeling about them. Her instincts rarely led her astray.

Mess made. All that was left was to fix it as best she could.

"You have two choices, Jyoti. You can either watch me kick these jerkfaces out and get some satisfaction from that, or you can go into the kitchen and wait there for five minutes to avoid the unpleasantness."

The waitress's shoulders sagged. "I'd rather wait in the kitchen, if that's okay."

"Sure thing." She knew Devi would see the girl's upset and feed her some happy-making food to cheer her up. Rana slipped the bill into a folio. "And, Jyoti." She waited for the girl to look at her. "You didn't cause any trouble. They did. We don't serve troublemakers here, got it?"

Jyoti didn't look entirely convinced, but she nodded and scurried away. Rana strode to the table o' dickheads and gave them a bright smile. "Gentlemen. Everything going smoothly?"

Demonstrating their general assholish tendencies, the blond checked out her breasts, the brunet her legs. "Sure thing," Boobs said, leering at her.

"Awesome." She slapped the check down on his full plate of food. "Now leave."

"Hey," Legs protested. "What's this about?"

"This is about being rude to the staff." Rana kept her voice low and measured. The nearest table was far enough away they wouldn't overhear, so long as everyone was civil.

"She's lying," Boobs muttered.

"Hmm, see, you say that a little too easily," Rana remarked, not letting her instant rage seep into her voice. "Makes me wonder how many times you've said it before."

"Look—"

"This isn't a negotiation. Pay your bill and leave."

"We're not paying for food we didn't even eat," Legs objected.

"Oh, no." She flipped open the folio and slapped a pen down on the check. "We'll absorb the cost of the food. You are, however, leaving a nice-sized tip."

Legs's lips twisted. "Or what?"

Rana smiled. She leaned down until her face was even with his. "Listen up, douchecanoe. You think I haven't dealt with men like you before? Here's what you're going to do. You're going to leave a forty-percent tip, and then you're going to quietly get up and leave and never come back. In return..." She picked up the chapati from his plate and slowly crumpled it in her fist. "I won't take your balls and play Ping-Pong with them. And in case you don't believe that threat? I won't tell your boss you're running around harassing underage waitresses." Jyoti was twenty, but she looked young. Let the men sweat.

Boobs tried to be brave. "You don't know our boss."

The sweet man baby. He was adorable. Rana sighed. "You're Bob. That's Martin. You work four buildings over. Your boss is Gerald. He likes to pick up his lunch every Wednesday. Usually lamb korma, medium spicy." Rana opened her fist and let the ruined chapati fall onto his cooling food. She wiped her buttery hand on her apron.

Honestly, did these men think she was new? She was an incurable gossip and incredibly nosy. There were few regular customers she *didn't* know way too much about. "Actually, let's make that a fifty-percent tip, hmm?"

"Is there a problem here?" Leena's pleasant voice came from next to her, and she silently groaned. The more people who stood around the table, the more attention they would attract.

"Yeah, actually," Legs started.

"Ping-Pong," Rana reminded him, barely above a whisper.

He clammed up, then shrugged awkwardly. "No. No problem."

Boobs was silent, but he had pulled out his wallet. He yanked out an impressive number of bills and dropped them on the table.

"They were just leaving." Her remembered annoyance at Leena rose up, and she bristled, waiting for her sister to challenge her, but Leena only glanced at the men, back at her, and nodded before walking away. Leena wasn't as comfortable with customers as Rana was. She tended to stick to the back office unless she truly had to deal with unpleasantness or Rana wasn't there.

She didn't leave the table until the men stood, and she followed them to the door, holding it open for them. As they passed, she looked at one angry face, then the other. "Ping. Pong." Then she tapped the doorframe and gave them her brightest smile. "Have a great night, boys."

* * *

"YOU'RE TENSE TONIGHT."

Rana rolled her neck. "Sorry." She was draped on the couch again, on her stomach, her head lying on her stacked arms.

His stool scraped across the floor. He did that a lot. When he wasn't moving her, he was moving himself. He studied her from every angle with an absorption she might have found unnerving from someone else. With Micah, she was fascinated.

"Did you have a bad day at work?"

Oh thank God. She still hadn't determined if he actually liked talking to her, or if he had figured out she loved babbling and simply wanted her relaxed. Part of her didn't care. She'd take any excuse to spill out her feels. "Had to boot some assholes out during dinner tonight. They were harassing the staff."

"They harassed you?"

The cool menace in the question made her smile. Aw. "Not really. Probably 'cause they knew I wouldn't take their shit. They said some stuff to Jyoti. The girl who brought you to the back office that day you came to see me."

He made an immediate disgusted noise, soothing her. "Assholes, indeed."

"Nothing new. Asshole's gonna ass."

"How poetic."

She sighed. "I'm not torn up over it. Sometimes I don't mind playing bouncer. Gets my aggression out in a healthy manner."

"So if it's not that, then what has your back all knotted up like this?"

She raised an eyebrow. The man was like Sherlock when it came to how attuned he was to body language. "Meh."

She rubbed her cheek against her arm. "I'm kind of annoyed at my sister. We're opening a second location."

"You had mentioned that."

"It's a smaller space, more like a bistro rather than a full sit-down restaurant. It was supposed to be another revenue stream, like our catering business." She pursed her lips, the tension headache reappearing at the base of her skull. "All it's been is an exercise in my sisters ignoring me." Rana realized she sounded like a pouty child.

She didn't care.

"That other woman at the restaurant, when I came to see you. That was your sister? You share some similarities."

"Because we're brown?" she snarked. Leena was almost a foot shorter than her and both she and Devi took after their mother, while Rana looked way more like their dad.

"No," he responded calmly. "Because your nose is distinctive."

Instinctually, she covered her nose, her least favorite of her features. "It's not that noticeable."

"It's not noticeable, but it is distinctive. You share it. You both also have the same hands."

She pulled her hand away from her face and studied it. The fingers were long, the nails medium length and painted a vibrant orange.

It was a hand. Didn't all hands look the same?

Riiip. Micah was creating a hefty stack of sketches. After she left, he'd pick them up and tidy them into a pile on one of his workbenches. While she was there, they pooled all over the floor like discarded pieces of her.

"Stay like that, please."

"Who the hell notices things like hands and noses when

they first meet someone?" she mused, talking to her hand.

"Someone who studies people's features for a living."

"Is that why you don't need a model usually? Because you're so good at recreating people's features?"

A pause. She twisted to look at him, but he scowled at her and jerked his chin down, so she returned to her position.

"I used to only use live models," he finally responded.

Huh. In all the time she had been spying on him, she'd never seen a model in this room.

Before she could ask, he ripped the paper out. "Can you roll over onto your back?"

She shifted and flipped over. His warm palm grasped her ankle, and crossed her leg over her other one. She rested her hand on her belly. He didn't rearrange her, so she assumed that was fine.

"So that one girl is your sister. Younger?"

"About a year, yes. We have another sister. She's the chef. She's four years younger."

"You're the oldest child."

Her smile was wry. "Whatever stereotypes you're thinking of that come with that designation, forget it."

"I'm thinking you should be able to boss your sisters into doing whatever you want them to do."

"Ah. That would work if anyone actually listened to me."

"Don't frown. That timid girl you spoke to when I was there. She listened to you."

She relaxed her brow. "Yes. No one really gets in my way with the staff. It's when I try to do anything else they shut me down."

"Why do they do that?"

She lifted her chin. "Because…well, I have sort of a reputation for being flighty. And impulsive. But I've never been a dumb screw-up when it comes to the business. I've always put it first. Always."

"Anyone who thinks you're dumb is foolish."

The certainty in his immediate reply warmed her. "Thanks. I don't think my sisters are foolish. Just…I don't know. Used to seeing me in a particular light? Sometimes it spills over into everything, even when it shouldn't."

The scratching of his charcoal slowed. "All families are like that." His voice was quiet, so quiet she looked at him. He had turned off all the lights tonight and lit about a dozen candles all around the room, saying only, "Shadows," when she asked him why. She understood it now, though. The lights flickered against his face, deepening the darkness of his eyes and sharpening the hollows under his cheekbones. He looked…different. Softer. She probably did too.

"I suppose so," she returned.

"Why did you fight today?"

"I showed Leena my pick for the paint for the new place. A lovely soft blue. She barely looked at it and dismissed me." Remembered frustration made her tense, until he leaned forward and stroked her instep. Her foot flexed.

"Relax. Why did she dismiss you?"

"Because it's so different from our current place. We're all red and gold. You know. Traditional. What any person would expect to see when they walked into an Indian restaurant."

"Why do you want to change it up?"

"One, for practicality. That place is small. Anything

darker would overpower it, so the color scheme should be kept light and airy."

He made an approving noise. "I would agree with that. My flat in London was about the size of this studio. Painted it a lovely ice blue. Lighter colors do tend to open up smaller spaces."

She glanced at him. He did this sometimes, sprinkled a mention or two of his life before he came here. It sounded so…different. Filled with friends and family instead of nobody, blue instead of beige. What had changed? Was it all because of the attack?

Since she knew he wouldn't elaborate, she refocused on her problem. "Exactly. Second, I know that area. I went to school there." She shot him a wry look. "My parents insisted on the best private schools, not that it helped me much."

"Mine were focused on academics as well. Until they realized I was spending most of my time in every class drawing."

She snorted. "I wish I'd been able to at least draw. Instead I…well. Never mind." It was impossible to describe the sheer soul-crushing experience school had been for her, to be told every day she wasn't exceptional at anything that mattered. Mediocre at sports, mediocre at academics, mediocre in art. Graduation had been the best day of her life, even if her mother had given her the silent treatment for a good portion of her senior year because Rana'd informed her college was off the table.

Rana rubbed her nose. Her dad had been okay with it. *Ah, Rani, you should do what you think best. I can always use your help at the restaurant.* "Anyway, the demographic in that neighborhood hasn't budged in twenty years. There's not a huge Indian population or Indian restaurants. One Asian fusion place, but it's super upscale."

"Your current establishment is hardly cheap looking."

Rana twisted so she could see him better. He'd stopped drawing to focus on their conversation. He'd never done that before. "What were your first thoughts, when you saw our place?"

He hesitated. "I feel like this is a trap."

"No trap. I won't be mad."

He considered his words. "I had a commission once, when I was in art school. Lovely woman, but she kept throwing around the word *exotic* for what she wished for her surroundings, and showing me pictures of Indian-inspired decor. That's what your place reminded me of."

She laughed loudly. "Good. That's exactly what we wanted. God, I can remember my dad coming home from work when I was a little girl." Rana deepened her voice, mimicking her late father so well, it triggered a pang of wistfulness. Someday, she'd probably forget what he'd sounded like. "These *goras* keep saying they like things to look exotic. How many elephants can we paint on the wall?"

The lines around his eyes crinkled. "So he gave them exotic."

"Yeah. And we continued it, only refining it. Our clientele likes the red and gold and the marble statue of the Taj Mahal on the bar. They find it charming."

"You don't think the population around the new place will want the same thing?"

She struggled to find the right words. "Strategies have to be tailored. The community isn't far from here geographically, but it's like a different world. A world where the dresses my grandparents brought me from India were weird, our décor was tacky, and the smell of our food gross."

"That was a while ago."

"Yeah, but attitudes don't change overnight." She fisted her hand. "It's a long con, Micah, getting people to embrace something new. We picked that site because Leena ran numbers and studied demographics and surveys, but running a business like ours depends on hooking customers as much as it does anything else. People there might *want* something different, but unfamiliar things are also scary. We have to be like…those trendy food trucks, where they serve exotic meats wrapped in burritos? We lure them in with something safe, then we give them different with our food."

When he didn't speak, she glanced at him. He was studying her with great fascination.

"What?" she asked.

"Nothing."

"You want to say something."

"You're…you're rather brilliant."

She scoffed. That was definitely a word no one had ever applied to her. "Uh, no."

"You are. Your understanding of human nature is impressive."

"Oh. Well. Hmm." Her cheeks heated, and she fumbled. "Thanks, I guess. I talk to people a lot, is all."

Micah shifted. "You explained all this to your sister and she laughed? These sound like valid arguments."

"Umm." Now that she thought about it, had she explained any of this? "No. I may have just showed her the color and gotten annoyed when Leena snorted, and then I got distracted by the assholes."

His smile was brief but sincere. "You should try explaining your reasoning to them. I can't imagine they won't be as impressed as I am."

She crossed her arms over her chest, trying to tamp down the surge of pleasure at his words. "They should trust me."

"Why? Blind trust is…" He rested his arm on the pad. "It's impossible."

"When it's family—"

"Family's the hardest. They might love you to an overwhelming degree, but you can't always trust they know what's best. If you both don't have the same goal in mind, you may be working at cross-purposes." He shook his head. "It's not enough to give someone the answer. You have to show the work, so the person can figure out if that's the right answer for them."

She stared at him, the intense speech taking her offguard. "Are we still talking about paint samples?"

His lashes hid his eyes. "Yes. Of course. All I'm saying is, your sisters should listen to you, but you should give them something more to go on than a paint swatch. Make the argument. Back it up. Be upset if they still dismiss you."

She wanted to pout, but her innate fairness made her realize his words were sensible. "Fine. I'll think about it."

Micah rose from his stool and came closer, kneeling in front of her. He wiped his hand on the rag draped over his shoulder, rested his finger against her chin and angled her head.

She had gotten used to this, him touching her and making minute adjustments. She brushed a kiss on his thumb. His warning, "Rana," dissolved as soon as she took his thumb into her mouth, sucking lightly on it. He smelled clean and woodsy, with a faint hint of paint. A combination she had never thought to find sexy until Micah.

"I haven't gotten nearly as many sketches as I wanted yet," he reproved. But he didn't move away, and she wasn't imagining the dilation of his eyes or the bulge growing in his pants.

She gave him a final suck and pulled away. "Sorry. You were right there."

"I need help if I'm going to keep this professional," he chided.

His stern tone had her shifting, her thighs tightening. His observant eyes missed nothing, not the perking of her nipples or her restless legs. "Can't we stop?"

He rubbed his thumb against his forefinger, his eyes heating. "I told you. I need you to inform me when you've had enough."

In that case, she'd had enough, and they could move right on to the entertainment portion of the evening. Apparently, being called brilliant was a turn-on for her.

Or Micah was the turn-on.

She opened her mouth to tell him they should call it quits, but he spoke. "I think we should do one more pose," he said quietly.

Damn it. One more pose could mean anything from two minutes to twenty minutes. "Okay."

His hand grasped her knee, and he pressed her leg up until it was bent along the back of couch, while lowering her other leg until her foot was flat on the floor. He opened her so smoothly, it took her a second to realize the lewd, vulnerable pose she was in.

The second she did, excitement raced through her. They hadn't played teasing sexy games yet, but it looked like they were about to start.

He pulled the space heater closer, so the hot air wafted over her spread legs.

"Good," he murmured. "Yes, this is how I want you. Hold very still."

He sat back on his heels on the floor and started to sketch, slower this time. She stared at the ceiling, her heart thudding, aware that his gaze was no longer distant or professional, but filled with hot, prurient lust.

"Micah. I'm cold." She wasn't. Between the space heater and her desire, she was burning up, but she hoped he would take it as the invitation she meant it to be. She flexed her feet and brought her leg up higher, hopeful she would be able to tempt him into forgetting his work.

The charcoal stopped moving. His lips covered her nipple. She moaned, and her back arched. He sucked as much of her into his mouth as he was able to, then switched his attention to her other nipple, massaging the one he had just left.

"Oh God, Micah."

She craned her neck to watch her nipple emerge from his mouth. His white teeth scraped the brown flesh as he pulled away, elongating the tip. He hadn't been careful about wiping off the charcoal on his hands this time, and his dark fingerprints smudged her skin.

"Fuck," she gasped.

He sat back on his heels and stared at her breasts. No, professionalism had gone straight out the window. So why the hell wasn't he mounting her?

"Fuck me."

He shook his head and started a new sketch, focusing intently on her breasts. "I have to get this. Wait."

"I can't. Goddamn it, take care of me."

"Take care of yourself. Let me see it."

She didn't even hesitate. She'd spent every day since their first night together in a state of vague arousal, unable to get this man and his talented fingers and cock and tongue out of her mind.

Giving herself an orgasm was always a welcome exercise, and if she was able to tempt him into mounting her in the process? All the better.

She coasted her hand down her body, over the plane of her stomach, until her fingers tangled in the hair between her legs.

"Spread your legs more. I cannot see."

He'd given her so many directions over the past few nights, she was conditioned to obey him now. *Turn your head. Hold still. Spread your legs.*

Anything he wanted. She knew he would reward her with pleasure. She slid her leg over the back of the couch so she was opened as far as she could go.

She dipped two fingers into her wetness, and moaned to the accompaniment of charcoal on paper.

This was so fucking hot.

Rana rubbed her clit in the circular pattern she liked and let her breath fall from her lips in increasing pants. His face was red, sweat forming at his temple. Still, he knelt in front of the couch, barely a foot away from her, and watched. Sketching in that quick, expert way he had.

Argh. This guy. "Fuck me, Micah."

"I'm not done yet."

"You said I should tell you when I'm done. I'm done."

He finally met her eyes, though his fingers didn't stop moving. "You're far from done, Rana." His voice was soft, matter-of-fact. "Look at you. You're hurting, you need to come so badly."

She rubbed her clit harder. "Then help me."

He considered that, but then his eyes were drawn to her moving hand. "I can tell you what I imagined doing that first time I saw you watching me."

She licked her lips, her nipples tightening more. "That sounds promising."

He ripped off the paper and started a new sketch, his eyes obsessively locked on her hand between her legs. Was he actually drawing her masturbating?

She should be sickened by this. It was perverted, for sure.

But then, she'd always been a damn pervert. Guilt flashed through her, guilt for not being a good, normal girl, but she shoved it aside.

Not now. This fling was to indulge her secret, selfish soul. No room for guilt here.

"I was going to come to your bedroom. Break down your door if I had to. I was so angry to catch someone intruding on my privacy. I fantasized about yelling at you." Before she could wince or apologize again, he continued. "I didn't stay angry for long. I saw you the next day, walking to your car. And my fantasy changed."

Her lips were dry, and she stopped stroking herself, more eager to hear what he had to say.

He shook his head. "If you don't keep fingering yourself, I won't tell you."

That was untenable. She whimpered as she resumed the circular stroke, bringing her other hand up to clutch her breast and squeeze it, hard.

"Yes, yes," he hissed. She froze when his hand covered hers, but it was only to adjust it so her nipple poked out between her fingers. "Keep fingering yourself, but don't move this."

"But I need…"

He pressed her fingers together until they formed a clamp around her nipple, and she squeaked from the pressure. "There. That way we both get what we need."

"Keep talking."

"I marched over and broke down your door. You sobbed, telling me you were sorry. And then I…"

He fell silent, his pencil stopping for a second.

"Then you what?"

"I made you show me how sorry you were."

The words carried a hint of self-recrimination she hated. If she wasn't allowed to feel it, neither should he. "I like that." She made her strokes more explicit, to demonstrate how much she liked it. "How did I show you?"

He let out a gusty exhale. "You bent over the bed. I pulled your pants down around your ankles. And then I…spanked you."

Jesus. Her ass clenched, as if she could feel his hand on her right now. "Micah?"

"Yes?" His voice was low, his head bent over the pad like he was ashamed to look at her.

"Did you finger me in between spanks?"

His head lifted. "Yes." The word was hissed out.

Rana ran her tongue over her lower lip, loving his undivided attention on her mouth. "Show me how. Your fingers are so much larger than mine."

He hesitated for a bare second. Then he dropped the pad to the side and slid his hand over her pussy, crooking his fingers so his palm could rub against her clit as he filled her. She grasped his forearm as he started fucking her, his muscles rippling.

She could barely talk. "What else did you do to me?"

"After you came, I made you get down on your knees and apologize to me." His voice was hoarse, strained.

"How did I apologize?" She knew very well how, but she wanted him to say it.

"With your pretty pink lips wrapped around my cock."

She imagined that, imagined having his cock inside her mouth, and she couldn't stop the freight train of lust that bore down on her. She came, loudly, her hand clutching his wrist.

She came back to her senses as soon as she heard the rip of paper. "You have got to be kidding me."

"You're beautiful like this."

She'd be offended he wasn't as undone as she was, but he couldn't hide the effort he was exerting to control his lust. His hand shook, sweat dripped from his brow, and his muscles were locked. It wasn't easy for him to focus on his work.

Lucky for him, it didn't have to be easy.

She sat up, conscious of the wetness on her thighs and the heavy weight of her breasts. "I said we were done today."

"We should..."

"No. We should definitely play. Work time is over." She

slid off the couch and onto her knees, facing him. He was mute as she took the pad and charcoal away from him and tossed it to land on the pile of other sketches he had made. She grabbed his rag and swiped at his hands before throwing that aside as well.

A sign of how far gone she was—her lust was outpacing her desire to poke at the drawings he had done of her. He hadn't let her see them yet. Her curiosity was killing her.

"Stand up," she said softly. "And let me apologize for spying on you."

"I told you…"

"Stop being boring, Micah, and let me suck your cock."

His Adam's apple bobbed, but he finally stood and unbuttoned and unzipped his pants. He pushed his jeans and underwear down low enough for his cock to emerge, and she almost sighed over the beauty of it. She wanted to grab him and drag him toward her. She wanted to be greedy and forceful. But that was his role to play.

"Make me suck it," she whispered.

He closed his eyes. A trickle of sweat worked its way down his temple. "You're killing me."

"Do it. Show me how you did it to me in your dreams."

He stepped closer, until the tip of his penis brushed against her mouth. His hand was shaking when he wrapped it around his cock and traced her lips with the fat tip.

"Cotton candy," he murmured.

"What?" His cock jumped at the puff of her breath on it.

"Your lipsticks. I like how you're always wearing a different shade. I imagine the color ringing my cock."

She splurged on mega-last lipstick, but she'd invest in

some less kiss-proof varieties, if that floated his boat. She slipped back into his fantasy and made her voice slightly higher pitched to account for manufactured fear. “Micah. Please. I’m so sorry. Let me make it up to you.”

His shudder was full body this time. “Fuck me,” he whispered, and ran his fingers through her hair. When he palmed her skull, some of the strands pulling painfully, she had to clench her thighs together to stop herself from pushing him down and climbing on top of him. “Show me how sorry you are.”

She kept her lips resolutely closed until his thumbs dug into her cheeks, forcing her to open. When his cock forged in, she whimpered, only half acting. He felt huge in her mouth, the thick shaft dragging over her tongue. He worked in an inch or two and then stopped, his fingers gentling in her hair.

“Take more,” he growled. He wrapped one hand around his shaft and stroked the part she hadn’t managed to fit in her mouth. “You were so bad, weren’t you? Watching me like you did.”

Her body trembled. What was it he’d said when they met? They brought out something wrong in each other? She had been bad. She’d been bad to watch him, bad to pose for him, bad to fuck him.

God, but it still felt so good.

* * *

MICAH BIT off a curse when she carefully nodded and thrust a little harder, his cock glancing against the back of her throat. If he’d had a hint of rational thought and muscle control left right now, he would grab his pencil and paper and sketch her from this vantage point. Her eyes were wide and dark as she stared up at him, playing the worried supplicant to the hilt. Her mouth was passive around him, as if she were merely allowing him to use her at his will—a fantasy he hadn't even been aware he fostered until this moment.

They were only a few days into this amazing arrangement of theirs, and he was learning all sorts of things he'd been ignorant of needing before. Her lilting laugh. Her chattering. Her sharp wit and intelligence. The way she pulled words out of him he found difficult to say to everyone else.

The way he felt when she was around him. Lighter. Calmer. Better.

Hotter.

He tightened his grip on her hair and used his thumbs to press against her face, shuddering as the smooth inner skin of her cheeks met his cock. "Suck. Hard."

She tightened her lips around him and sucked immediately. He pressed forward, fucking her shallowly, then harder when she seemed eager to take it. He picked up speed, his hips swinging, hammering his cock into her warm, wet, willing mouth.

He allowed all his most barbaric fantasies to surface: her, attached to a chain in his studio, watching him while he painted, servicing him when he needed it. Her, dragging him away from his work because she was too aroused to wait a minute longer.

Her, here. For as long as he could keep her.

He shoved the dangerous thought away. She gagged, and he jerked back to reality. He pulled back instantly, letting her breathe. Tears had trickled from her eyes, making her eyeliner run.

Alarm pierced through his lust. "Are you okay?" As soon as he said the words, he knew she was. Her hand was working fast between her thighs, her cheeks high with color. "This is turning you on," he growled, his lust kicking up another notch.

She panted, her eyes on his cock. She looked wrecked, her pink lips wet, her makeup smudged. The debauched party girl, after the party.

He ran his hand over his dick, making it slick and shiny from the combination of his pre-come and her saliva. "I want to watch you fuck yourself," he rasped, giving himself over to his filthy fantasy entirely. "And after you do, you're going to drink me down, is that clear?"

She watched his fist stroking his cock. "And then you'll believe how sorry I am?"

Her words were pleading, but her tone was a demand. His erection pulsed. "Yes."

Her fingers picked up speed, in time with his own jerks on his cock. Her body flushed a charming red, her breasts shivering as her orgasm rushed over her. Her eyes closed, a series of breathy moans falling from her lips. "Oh, oh, oh."

He waited for her to look at him before he directed his cock inside of her slack mouth. She gasped but quickly got on board, sucking him while he set the motion, fucking her face harder than he had dared the first time.

When he felt the orgasm spilling over him, he tugged at her hair, trying to do the gentlemanly thing, despite his earlier demand. "Rana. I'm coming."

She only tightened her lips around him and sucked

harder. Unable to resist the invitation, he came in giant shudders, spilling down her warm, willing throat.

He staggered when he was done, his cock leaving the seal of her mouth with a pop. Unable to stand, he collapsed backwards, landing on his ass, and stared at her.

What kind of spell had she cast on him? He'd never had trouble maintaining professionalism in a model's presence, his thoughts no more prurient than a doctor's would be upon seeing a naked patient.

Rana wasn't like any other model, though.

She made a show of wiping off her mouth. His cock stirred as she licked her thumb deliberately and smiled a confident, seductive smile. "Well. I would say this session was highly productive, wouldn't you?"

He glanced at the pile of sketches. He'd never worked so slowly before, but he spent a good chunk of their sessions talking to her. What had started out as a way to get her to relax had become a nearly vital part of his day. He wanted to hear about the TV shows she liked or the fights she had with her sisters. He wanted to know her, inside and out.

At this rate, she would be his model for a hell of a long time. Funny how he didn't mind that.

He cleared his throat, fearful that the rasp in his voice would give away his feelings. Feelings he was nowhere close to understanding. "Highly productive."

CHAPTER 15

"Rana?"

"Huh?" Rana looked up from the pad she was doodling on to find both of her sisters watching her. She blinked at them, remembering where she was. "Oh. Sorry. Daydreaming."

"As usual," Devi teased with a fond smile.

She internalized the dig that wasn't meant to be a dig. She couldn't help being a space cadet today. If either of her sisters had spent the last week naked in front of Micah Hale in one capacity or another, they would be daydreaming too.

Rana cleared her throat. "What were we talking about?"

"The decor," Devi said.

"Can you call the people who made the couches for us, Rana?" Leena inquired. "We can order two more."

Rana took a deep breath. "Actually, I thought maybe we could revisit my idea from earlier in the week. To change things up in the color scheme."

Leena was already shaking her head. "We know what works. People like the way this restaurant looks. We'll keep it the same."

Show your work. "Just...hang on a second." Rana leaned over and pulled out a book of paint samples from her giant bag, flipping to the page she had tagged. "Look at it again."

Leena accepted the book Rana passed her. They were sitting at an empty table in the restaurant, which was currently closed to the public, since it was between the lunch and dinner shifts. Officially it was Rana's day off, but this was the only time and day all three of them had been able to get together to talk and make decisions.

Leena was frowning down at the paint swatches. Devi scooted her chair closer, so she could see. "That blue is pretty, Rana," Devi said, "but I think Leena's..."

"It's a smaller place." Rana had always felt vaguely awful over her tendency to chatter, but she used it now, eager for her voice to be heard. "Red and gold will be overpowering. Plus, we're targeting a more upscale market. We need to go less kitsch." Rana pointed to the light blue she had picked out. "On the walls, this is soft. Calming. It won't overpower the small space."

Leena pursed her lips and flipped to the reds. She found a red similar to the color currently on their walls and tagged it. "Okay. Let's get samples of both these colors and take them over tomorrow. See how they look."

Rana inhaled. That was an unexpected concession, but she wasn't done yet. She grabbed the binder she'd spent the previous evening creating. "Here's some ideas for what to do with the space if we go with the blue. Fabric and whatnot."

Leena glanced at the page Rana had opened the binder to, then came back for a second look. Her eyes widened and she accepted the binder. "Oh."

"Let me see?" Devi scooted even closer, craning her

neck. "Oooh. Rana, this is lovely. This isn't so different from what we have now."

They saw what she saw. She had to restrain her squeal. "No, it's not so different. Our brand will be all over that place." She used the word "brand" because she knew that would catch Leena's attention. "It simply won't be a carbon copy. This place is over-the-top kitsch. That place will be like..."

"Elegant kitsch." Leena's eyes lit up.

"Yes. Exactly."

"We'll still get both colors," Leena said, making Rana's heart plummet. But then she beamed at Rana. "But I'm excited about the blue. I didn't really think it mattered, what went on the wall. You changed my mind."

Such a tiny, silly, inconsequential thing to be excited about, them listening to her, but she couldn't help it. Flushing hard, she pulled out a file folder from her purse. "I've also gone through the staff applications we've received. I know we agreed to all oversee, but there's a couple in there that might make a promising manager for when we—"

The bell over the door rang, cutting her off. The three of them turned their heads, Leena frowning. "I'm sorry, we're closed right—Oh. Mama."

Devi stiffened, and Rana cast her a sympathetic glance. Since the poor girl had no choice but to keep her polyandrous lifestyle secret, Rana had noticed she was often ill at ease in their mother's presence.

Someone else might tell Devi that the truth would set her free or some such pap. But Rana knew better, and no matter how the lies weighed on her little sister, she hoped Devi would keep her mouth shut for the entirety of her relationship with Jace and Marcus. Rana knew far too well what it felt like to be on the receiving end of her mother's displeasure. She'd had a lifetime of it, after all.

Devi mumbled a greeting. Leena stood. Though she was unarguably their mother's favorite, a subtle tension vibrated through her. Who knew why, though. "Mama. What are you doing here?"

"You said you were talking about the new restaurant." Short, plump, and still handsome, their mother strode to the table where they sat. "I thought I would come help."

Rana tried to hide her wince. After their father had died, Rana had stepped in, and for a few years before Leena and Devi were finished with school, had run the restaurant with her mother. The greatest day of her life had been the day Mama retired.

The older woman meant well, but she also had an arch attitude that put all of them—including the customers and employees—on the defensive.

"We're doing pretty well," Devi piped up, her fingers twisting in her lap.

"We were almost finished, Mama," Leena agreed smoothly.

"Hmm," their mother muttered skeptically. "Well, then, Leena, you and I can go over the plans and have some tea."

"I have a meeting with the contractors," Leena said quickly. Rana narrowed her eyes at her sister, certain she wasn't imagining her unease now. When had Leena ever turned down an invitation to chat and gossip with her beloved mother? They liked putting their heads together and giggling.

For an instant their mother looked disappointed at this

rejection from her favorite daughter, but then her face cleared. "Well, you run along, and Devi can tell me about the plans for the kitchen then."

With the ease of long practice, Rana kept her face neutral. Of course Devi would be able to tell their mother about the kitchens, and Leena would fill her in on everything else. Rana's contributions were minimal, at best, so she couldn't be trusted to report anything.

She'd been excited about the color of the walls, for crying out loud.

Devi slid out of her chair. "Sure," she trilled, too eager to be convincing. "I'll go make some chai, Mama."

Leena made her goodbyes, leaving the room so fast Rana could have sworn her sister's feet were on fire.

Rana began gathering her stuff together as their mother slid into the chair next to her. "Where are you going? You'll have chai with us."

She glanced up at her mother, surprised and pleased. Until the other woman continued. "I have some boys I want to show you."

Heaven help her. "Actually, today's my day off, and I wanted to run some errands…"

"There is no such thing as a day off when you own your own business," her mother reminded her, something she'd been telling Rana since she was a toddler.

Rana bit off her usual response. That she knew that, damn it, since it had been eons since she'd actually had vacation. At the very least, someone called her to address some crisis or mediate a dispute. "Right."

The older woman fiddled with her phone before handing it to Rana. "Look at this boy. He's perfect."

Rana dutifully took the phone and looked at the man in question. Indian and handsome, with perfectly styled hair and a gleaming white smile. "A doctor?" she guessed, resignation weighing her down.

"Of course. You know I only filter by lawyers and doctors who earn over six figures."

The fact that there was a way to filter by income, and that matchmaking mamas used it, made Rana's head hurt. She handed the phone back to her mother, hoping Devi would return soon. "I told you, I think I got this handled…"

"I talked to him. He's so sweet."

She gaped at her mother. "You *talked* to him."

"I accepted his interest on your behalf. That makes my phone number visible to him," her mother said with a touch of defensiveness. "He called, and we spent a lovely fifteen minutes chatting about his family. His parents are both doctors, Rana."

What that meant, Rana still wasn't sure. That the successful gene was strong in this dude? She rubbed her forehead. "Mama. Please don't talk to anyone for me. And please take down the profile you made for me on that matrimonial site. I don't feel comfortable with strange men calling you."

Her mother frowned. Rana knew her mom wouldn't mind her bringing home a man of any ethnicity—his profession and income level would get a far harder scrutiny—but a successful Indian son-in-law would be the holy grail. Hence, her "help." "I'm *trying* to help you, Rana."

There it was. "I'm doing okay without help." She took a deep breath, not eager to have this conversation. "And anyway…I'm taking a break from dating right now."

Her mother reeled back, looking at her as if Rana had announced her intention to be a professional mud wrestler. "What? Why?"

Because I'm posing nude for this artist and we're also having sex, and I promised him I wouldn't see any other men while we're involved. How long will we be involved? No idea. Whee!

She lifted a shoulder. "I needed a break. It was getting exhausting."

Her mother leaned in, her face very grave. "Rana. I know it is exhausting. I told you in the beginning that it wouldn't be easy. I was lucky enough to meet your father in college, but I had friends who waited until their thirties to start this search, and it was incredibly hard for them. But you *must* stick with it. You are already thirty-two. You have no time to waste."

Rana studied her hands, the goddamned pressure weighing down on her on every side. She had heard some variation of the above for longer than she could remember. She was nearing some indefinable mark which made her an old maid, a desperate spinster on the marriage market.

She wasn't even particularly set on marriage, though everyone had automatically interpreted her "getting serious" as needing a ring. All she wanted was to find someone who loved her desperately. Maybe someone to cuddle with when it was cold out and who would be around when she wanted sex and who wouldn't mind her obnoxious chattering. Someone kind and dependable.

The pressure of tears against her sinuses made her eyes sting. She knew, intellectually, her mother had a skewed vision of marriage and men. But she couldn't quiet the little voice that told her the older woman was right. She was racing against a clock no one could hear or see, but it would sound an alarm and she'd be alone forever.

Her mother tucked her hair behind her ear, the touch devastatingly gentle. "You are so beautiful, Rana. Any man would have you right now."

Rana hunched her shoulders to hide the body blow her mother had just delivered. Yes, any man would have her. Right now. Before her beauty faded.

Because that was all she had to offer a man.

She made her hands into fists and dug her fingernails into her palms to keep from screaming. When she saw Devi return from the kitchen, a tray of steaming drinks in her hands, she stood and snatched up the papers and binders she'd brought with her.

"You're leaving?" Devi asked, a hint of betrayal in her voice.

"Yup," she said, as cheerfully as she could. Devi was still young, and as far as their mother knew, involved in a committed relationship with Jace Callahan, a successful, attractive attorney. Her baby sis could handle herself.

Rana wasn't sure that she could.

"Rana," her mother called out after her as she scurried away. "Think about what I said."

As she drove home, Rana wanted to release a hysterical laugh. Of course she would think about her mother's words. How could she do anything but think about them?

Any man would have you right now.

Her looks wouldn't last forever. And then what would she have to offer a man? Her stimulating mind? Her stunning academic background? Her innate classiness?

She was breathing hard when she entered her bedroom. Feeling stifled and repressed, she stripped out of her shirt and pants before sitting on her bed in her bra and panties. Since it was her day off, she had things to do, but she needed a moment to get her temper and her emotions under control.

So overemotional, that Rana. She pressed her lips together to stifle her cry of pain. No. Old Rana had been overemotional. New Rana was composed. She wasn't about to fly off the handle or fling stuff around or destroy a pillow in rage.

Even if that was exactly what her body was clamoring to do.

Rana took a few deep breaths, counting to a hundred, and then again, slower. She didn't have time for this. She had promised Micah she would come over today when it was still light out so he could see her in the sunlight.

Her heart automatically calmed, thinking of her neighbor.

After their third night together, he had brought in a timer and set it for two hours, explaining to her that he didn't trust either of them to get any significant work done if they started pawing at each other not long into every sitting.

That hadn't kept either of them from getting aroused though. The second the timer went off, she pounced on him, or he on her. Except the night before, when thanks to the space heater and the comfortable position he had asked her to hold, she fell asleep.

She had awoken to Micah carrying her home. He had somehow dressed her in a T-shirt of his and then bundled her robe around her, all without waking her.

She'd snuggled in, enjoying the novelty of having a man making her feel small and breakable, only protesting when he eased her into her bed and tried to move away.

She clutched his shoulders and puckered her lips. "No. Stay."

"You're exhausted," he said in that clipped, fantasy-inducing voice.

She was, but she wasn't about to admit that. Admit it, and refuse his penis? Never. "No." She tugged harder on his shoulders. "Need you."

He hesitated, and then he was over her, his fingers sliding over her wet pussy. He shushed her. "Relax. God, how wet you are. I make you like this? My looking at you?"

"Mmm." She jerked when his finger entered her. "Fuck me."

"I think you need this more than you need me rutting on you." His fingers found her clit and squeezed. "Relax. Let me give it to you."

The memory made her thighs clench, and she dragged her hands over the bedspread. She remembered the orgasm he had given her, but vaguely, like it was something in a dream. When she'd woken this morning, she'd been alone, still wearing his massive T-shirt.

She hesitated. They never set a time for her to come by. He had said he was almost always home, so she'd assumed it was up to her schedule. She glanced at her closed curtains.

She stood abruptly and made her way to the windows, yanking open the curtains and the blinds. Ah. Yes.

There he was, standing in his studio, a huge stack of papers in his hands. He hadn't actually started painting her yet, so these were probably sketches of her.

She tapped lightly on the window. He didn't turn around.

Of course not. He wouldn't hear her. And though he knew today was her day off, she hadn't said she would be home at mid-day.

She stroked her finger over the glass, thinking. And then, before she could talk herself out of it, she strode to her discarded jeans and fished out her phone, finding the number she had programmed into it. She hit send and held it to her ear, returning to the window.

She knew it was ringing on his end because his head came up, and he cast a glance at his worktable. Then he returned to studying the sketches in his hand.

He was ignoring her…for her.

She huffed a sigh of annoyance, hung up, and dialed again.

This time, he was the one who was sighing. He strode to the worktable, tossed the sketches down, and picked up the phone. She held her breath as he looked at the display.

Her heart leapt when he instantly answered. "Rana."

Now that she had him on the line, she felt silly, like she wasn't sure what to say to him. "Hey."

"Hello."

She licked her lips, amusement at herself making her smile. "Nice shirt."

His head came up, and he turned to look out the window. His eyes widened, and he came forward to stand in front of the glass. "I like your lack of shirt."

Oops. Rana looked down at her body, clad only in her bra and panties. In her emotional upheaval, she had forgotten about her instinctive response to feeling stifled—going pantsless.

Well. At least her underwear matched. She looked damn cute in the mint green. "You said you wanted to see me in sunlight."

"That I did." His voice had grown hoarse as he studied her body.

Confidence made her shoulders straighten. Prettiness might be all she had going for her, but Micah didn't make her feel pretty. He made her feel like a goddess. Like he was starving in a desert, and she was the only thing that could save him. She shook off the fanciful thought and ran her finger over her cleavage. Distraction. That was why she had called him. "What are you up to?"

"Organizing sketches."

She traced a heart over the window. Realized what she was doing. Dropped her hand. *Distraction.* "Do you like what I'm wearing?"

"Yes."

His immediate response was like a balm to her soul. "Do you want to see me in less?"

He grunted. "Always."

She placed the phone on the windowsill and reached behind her to unhook her bra. She teased him for a second, holding the cups over her breasts, and picked up the phone. "Take your cock out. You know I like to see it."

His breathing had roughened. With one hand, he unzipped his pants, the bulge of his cock immediately filling the open vee of his pants. He released it from the prison of his boxers and stroked it from root to tip.

"Mmm. Have you been hard all day thinking of me?"

She wanted his answer to be yes. Wanted him to confess that he spent the day in constant arousal, waiting for the few hours a night when she lay stripped in front of him.

"Yes."

It wasn't the grand statement she was hungry for, but it would do. She let the bra slide down her arms. He moaned, helpless.

"Lick your hand. Get it wet. Now stroke your cock for me, Micah."

He did just that, spitting in his palm, then wincing when he grasped his dick. He always touched himself far rougher than she could, and she worked him over hard when she had him in her hands, letting the calluses on her palms rasp over his sensitive skin.

"Come over," he gritted out.

She pressed her breasts against the glass, needing the bite of cold to stop her body from finishing this game before she intended it to end. "Later."

* * *

HE WAS DYING. She was killing him, and Micah didn't care.

He wanted to close his eyes and focus on the harsh feeling of his cock in his hand. He hadn't masturbated much over the past week. His own palm simply wasn't as good as her hands, her mouth, her pussy.

What are you going to do when this is over?

He shut out the cloying, annoying voice in his brain, the voice that got louder every time they were together. "Lick your finger for me, then," he bit out. "Rub your little clit the way you like it. I won't be the only one losing my goddamn mind."

"You never are," she purred in his ear. She did as he asked, sucking on her finger and popping it out of her mouth. She stroked her hand down her body, teasing them both, until her fingers slid under the waistband of her light green panties.

He wanted to tell her to lose them, but something about watching her hand moving beneath the silk was erotic as hell. "How does that feel?"

"So good." Her head tilted back, and she closed her eyes.

"No. You watch me," he snarled. He tugged on his cock viciously. "You watch what you do to me."

She opened her eyes, and even from this far away, he could see they were blurry with need. "Micah."

"Come over here," he cajoled, "and I'll put you on my face. You can ride my mouth. I'll rub my tongue against that spot you like deep inside you."

There was no hiding the shudder that ran through her. With her breasts rubbing against the glass, she was certain to have lewd imprints there later. "No. Like this."

He pushed his cock through the circle of his fist, twisting it on each upward stroke, matching the motions of her fingers working between her round thighs. His hand was suddenly too big and clumsy. He wanted her palm around it, delicately roughened from the work she did. "Rana. You can't come standing up. Get over here and I'll help you."

She focused on him. "You're right. I can't. But you can."

No. He shook his head, his lips barely making the word.

Rana gave him a siren's smile. "Let me do this for you. I'll get mine later."

"Then I wait too," he gritted out.

She pouted. "Don't be so boring. You don't want to wait." She leaned back, and her fingers strummed her nipple. "What do you need from me?"

He wet his lips and stroked his cock. "You're already doing it."

"What would you do to me if I was there?"

"Oh, God. Everything. I'd lick you…" He shook his head, aware that he was close to dropping the phone. "Everywhere. I'd lick you everywhere. Your tits. I want to live with them in my mouth."

"Would you fuck me?"

"I'd make you wait for it. The same way you're making me wait right now." He stroked his cock faster. She was enjoying herself, her fingers playing over her body. He wanted that to be his hand, damn it. "I love how wet you get, how tight you are."

"What if I begged you?"

"On your knees."

Her lips curled up. A deep shade of raisin stained them today. "You do like me on my knees."

"I love it."

"Would you give it to me?"

"Yes." His fist moved faster, and he shut his eyes. He'd had her here, in his studio, her pretty lips parted for his cock. Later today, maybe he would put her on all fours and enter her from behind. He wanted to see her ass jiggle as he rammed into her.

There were so many things he could do to her. He'd never get bored.

"I'd fuck you so hard." His testicles were pulled up tight

to the base of his cock, and he rubbed the head, spreading the wetness around until he was slick from root to tip, the moisture easing the path of his fist. "Take it harder," he rasped, and fucked his fist like he wanted to do to her tight body.

She moaned, this time louder. "Deeper."

"Yes. Yes." His body arched, and his come spurted from his cock, trickling over his fingers. He braced himself against the window, staring out at her, his brain lost in the fog of a perfect climax. "God."

"Mmm," she purred. "Nope. Just me."

His fingers curled against the glass. He wanted to march over to her home right now and kidnap her, bring her back to his lair. Not so he could torture both of them for a couple of hours while he sketched her, but so he could get right to what he needed from her.

It wasn't sex, though he worshipped her for giving it to him. He wanted to hold her close while the afternoon sun rolled over their bodies. He wanted to nuzzle his face against her neck in the hope he might actually sleep a whole night through. When they climaxed, it was the only time in recent memory he could remember feeling at peace. Maybe, if she stayed the night or he slept at her place…

He made a fist and bowed his head. He could see her mouth moving, but he'd dropped the phone. He fell to his knees and grabbed it, not getting up again. It was better this way. If he was having thoughts of sleeping in her arms—when he knew damn well and good that was a terrible idea—God knew what was visible on his face. "Sorry," he said gruffly.

"That's ok—"

"Come over." He scrunched his eyes tight in dismay,

but the words were already out there. Though he hadn't told her his cuddling fantasy, he hurriedly clarified. "You didn't come. Let me take care of you."

Her laugh was lighthearted. "That's really okay." There was a rustle of fabric in his ear. "I have some errands to do first. I have to get to the bank before it closes or I'll be in trouble, and I'm practically out of food."

"Ah."

"But, um…" She hesitated. "Do you want to, maybe, I don't know. Grab dinner?"

He froze. "Grab dinner," he repeated, like some sort of fool.

"Yes. Out. Not at my family's restaurant, of course, but maybe some other place?"

Dinner. He didn't fool himself. Dinner was perilously close to a date.

She sounded unsure and nervous, something he was certain she never felt when asking men out. She was too confident and self-assured. She shouldn't feel nervous, not with him. He wasn't worthy of her nerves.

He didn't know how to have dinner with a beautiful woman anymore. Hell, the only time they'd been in public together he'd behaved like a barbarian, told her to go back to her house and wait for him naked.

He was silent for too long, because her voice came over the line, her words tripping over each other. "That's okay. I'll eat something quickly, and then I'll come over after for our session."

If he'd hated her nervousness before, he despised the embarrassment now coloring her tone. Somehow, over this past week, they had gotten to know each other a little too well, so he wasn't surprised she knew he wanted to decline this invitation.

He rose on his knees and looked through the window. She'd drawn on an oversize shirt. His shirt, which he'd slipped on her last night before taking her home. It was falling off her shoulders, helped by the way she was hunching over.

He glanced at the sketches in the corner. He was having a hard time deciding what pose to paint Rana in, because he was enamored of her body from all angles and positions. One thing every sketch had in common: strength.

He looked at her bowed shoulders and thought of the tremulous way she had asked him to dinner. Defeat wasn't something he was interested in cultivating in any woman, but especially not Rana.

"I was only thinking I don't know of any restaurants in town," he said flatly.

Her head came up, and she looked at him. "I know lots of places. What do you like?"

"Anything." He hesitated. "I don't much care for sushi."

"I can find a place," she said, her happy chirp far too bright for his conscience. "Let me think while I'm running my errands. I'll text you the perfect place. Say, six?"

She had promised he would get to sketch her in sunlight today, something he'd been anticipating. But he supposed only geriatrics would request they eat at four.

If he'd had any inkling of protesting, it would have gone out the window when she smiled at him. Fuck it all to hell. Who needed the sun when they had that smile?

This is dangerous. Highly dangerous.

Still, he nodded like a marionette on a string, even while dismay made his stomach churn. "Perfect."

CHAPTER 16

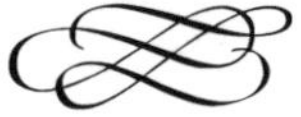

It's not a date.

Rana had chanted those words so many times over the course of the day, they were practically on an infinite loop in her brain. It was not a date. This was…an encounter between two people who happened to be sleeping together wherein they would eat a meal. And then probably sleep together. Hell, this was basically foreplay in a public setting.

That didn't stop her from tugging at the hem of her tight shirt. She'd paired it with a miniskirt. To keep from scandalizing the other customers, she'd slipped on a lightweight trench-style coat that hit her mid-thigh, covering the clothes up completely. Her stilettos finished the outfit.

Panties, yes, but no bra. Because foreplay.

Her phone buzzed in her purse, but she ignored it. She knew it was her mother texting her pictures of more eligible men. That was literally all her mother texted her anymore, and she'd already sent over three pictures and profiles of possible suitors today. Rana supposed she wasn't the only one who had been upset by their conversation.

Not thinking of that. Foreplay.

The hostess smiled when Rana came in. Like The Palace, Finnigan's was a family-owned affair. When her father had been alive, he'd done his best to encourage a spirit of cooperation instead of competition, so the little guys often traded having their dinners out at each other's places. Rana hadn't come here in a while. Her string of first dates were usually at chain restaurants and bars and coffee shops.

Unfortunate, because Rana was rather fond of this particular family. She had known Mia since they were in kindergarten. They exchanged a quick hug, and Mia leaned back to look at her. "Don't you look cute tonight. A date?"

Rana hid her flinch. "Meeting a guy," she hedged. She scanned the restaurant. "He may not be here yet—"

"Wait. The hot English dude with the long hair? He said he was waiting for someone."

Maybe he had beaten her here. "Uh, yes. Unless there are two of them."

"Dear God, please let there be two of them," Mia joked, fanning herself. "I put him in a booth in the back. Figured if his date didn't show, I would mosey on over and have a drink with him." She dropped her voice. "Have you seen his butt?"

Yes, she had seen his butt. Better yet, she had felt it.

She adored Mia. Which was why she tucked her hands in her pockets, lest she smack the other woman's eyes for daring to peek at her not-date's butt, and followed her to the back of the dimly lit pub.

Micah was studying the art on the wall but looked at her when they approached. He stood.

She'd seen him in a suit the night they had first met, but

she'd grown accustomed to his paint-spattered shirts and jeans. She abruptly forgave Mia for lusting after him. He cleaned up nice in a crisp blue button-down and a pair of gray trousers. She smiled, her blood pumping faster at the sight of him.

He nodded once but didn't make any move to kiss her or otherwise greet her. She suppressed the surge of disappointment. They were in public. He was so reserved, he probably didn't like PDAs.

"Malbec, Rana?"

She smiled at Mia. "Please."

Rana slipped out of her coat and into the seat. She placed her palms on the rough table. "Hey, you." She nodded at his beer, weirdly nervous. "Good?"

He sat down opposite her and curled his palm around the pint. "Very."

"They have excellent beers on tap here."

"You didn't get one."

A server came and placed a wineglass on the table in front of her. She gave the young boy a grateful smile. "I don't much care for beer."

"I was surprised when I realized what spot you picked. You don't seem like the type to frequent pubs."

Because she was…what? Too high-maintenance? She battled back her irrational surge of temper, aware her earlier encounter with her mother had put her on a hair-trigger. "I prefer wine. But I thought you might like this place. I understand English people spend approximately 78% of their life in pubs."

He smiled. She'd lost count of the number of smiles she'd drawn from him over the past week. They were like quicksilver—fleeting, gone with a flash. But her heart still accelerated every time she received one.

True to form, the smile faded. "Approximately, yes."

"Do you miss it?"

"Pubs?"

"England."

His face tightened imperceptibly. "Sometimes. Not much."

"Your family. Your friends? You must miss them."

"Occasionally. I can call them when I do."

She nodded and reached for the menu in an attempt to normalize her probing questions. Why she was probing, she wasn't sure. She was well aware they weren't in a relationship where probing would be okay.

He shook his head. "I already ordered for us."

She blinked at him. "How did you know what I would want?"

"You said in your text the burgers here were good." He shrugged. "I ordered you a burger."

She hated it when men ordered for her. But this time, her temper was eclipsed by disappointment.

Reading people was something she did and did well. So she didn't think it was a stretch to state the obvious. "You didn't want this to take any more time than it had to, did you?"

She had her answer when he studied his beer and wiped at the condensation on the glass.

"Micah."

"What do you want me to say?" He pinned her with his gaze. His eyes were stormy, his lips compressed in a thin line. "Dates weren't a part of our agreement."

Ouch. His pointed jab was made far more painful by the fact she'd had to tell herself multiple times that this wasn't a date.

She repeated her mantra. "This is not a date."

"You're dressed up. So am I." He shook his head, as if there was nothing more to say.

She clenched her fingers around the glass. "Nobody asked you to dress up."

"I knew it was expected."

"I didn't dress like this for you."

He raked his gaze over her. For the first time, she didn't feel desirable and sexy in his eyes. She felt cheap.

He looked away. "You knew I would like it."

"Of course I did," she said, with a calmness she wasn't feeling. "I know what turns men on. But I don't dress like this for men. I dress like this for me because I like it. If I didn't like it so much, I would have been able to trash my wardrobe when I trashed everything else about myself."

His eyes narrowed. "What do you mean by that?"

Stupid. "Nothing." She grabbed her trench and scooted out of the booth. He followed, looming over her, his frown massive.

"Sit down, Rana."

"Why? So we can soldier through a silent dinner while I try to play jester and make you smile even though you clearly don't want to be here?"

"You're creating a scene," he said through gritted teeth. "I won't have it."

Calm down, Rana, came her mother's voice in her head. *You don't want to make a scene.*

"Oh no," she retorted with vicious sweetness. "This

would be a scene." She grasped her full wineglass. With a flick of her wrist, she tossed the contents.

The red wine trickled over his astonished face, running down to stain his shirt purple. An unholy, inexplicable urge to giggle came over her, mixed with the need to sob. Before she could do either, she carefully placed her glass on the table and walked away, yanking her coat on as she went.

"I'm so sorry," she mumbled to Mia as she passed, but Mia only waved at her cheerfully, her eyes wide.

"I'm sure he deserved it."

"Send me a bill." She couldn't dig in her purse right now.

"We'll figure that out later, honey."

She took great, gulping breaths of air when she was outside, quickly jogging to her car as fast as her heels would let her. Feeling suffocated in the small space, she lowered all the windows as she drove, letting her hair whip around her.

She had no conscious recollection of getting home. One minute she was driving and the next she was in her driveway, struggling to calm herself. There was no reason for her to be so irrationally angry.

Yeah, okay, maybe it had been a date. And he was right, dates *hadn't* been a part of the agreement. That didn't mean she'd expected him to get down on a knee and propose to her.

She'd just wanted to go to dinner with a man she liked.

She lowered her head to the steering wheel and let the tears come. She wasn't sure why she was crying, exactly. Because she was alone? Because Micah liked banging her but was wary of having dinner with her, though she was the one to put that don't-fall-for-each-other rule in place?

If you hadn't spent your life cultivating shallow relationships with unsuitable men, maybe you wouldn't be alone right now.

She practically snarled at her mother's voice in her head, and thumped her fist against the steering wheel. Fuck, hadn't she been trying to change all that? Hadn't she been so fucking good lately, doing her best to find love with the right kind of man?

Micah wasn't suitable.

He was purposefully unsuitable. He was her muffin. They had no future. So there was no reason for her to be so upset.

She wasn't sure how long she sat crying, but Rana jumped when her door jerked opened. She relaxed only a bit when she realized it was Micah standing there. She straightened, hastily brushing the tears off her cheeks. Her scowl was automatic, a reply to Micah's frown. He'd wiped off his face, but his shirt was ruined.

"What do you want?" she asked.

"I want to talk to you."

She sniffed and tugged her key out of the ignition. She ignored his hand and shoved at him to get him to back up. Only then did she clamber out of the car. "Go to hell."

"Rana."

She ignored him and pressed the button on her key fob to lock it. "I don't want to talk." She moved around him—God, did he have to always take up the most space?—and started up her pathway.

"I haven't been out to dinner with a woman since the attack."

She froze, his voice piercing through her fog of self-pity

and anger. She didn't turn around, but she didn't walk away.

He came a couple steps closer. "I went to a pub with some mates a few months ago. I—I couldn't even make it through a full meal. I thought I could, tonight, with you. I managed to muddle through the show at the gallery. I could do this. But something about that place made me feel like the walls were closing in. I took my unease out on you."

She swiped under her eyes and turned to look at him. "I don't appreciate being a punching bag."

"I'm…" He rolled his lips in, as if the words were paining him. "I'm sorry."

"Why are you telling me this?"

"Because…" His face was strained. "We're not done yet."

"With the painting."

"With each other."

She steeled her heart and crossed her arms. "I know this can't go anywhere, you know. It really was only dinner." That was a half-lie. She did know this couldn't go anywhere. But it hadn't been only a dinner.

He didn't challenge her, though. "I know." He paused. "And I love the way you dress. Always. I know it's not for me, either."

She studied his purple-stained blue shirt, annoyed at her twinge of guilt. "Sorry about your shirt. Maybe that was an overreaction." She'd never been so melodramatic as to fling a glass of wine at someone, not even in her most emotional of moments. "I've been annoyed at my mother all day. Then you said what you did, and I sort of lost it."

He thrust his hands into his pockets. "Do you want to

talk about it?"

"Nah." She gave him a wobbly smile. "She keeps trying to set me up with dudes."

"What?" His eyes narrowed, nostrils flaring, and she couldn't deny a part of her thrilled at his possessive sneer. They both had some jealous tendencies, it seemed. "We agreed you wouldn't see anyone while we're together."

She rolled her eyes. "I told her no."

"Because you're with me."

"No. I didn't tell her no because I'm banging my neighbor. I told her no, because no."

He reached her in two strides and sank his hand into her hair. He used his grip to drag her closer and lowered his head, his lips brushing against hers. "It's going to stay no. As long as we're together."

Surely that wasn't her heart going pitter pat. "Well, we won't be together forever," she said quietly, needing to hear it more than he did. "So when we're finished—"

She never got to complete her thought because his lips covered hers, demanding and forceful. He angled his head at the last second, and the kiss exploded beyond either of their capabilities to control it. With a rough moan, he tightened his grip on her hair to hold her still while he ravaged her mouth.

His tongue was so…perfect. Rana considered herself a connoisseur of kisses, particularly French kisses. Micah was possibly the best kisser she'd ever come across, not too wet, not too dry, just the perfect amount of saliva and tongue and lips and—he nipped at her—teeth.

She would've started ripping off his clothes right there, but a sharp whistle and a roar of laughter broke their spell.

They tore apart to find a trio of teenagers driving by in a rusted Chevy. "Damn kids," she muttered.

She squeaked with surprise when he wrapped his arm around her waist and brought her to rest flush against him. "You make me forget who I am."

Her knees went weak. Fair enough. He made her forget who she was too. Or who she was trying to be.

He dipped his knees, and suddenly she was hanging upside down over his shoulder. "What are you doing?"

"Making sure I have you where I want you."

She studied the ground as he strode to his house. "I would have come with you."

"I can't expect you to ever do the expected."

Her heart swelled. Other people had called her unpredictable before, but no one else had ever sounded so fondly exasperated over her nature. Exasperated, yes. Not fond.

She was laughing by the time he set her on her feet in his foyer. He frowned at her and started unbuttoning his shirt. "What's so funny?"

"Nothing." She grinned at him, unexpectedly light.

He might be wholly unsuitable, but right now he was exactly what she needed. Everything and everyone else could get back-burnered for a while.

His shirt fell to the floor, his skin begging for her touch. "You won't be giggling when I get you."

She smiled, even with the predatory gleam in his eyes shining at her. "Is that right?" She turned and bolted up the stairs. "You'll have to catch me first."

He growled, but he didn't immediately follow. She heard the rustle of fabric as he dropped his pants.

Fun sex games were exactly what the doctor had ordered.

A primal urge screamed at her to run. Run because she wanted him to chase her. Run because she knew it would make the capture more exciting. Run because she wanted to submit.

The heavy footfalls on the stairs made her adrenaline pulse, though she knew he intended for her to hear them.

She bypassed the open door of his studio. Too obvious. He had to work for it.

The room next to it contained only a treadmill and a gleaming set of weights, which meant there was nowhere to hide, but more importantly, no place to fuck. She jogged to the last door in the hallway and closed it behind her with a quiet snick.

Her breath sounded loud in the stillness of the home. Enough light shined in from the slits in the blinds that she was able to see this room was as sparsely furnished as the rest of the house. There was a queen-sized mattress and box spring on a frame, the sheets and comforter mussed.

Rana backed up to stand in front of the bed.

She knew the instant he stepped foot on the landing upstairs; he made no effort to be quiet. His measured footfalls came closer to her, pausing once as he threw open the door to his studio.

Finally, he paused in front of this room. "I know you're in there."

His soft voice and the sensual threat it contained made the agony of excitement swell. Her thighs felt too sensitive, rubbing together under the short skirt.

The doorknob turned. Tall and imposing, he stood in the shadows. His shoulders filled the frame.

He was completely naked.

"Oh no." She blinked twice. "You found me."

Micah maintained his grim expression, though she caught what she might call an actual twinkle in his eye. "Take off your clothes, Rana."

She lifted her chin. "What if I don't want to?"

He took a step closer. His cock grabbed her attention, and she had to fight not to lick her lips in anticipation. It was so damn thick and curved, the tip bouncing off his belly button when he moved. Yummy.

He slapped something in his hand against his palm. She almost died when she recognized the leather belt from his pants wrapped around his fist.

"You're going to be punished for running," he said, still in that soft, dark voice. "If you don't want to make it worse, you'll strip right now."

Hmm. Rana briefly contemplated calling his bluff. But what if the punishment entailed him leaving her high and dry or prolonging her tension? Nah, she wanted to get off, and quick.

She crossed her arms in front of her and grasped the hem of her snug shirt, pulling it up and over her head. She dropped it to the floor, savoring his swallowed groan. It didn't hurt her ego to see the hot need in his eyes as they flicked over her bare breasts.

"Leave the shoes," he ordered, when she was about to kick them off. Oh good. He liked her heels as much as she did.

She unzipped her skirt and let it fall to her feet, stepping out of it.

His cock twitched, impossibly growing larger. He

groaned and wrapped his palm around it.

The sheets on the bed were scratchy against her legs. He prowled closer. “Turn around.”

She obeyed, a shiver working through her at the command in his voice. His hot palm came to rest on her back, and she jumped. He slid it up her spine, under the fall of her hair, where he gripped her neck. Inexorably, he pushed her forward to bend over the bed, her forehead against the cool sheets.

“Put your hands behind your back.”

She twisted enough to speak. “Micah…”

“Don’t talk.”

She clammed up, so wet her thighs felt slick, and complied. The thick leather of his belt surrounded her wrists. He tightened it until she couldn’t move. She gave an experimental tug.

The sting of his fingers connecting with her ass had her jolting with pleasure. “Don’t mess with it,” he snapped.

“Again,” she said, fully aware she was inches away from begging. “Spank me again.”

He paused. “Are you sure?” His voice was hoarse.

She didn’t answer, only raised her ass, and she felt another swat against her other buttock. He rubbed the flesh, his touch soft. “I want to paint you like this.”

She bit the inside of her cheek, imagining how lewd and wrong that painting would look.

“Don’t move.” The wood floor creaked as he walked away. Out of the room? Where the hell was he going?

Maybe to grab a condom. Funny, but for all the sex they’d had, they hadn’t made their way to his bedroom yet. She pressed her fingers against the heated skin of her ass and shifted on her high heels, feeling vulnerable and open. The sun had set outside, filling the room with shadows.

He returned, his size making a quiet approach impossible. She tensed, eager and vibrating with anticipation.

A featherlight, prickly touch over her lower back had her squealing. "What the hell—"

He shushed her, stroking her hip. "I told you. I want to paint you like this."

Something cool and bristly—oh God, he'd brought a *paintbrush*—dragged over her ass.

At least he wasn't actually smearing paint on her. Not that she was opposed to that, but the bed would get filthy. She breathed out a wheezy laugh as her inner muscles clenched. "Micah Hale, you're a dirty bastard."

* * *

MICAH DIDN'T RESPOND, his attention occupied. The room had grown dark with the dusk, but he could see well enough to enjoy the sight of the flat, wide brush coasting over the curves of her bottom. Long ago, he'd attended a show where the artist had covered the models with paint, and they'd silently posed for hours. He wanted to do that to Rana one day. He'd use passionate reds, hot coral, deep purples. She'd only pose for him, though.

The way she looked, hands bound, bent over the bed, ready for the demands of his body… If he came on her ass, would she forgive him? She would. She'd smile that sweet smile, roll over, and wrap her long legs around him, guiding his fingers to her pussy to ensure he gave her what she needed.

So tempting.

He tapped her cheek with the brush, and she jumped. Her skin was lighter here, her resilient flesh reddened by his hand. He traced a thumb down the crease and separated the curves. The little rosette of her anus winked at him.

Obeying his instincts, he traced down the crease until his finger rimmed the pucker. Rana gasped. "Micah, no."

He eased away immediately. She twisted around to look at him over her shoulder. "I mean, your finger's fine, but nothing else. Unless you have lube."

The caveman within him roared to life at the realization she wasn't denying him. "Later. I don't have any here."

She chuckled. "Oh most definitely later."

He groaned and dropped to his knees. "Widen your legs."

She did, her heels slipping on the hardwood floor. He placed his hands on her thighs and shoved them even farther apart, until he had room to kneel between them.

Micah had had some vague fantasy of Rana tied up and at his mercy. One where she sucked on his cock until she was ready to blow. Then maybe he fucked her until they were both spent.

He was hard enough to drive nails, though, and if she put her mouth on him, he wouldn't be able to retain a hint of rational thought. That didn't mean he couldn't play with her, though.

He leaned in closer to her sex and inhaled the scent of her arousal. She smelled delicious, and the sight of the plump lips, the hard bud of her clit peeking out in between, made his mouth water.

He didn't bother with a slow lead-in. He swept the brush over her clit, her response instantaneous. She gave a low cry, her legs widening. "Oh God, Micah, please...please, more."

He pressed the bristles harder against her, rotating the handle in a wide circle. The muscles of her thighs trembled. "Like that?"

"Yes."

Micah drew the brush away and slapped it against her pussy, loving the wet smack, her sob of pleasure. "Do you want to come like this?"

"No."

He dragged the bristles through her wetness, letting them abrade her aroused flesh. Back and forth. Again and again, until she was shaking. "No? You don't like me painting you?"

"I want you inside me."

He hadn't thought it possible for his dick to harden more. He dropped the brush on the floor and drove two fingers into her wet pussy. "Is that good enough for you then?"

Her entire body trembled at the sudden invasion. "No, let me... Fuck me with your mouth at least."

He couldn't stifle his groan. He pulled out of her swollen sheath and widened his fingers into a vee, holding her open. "Why don't you show me what you like? Ride my face."

Micah stiffened his tongue and rested it against her pussy. She froze for an instant, and then seemed to understand exactly what he wanted her to do.

She braced her legs and ground down on his face, her hips jerking, soft cries of ecstasy breaking from her mouth. Micah had to clench his hands to let her continue to take what she needed without interfering.

"Oh, I'm so close..." she moaned.

Understanding the desperation in her tone and the cues of her body, he groped for the brush on the floor. He flipped it over, pressed the tip of the wood handle against her clit, and twisted, agitating the nubbin. She stiffened above him, the flutters in her pussy intensifying until she was milking his tongue. He gentled his touch as the spasms faded and she lay still, half on the bed.

He couldn't wait any longer. Rana didn't move when he stood and grasped her hips, though she roused when he slammed his cock inside her.

He froze, realizing his mistake immediately. He'd never had sex without a condom in his entire life. God, it felt so good. Her wet heat and soft tissues surrounded his dick in a tight clasp. "Rana...I forgot the condom."

Her head lifted.

Micah swallowed, his brief selfish hope that she would say it was okay, that he could stroke in her, shaming him. "Sorry. I...sorry." He pulled out, the hot drag of her pussy making him want to weep.

"It's just that—"

"Don't explain." She shouldn't ever have to compromise, not with him, not on this.

He wanted that wet heat, though, without anything in the way. He pressed his cock against her, rubbing it in between the wet warmth of her folds. "Like this. Let me fuck you like this. I'll make it good for you." She was bound, but she was never helpless. If she shook her head, he'd stop. Even if he was perilously close to begging.

"Yes." She shoved back, and he gritted his teeth, fucking

her farther up the bed. He grabbed her hips, trying to hold her steady, but his sweat-slick hands skimmed over her flesh.

Her rising moans drove him to shaft her harder, making sure he tapped her clit with every stroke. He looked down, watching the red, angry flesh of his dick as it tunneled between the folds of her cunt, her hips churning back against him as if she couldn't bear for them to part, her hands clenched, the elegant, long line of her spine and back. Her hair fell over her face, and he leaned forward to gather it, grunting as she screamed at the increased pressure.

He wouldn't last much longer. Micah fisted her hair, and she gave a broken sigh. She liked the sting of his fingers grasping her hair as much as he liked her ripping the elastic out of his. His hips hammered against her with fast, hard jabs. "Who's fucking you?" he demanded, barely recognizing the rough snarl as his own voice.

"You are, oh God, yes."

"Say my name."

For a second, he wondered if she would refuse, and he tensed in anticipation of securing her compliance. "Micah. Please. Harder, faster."

He obeyed and gritted his teeth to keep from coming. He used his grip on her hair to arch her neck, and leaned over her until his lips were by her ear. "Who do you belong to?"

Nothing.

He bit her neck, and then sucked at the bruise. "Tell me," he demanded, even as he cursed himself. This was terrible. A terrible, horrible question to be demanding from her.

She was silent but for her uneven breaths. Her lips

worked, but no sound came out.

He growled, his frustration making his hips pick up a brutal speed. Her feet left the floor as he grabbed her by the hips and fucked the folds of her pussy.

She screamed, a high sound, as she came. At the last possible second, he pulled away and grasped his cock, his come spilling on her upturned ass.

His legs nearly gave out on the aftermath, and he braced himself by resting his hands on either side of her body, which was draped lax over his bed, bound and destroyed, his release standing out on her soft brown flesh.

Mine.

CHAPTER 17

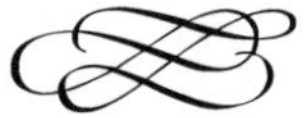

Who the hell was calling her?

Rana rolled over and groped for the offensively ringing phone. "'Lo?"

There was silence on the other end, and then a tentative female voice. "Hello?"

She yawned. "Yes?"

"Pardon me. I'm looking for Micah… Do I have the right number?"

Rana's eyes popped open. Oh God. She wasn't in her room, she was in Micah's. And she'd just answered his telephone.

Her eyes narrowed. For some woman with a crisp British accent, who happened to be calling at the ungodly hour of… Rana checked the clock. Four a.m.

Which made it a perfectly decent time to call in the UK. Rana tamped down her unhealthy surge of jealousy. "Um, I'm sorry." She sat up straight. She was alone in his bed, the blinds closed so tightly it was dark. His side was rumpled but empty. "He's not here right now. I can go try to find him though…"

"No. No, that's okay." The woman cleared her throat. "This is his mother. May I ask who this is?"

Rana winced and dropped back to the pillow. Oh God, his mother. Mortification made her mute.

She had no idea what kind of parents Micah had, but she could well imagine what her mother would say if a strange man answered her phone in the middle of the night.

Did you kill my daughter?

Or, alternatively, and far more likely: *Give Rana the phone. Rana, really. No boy is going to respect you if you bring them home with you.*

Rana made a face. *What are you worried about? It's not like he's ever going to take you to Sunday brunch with his mom.*

Still, it was his mother.

"Hello?"

"Um. Sorry. I'm…um. I'm his…his model."

"His model."

Well, fuck, she *was* his model, but she barely believed that stammered explanation.

Rana got up and swung her legs over the edge of the bed, tugging on the sheet. It was all kinds of icky to be on the phone with Micah's mother when she was nude. "Let me see if I can get him. I mean. I'm sure he's in the house." She winced. Wouldn't his model know where her employer was?

"If you two are in his house, he's probably in his studio," his mother said, and this time Rana didn't imagine the thread of laughter in the other woman's words. "Don't bother disturbing him. What is your name, dear?"

She swallowed. "Rana."

"Rana. Leave him be. I'm sorry to have woken you. I

know Micah's always awake at this time, which is why I called. Tell him to call me back as soon as he can. I haven't heard from him in a while."

Micah was always awake at four a.m.? Rana murmured her goodbye and hung up. She sat there for a minute before taking a deep breath and coming to her feet, tucking the sheet around her like a toga.

Rana used Micah's phone as a flashlight to guide her way out of the room, but she didn't need it in the hallway. The door to the studio was cracked, letting out a sliver of light.

She pushed it open slowly, trying not to startle him. He sat in front of a canvas with his back to her. He'd put on a pair of jeans, but he was naked from the waist up.

She stopped a couple steps in. He hadn't turned on the brightest of the lights, but there was enough for her to clearly see his back.

She'd felt the scars on him a couple of times but had moved her hand away quickly, mindful of the condition he had placed on their getting together. The last thing she ever wanted to do was trigger some sort of awful flashback when he was with her. Not when he was giving her so many delightful memories to tuck away.

She felt so guilty, but she couldn't stop looking. She couldn't count them. Over half a dozen? They were spread all over his lower back and right flank, shiny, two- to three-inch silver scars.

Artist Knifed in Limehouse Studio. Jealous Lover Leaves Rival for Dead.

She clenched her sheet tighter in her fist. Though she'd always preferred working in the front of the house, she'd spent enough time in a kitchen that she could estimate which sized knife could make cuts like this. Her throat went dry at the thought of someone plunging a blade into his back and side, again and again.

"You're awake."

She jerked at his low voice. He didn't turn around but continued to sketch on the canvas.

"Yeah. You working on my painting?"

"Not really. Messing around. I'm sorry if I woke you," he said absently.

She drifted closer, trying to look somewhere else, but she couldn't. His back was gorgeous, long and brown and strong, the scars doing nothing to detract from that. They only…made her hurt. To think of the pain he must have been in. How close he had come to dying.

But for those scars, you would have never met him. She shivered. Such a selfish thought, but she'd always been a selfish person. "You didn't wake me. Sorry I fell asleep." She'd been so tired after they'd had sex. She had a vague recollection of him readjusting her on the bed and tucking the blanket around her. They hadn't talked about a ban on sleepovers, but she assumed that went with the whole casual-affair thing. *Don't get attached because he didn't kick you out of his bed as soon as you both orgasmed.*

"It's nighttime," he said, as if that explained everything.

She came to stand behind him and placed his phone on the table next to him. "Your mom called."

"You talked to my mum?" That brought his head up. He looked over his shoulder, eyebrow cocked.

She grimaced. "Yes. So sorry. I was asleep, and the ringer sounds like mine, and I guess I answered it accidentally."

He picked up the phone, his lips compressed. "Don't apologize. She likes to call me at unpredictable times."

"She said you're always awake at this time." She paused. "Are you?"

He only grunted, which she guessed meant yes in Brooding Manspeak. "She must have gotten off her shift."

"Oh. What does she do?"

"Nurse," he said shortly. "Do you mind, I have to call her."

"Nope." She shook her head and tightened her hand on the sheet. "Go right ahead." To give him privacy, she turned and walked over to the window. Of course, there was nothing to look at but her own bedroom, so she feigned interest in the peeling paint around the windowsill.

"Mum," came his low voice. "You called?"

A burst of chatter came from the other end, audible even to Rana. She peeked over her shoulder to find him massaging his forehead. "Mum, she's…no, she's…Mum. Stop. No. She's…my model, okay?"

She returned to examining the paint, tucking away the twinge of annoyance that description caused. Stupid to feel annoyed. She hadn't *wanted* his mother to think they were sleeping together. Yes, she was his model. Okay. Fine.

"Is there something you needed?" A pause. "I'm good. As you can tell. Everything's good. Look, why don't I call you later. Ah…yes. I'll tell her. Thanks."

He ended the call and placed it on the table. "Mum says you have a lovely voice."

"That's nice of her." Rana walked back to him, hitching the sheet higher around her. Deliberately, she brushed her arm against his, raising goose bumps all over her.

Would there be a time when this man's body failed to arouse hers?

She felt a creeping fear she knew the answer to that. *You can't make me fall in love with you.*

He hadn't. He wouldn't.

"Is this an only-child thing? Parents calling in the middle of the night?"

"This is a parents-of-an-only-child-who-was-almost-killed-once thing," he said, and the bitterness of his honest response caught her off-guard. A muscle in his jaw ticked. "Sorry. When I said I had to call her back, I wasn't kidding. If she doesn't hear from me, she gets anxious."

Unsure of what to say, she leaned against his side. His muscles relaxed for an instant. Then he straightened, his body snapping to attention. She watched his eyes dart furiously from side to side, as if he was looking for something.

His shirt. Which he'd left on the floor of the bedroom.

Her heart almost exploding, Rana loosened her hold on the sheet and let it slip from around her body. "Since we're both awake, maybe we should work?" Without waiting for a response, she dropped the fabric over his shoulder and strode naked to the couch. She sat down and curled her legs up under her. It seemed to be the position he liked best.

He stared at her for a long minute. He was facing her now, but she could see the reflection of his back in the mirror. The sheet hid his scars.

He wasn't stupid. She knew that he knew what she'd done.

If she'd expected him to take the easy way out she had offered, she would have been surprised. He stood and stripped off the material covering him. Holding it in his hands, he walked over to her and dropped it in her lap. "I don't need this. You've already seen it all."

* * *

RANA WORRIED her lip between her teeth. She didn't move to conceal her nudity. Her nipples were perky, erect in the cool air of the room. "Don't be mad," she said quietly, instantly making him feel like a monster.

Scratch that. Like *more* of a monster. "I'm not."

Bone-deep tired, and not the kind that resulted in restful sleep, he dropped down on the couch next to her. The scars on his side were facing her. She could touch them, if she so desired.

"I'm not mad at you," he repeated, partially to reassure her, but mostly to remind himself. Rana wasn't the problem. She could never be the problem.

He was the problem, forever and ever, amen.

She took the sheet and smoothed it over her until it covered her thighs, her breasts. "Okay."

She didn't believe him. He rolled his lips in, trying to figure out how to reassure her when he could barely articulate anything anymore. "I don't like anyone seeing my back, but especially not you."

"Did you think I would find it unattractive?"

She'd asked him that before, and his answer hadn't changed. No. Not the way she meant, at least. He shook his head.

He didn't want to talk about this. But then he thought of the way she so sweetly trusted him with her body. The way she made goofy jokes to make him laugh. The way she'd just pretended to want to be naked so he wouldn't feel ill at ease.

The way he had inadvertently hurt her earlier in the evening because he couldn't do something as normal as take a girl he liked out to dinner. "You know what happened, right?"

"Someone stabbed you." She paused. "A lot."

The words crawled up his throat. Everyone who had been close to him had known what happened. The news articles had rehashed the story a million times. His therapist had encouraged him to talk about it, claiming he would feel empowered if he could choose the language to describe it himself. He'd scoffed.

But right now, right this minute, with Rana curled up next to him in his sad house, he wanted to tell her. A first. "I had a model. A sweet girl, Paige. I liked her a lot." He gave her a sideways glance. "We never… It wasn't like that. She was a student at uni. The modeling was purely a job."

She nodded, her expression open. "Her boyfriend was the dickhead who did this."

Of course she had managed to piece that much together, even if she hadn't read the articles.

"Yes." He thought back to the week or so before the attack. The things he could have said or done to avoid it. "I noticed a bruise or two on her wrists. One on her thighs. We had become friends, but I didn't think to ask her if she had a problem at home." His chest expanded and contracted. "I used to rent this space in a warehouse for my studio. I'd left the door open downstairs. I was looking through some sketches. Paige was wearing her robe, taking a break, playing with her phone. She saw him first, screamed.

"I was even bigger then. But I didn't have a chance to so much as turn around before he stabbed me the first time." He was aware of Rana sitting next to him, watching him with her deep brown eyes. But in his head, he was back in that cavernous warehouse, falling face forward, his nose smashing against the concrete hard enough to break it. After the first couple of wounds, his body had checked out, all of him going numb, even when the bastard had kicked him over to lie on his back. He'd played dead, but still his attacker had sliced his face.

He'd opened his eyes long enough to see the smaller man hoist Paige over his shoulder. As much as he'd wanted to, he couldn't move a single muscle, though he was certain she was dead or dying too. He'd discovered later her boyfriend had knocked her unconscious when she'd heroically tried to stop him from hurting Micah.

He came back to the present to find Rana's hand resting on his shoulder. Grounding him. "I don't remember much else of that day. Except I knew the wounds in my side and back were going to kill me, but I was insanely upset over this." He fingered the scar bisecting his lip and gave her a wry smile. "I was a vain man, you see. Quite proud of the way I looked. I could feel the blood running down my face."

"Your model…"

"Barely a scratch. She managed to escape and get help. Smart girl." Paige's eyes had been haunted when she'd stood in his hospital room and emotionlessly told him of how she'd manipulated her boyfriend so she could get someplace safe. The man had killed himself before the authorities could find him.

"Thank God for that. I don't know how you survived."

"Neither do the doctors. I should have died from the blood loss, if nothing else." He shrugged, still boggled himself. "They called me a miracle. If you didn't know, that guarantees more articles will be written about you."

She ignored the quip. Her fingers skated over his arm. "Would it be bad if I touched you?"

Touched his injuries, she meant. She'd brushed them before, brief glances while they were having sex. He hadn't been triggered, though he'd worried over that possibility. After a brief moment, he nodded, but caught her hand before she actually could.

"I don't have to," Rana said. It was amazing, how she knew exactly when he needed her to be aggressive and when he needed her to be gentle.

"No. Just…let me control it." He dragged her hand down, until her fingers rested against a scar. Holding his breath, he let go. He was braced for flashes of pain and fear, but there were none. Only the touch of her calloused fingers stroking over him.

He relaxed one muscle at a time. This wasn't different from any other time she explored him.

This is fine. This is good. He repeated those words in his head as she traced the white lines. "It must have hurt so much. I'm sorry."

No, he'd been in shock through most of the attack. The pain had come afterward. The pain of recovery, and then hearing the story rehashed, again and again. The pain of realizing his parents couldn't look at him without fear in their eyes because they were suddenly aware of his mortality in a way they never had been before. The pain of feeling like an outsider amongst his friends. The pain of secluding himself away, unable to share himself with anyone. "I didn't want you to see them because...well, like I said, I didn't want the memories to intrude and ruin our time together, but also because you're the only person who...who doesn't watch me and carefully gauge everything I do." His laugh was humorless. "God, everything's a *step*. A step forward or a step back. No one lets me simply exist anymore. Except you. You see me. Not what happened or what I need to do to get over what happened. Not the scars. Me."

Her fingers stilled against him.

Her voice was matter-of-fact when she spoke. "Micah. That's because you're so much more than a bunch of scars. You know that, right?"

A bunch of scars.

His attack, reduced to a few meaningless words. A weight he wasn't aware he was carrying lifted. They were only scars, were they? But his life had revolved around them for years. Even people who couldn't see his back looked at his face. They read the papers. They compared his old art to his new art. They studied him with a mixture of weariness and pity and sympathy. No one else thought they were only scars, some marks he had happened to pick up on his body over the course of many years on the planet.

You can't fall in love with me.

For the first time, he doubted his cocky reaction to her condition. How would he be able to stop himself?

Micah knew he should be unnerved, but he couldn't bring himself to be, not when the two of them were sitting together so comfortably. Besides, his feelings didn't matter.

Tomorrow. He would panic tomorrow.

He tugged her closer, coaxing her legs to stretch out until he could grasp her foot. He ran his thumb over the arch. He'd noticed the way she sighed when she kicked off her shoes after work.

Her nails were painted a cheerful turquoise with a frivolous white flower decorating the center of each big toenail. Micah focused on that flower, counting each petal as he savored the feel of her slender foot in his hand. Then he dug in, massaging.

She groaned and instantly slipped her other foot into his lap. "Be warned," she said playfully. "I'm on these puppies all day, every day, so if you don't want to get into a habit, you should probably stop right now."

He didn't mind a habit like that.

He pushed the thought out immediately. This wouldn't continue much longer. He'd realized that today, while going through his sketches of her. The preliminary work took him the longest. Another couple weeks, tops, and he wouldn't need her modeling for him at all.

Her stomach rumbled, and his head came up. He was used to missing meals, but Rana hadn't eaten anything for dinner after their aborted attempt to sit down for a meal.

"I ruined dinner," he said. He had quickly paid for the food and drinks after Rana had stormed out. He would have had the pub pack up their burgers, but he'd been eager to track Rana down.

She wiggled her feet, and he obligingly moved to her other foot, rubbing the tender flesh. "That's okay."

He looked at her. Her hair was tousled and her makeup long gone, save for a bit of black liner smudged under her eyes.

It was the middle of the night, she was naked, and he

had just bared his soul to her. This wasn't the time for them to recreate their failed attempt at dinner. And yet… "Get dressed. I want to take you somewhere."

*   *   *

MICAH DIDN'T MISS the way Rana eyed him skeptically as they slid into the cracked vinyl of the diner booth. He was a true hermit, but one night he had gone out wandering and stumbled across this restaurant.

"I've lived here all my life, and I didn't realize this place existed," Rana remarked. Her tone was carefully neutral.

He glanced around. He liked this booth, where he could sit with his back against the wall and study everything. It was a '50s-style diner, not due to theme, but because the decor had stopped being updated sometime in the '50s. The lighting was harsh and garish, everything painted a bubblegum pink or a bright yellow. A dented jukebox stood in the corner, its lights off. Somewhere in the back, an AM radio station was playing, giving traffic updates. Only two other patrons sat at the long counter.

"I think this place looks exactly like I always imagined an old American diner would look," he confessed. "Like a diner in *Back to the Future*, only more rundown."

She squinted at him. "You watched *Back to the Future*?"

"Why do you sound so surprised? We do get American movies in England. Plus, I visited America often enough. *Back to the Future* was a staple amongst my cousins."

"I'm not surprised English people have seen *Back to the Future*. I'm surprised you have. You're so…"

"What?"

"Artistic?" she ventured.

He was equal parts amused and insulted. "Are you calling me pretentious?"

Rana wrinkled her nose. Wearing a gigantic sweatshirt of his, with her hair in a high ponytail, she looked so cute it hurt. "Not pretentious. Okay. Maybe a little pretentious. You don't seem like the type to watch eighties movies."

"You Americans think anyone with an English accent is pretentious."

"Hey, like you reminded me, you're an American too."

He sniffed. Loudly. "I used to go to the movies quite a bit. Having an appreciation for art does not mean you automatically condemn all other forms of media."

"Yeah, yeah." She picked up the plastic menu and skimmed it. "So what you're saying is I get to pick a movie for us to go to and you won't be all snooty about it…even if it is a cheesy horror flick?"

He opened his mouth, but stopped. She had called it—he had always been a bit judgmental of certain films, often avoiding the big-budget blockbusters for smaller, independent movies. Like everything else in his life, he hadn't gone to a movie in years. He imagined sitting in a theater now, his arm around Rana as she squealed and burrowed closer to him.

Micah didn't care what movie she picked. He wouldn't dare criticize it. As long as she was there.

He was saved from having to articulate that when the waitress came by and gave them a bored nod. "What can I get you two?"

"Ah…" Rana looked down at the menu. "Waffles? With extra whipped cream please. And a glass of orange juice."

The waitress turned to him, and he balked. He usually

only got coffee here, but it seemed rude to do that while Rana was eating. "Coffee, black. And the same, please."

"Oh my God," she whispered as the woman poured his coffee and then left. "You're right. It's such an old-timey diner. She was popping gum *and* apathetic."

He had to smile, and he didn't miss the way her gaze dropped to his lips. She didn't make a big deal out of it, but he noticed that she liked amusing him. Made sense. He was growing addicted to that peal of laughter she rolled out.

She moved the menus to the side of the table. "I hope you're going to tell me the food here is amazing."

"I have no idea if the food is good or not," he said. He was fond of this place because it was like being around people without being around anyone. Normalcy he could tolerate. "It's quiet and there's no one here. That's all I care about."

They were silent for a few minutes. Rana fiddled with a napkin before glancing up at him. "The pub was a mistake."

Micah cocked his head. "What?"

"The pub was a mistake. I should have picked a place less like something from your past. That wasn't crowded." She nodded at the diner. "You have no memories attached to a place like this, I bet."

"I don't know what you mean."

"Uh-huh." Her tone made it clear she didn't believe him. "Well, I'm sorry about that. I should have thought about it."

She was apologizing to him? When he was the problem? Unacceptable. He wrapped his hand around his mug to disguise its shaking. "You should have been a psychology major."

She chuckled, but it carried a tinge of bitterness. "Oh, God no. As my mother will so fondly remind everyone, I barely graduated high school. No majors for me."

It didn't take a genius to pick up on Rana's strained relationship with her mother. "Do you regret not going to college?"

"Not really. I was so terrible at sitting still in school, my parents had me tested me for ADD. Negative, by the way. Which I think only made my mom sadder, because to her that meant I was just flighty and dumb."

"You're neither of those things." Thanks to the attack, he'd spent more than his share of time with people who presumably understood brains and how they worked. When he said she was brilliant, he meant it. She had an uncanny grasp of human nature.

She lifted her shoulder. "Anyway, I barely made it through high school. My dad died not long after graduation."

"I'm sorry." His chest tightened to think of his big, gregarious father dead. He may not be able to live near his parents right now, but he couldn't imagine them not in the world.

"It's okay. It was a while ago. But with him gone I knew my mother would need help. Both of my sisters were planning on higher education. And I…I adore that restaurant." She gave him a vaguely sheepish smile, as if she were confessing something shameful. "I like waiting tables. I like talking to everyone who comes in and making sure they have a good time. The restaurant being one-third mine is like an added benefit, not the main reason I work there. If we closed tomorrow, I'd go be a waitress somewhere else."

"There's nothing wrong with that."

Her smile grew brittle. "You know when someone says they were the first person to go to college in so many generations? I was the first person in three generations *not* to go to college."

Academics had been important in his family, but his father had tempered his mother's tendency to push him. Papa was a teacher by profession, but if he'd had his way, he would have spent his entire life surfing and chatting with tourists. He'd been happy to have a son who wanted to explore art.

Rana shifted. "Most of my extended family thinks I'm cashing in on the family business and coasting through, not working at all."

"Coasting?" He was vaguely insulted on her behalf. "I've seen how physically tired you are every day. I can't believe you aren't mentally exhausted as well."

"Eh. They don't get that. Education's like a..." she made a helpless gesture, "...like an asset in my family. So of course I get flack for not having it."

"I tried to get an art degree," he confessed. "I quit after a year to focus on painting full-time. I suppose I have no assets either."

Her smile grew stronger. "You have plenty of assets. I mean, honey. Really, that ass alone."

"I could say the same," he growled, her silliness awakening a frivolousness he'd thought long dead. "Your buttocks are worth two diplomas, at least."

The waitress chose that moment to arrive with their food, her face carefully impassive. Micah avoided looking at Rana, certain she was watching him with dancing laughter in her eyes over what the older woman may have inadvertently overheard.

The waitress placed two plates with waffles and mounds of dripping whipped cream in front of them and left without a word.

Rana unwrapped her silverware from the napkin. "That's what my family says," she responded lightly. "At least I'm pretty."

Micah knew he should turn the conversation to more shallow topics. They were getting in far too deep. Yet he couldn't stop. He could tell himself he merely wanted to learn more about Rana to aid his painting her, but that was a stone-cold lie. "You have more going for you than your ass."

"Says the man who wants to paint my ass."

Her words remained joking, but he caught the bite under them. "I may not have the clout I once did, but I could make a few phone calls and find supermodels who would be happy to pose for me. For free."

Her eyes narrowed, and her fingers tightened over her knife. "Your arrogance is showing, Micah."

When he chose a model, Micah did so only partially on looks. The rest of his selection was based on some mysterious combination of qualities he couldn't begin to verbalize. "My point is that I didn't want you to pose for me because you have a pleasing face and body." He leaned over the table and tucked a lock of her hair behind her ear. "I wanted you to pose for me because you're you. You have this…intriguing mix of good and naughty. Silly and sexy."

She froze as he touched her, her eyes deep and soft and wary, as if she wanted to believe him but couldn't. "Good?

I'm not a good person," she blurted out.

His lips turned up. "Okay."

"I'm serious." She shook her head, suddenly looking upset. "You know that, right?"

She was serious. "No. I don't know that." She wasn't a good person? He had seen the worst of humanity, the very bitter dregs.

Rana was so far away from that, it was laughable.

"I'm shallow and vain and blunt and flighty. I've slept with more than my share of men. I…" She looked down at her knife.

She could have been describing him, before the attack had changed him. He'd been all of those things. Shallow, vain, blunt, something of a player with women. Only people had praised him for those qualities. "What?"

"Nothing."

"Tell me."

Her voice was so low, he had to lean forward to hear her. "I almost slept with my baby sister's boyfriend."

He absorbed her confession. Did she honestly think he would tsk at her and walk away, certain she was a terrible human being? "Why?"

Rana didn't look at him, but scraped some of the melting whipped cream off the waffle. "Why what?"

"Why did you almost sleep with your sister's boyfriend?"

"There's no good reason—"

"Certainly there could be. Why?"

Her cheeks puffed out, and she exhaled so hard her hair fluttered. "I knew the asshole was cheating on her, and I didn't think she would listen to me. I set it up so she would walk in on us. I didn't sleep with him." Her lips compressed. "But I can't promise I wouldn't have. I was panicked. Not thinking straight."

"That must have…strained things between you two."

"Devi's super forgiving, the jerk." Rana forced a smile. "She said she understood why I did what I did. Now she's in a great relationship with someone else and incredibly happy. But, yeah, it made things kinda awkward for a while."

He considered what he knew of Rana. "You're a fixer."

"What?"

He took a sip of his bitter coffee. "You're a fixer. You like fixing things for people. Keeping everyone happy." Even as he said the words, he experienced a sinking sensation in his belly.

God, she wasn't trying to fix him, was she? That was a lost cause. What if her emotions became engaged and…

Then you'll end it.

She gave a short laugh. "Yeah, okay. That's better than calling me an impulsive moron."

"Maybe your actions were a bit impulsive," he began.

"My life was a bit impulsive," she interrupted, so much self-loathing in every word, he scowled. He didn't like anyone hating her. Even her. "I've always looked before I leapt. And that time, I almost irreparably damaged my relationship with my family." She shook her head. "Anyway. I learned my lesson. I've been working hard at changing myself. For the better, you know?" Her eyes glimmered. "I ask myself, what would Old Rana have done? And then New Rana does the opposite."

I dress like this for me because I like it. If I didn't like it so much, I would have been able to trash my wardrobe when I trashed everything else about myself.

One of the many puzzle pieces that made up this complicated woman slotted into place. "Is that why you haven't slept with a man in a year? Because it's what Old Rana would have done?"

Her flinch was slight. "Not exactly." Her words were halting. "I always liked men, keeping it casual. And then I saw my sister fall in love and...I don't know. Suddenly I wasn't happy with what I had. I wanted permanency."

"Marriage."

"That's what everyone else interpreted it as, especially my family. I wouldn't be opposed to getting married. But really I want love." Her tone grew defensive. "No one thinks it's weird when a playboy wants to settle down. This isn't so different."

He'd been something of a playboy. Maybe he would have gotten to the point where he'd wanted to be reformed, if the attack hadn't thrown a wrench in his whole life. "I don't think it's weird."

She played with her fork. "Since Old Rana wasn't so good at the whole dating-a-guy-more-than-twice thing, I figured I needed to change my methods to get the perfect man. No going out to clubs, no partying, exactly one date a week."

Did she hear how wistful she sounded? He didn't like clubs or parties, but Rana was a social butterfly.

He wanted to poke at all the things she'd said. What made up the perfect man? Who was defining that perfection, her or her family?

He couldn't though. He didn't have the right.

She shook her head ruefully. "I honestly think I would

respond to my dating profile username as well as I would my real name right now."

"What is it? Your username."

"QueenofHearts," she mumbled, and then shot him a mock glare. "It's because of my name, okay?"

He bit the inside of his cheek to keep from smiling. "Does your name mean Queen of Hearts?"

She brightened, her mood changing quicksilver fast. As always, he found her unpredictability utterly fascinating. Strange, and fascinating. "Yesssss," she hissed.

"What?"

"You walked right into that. You've asked this desi girl what her name means." She pointed her fork at him. "Strap yourself in, sir. There's a story. There's always a story."

His fingers itched to grab a napkin and pencil and sketch her expressive face. Every day he grew more frustrated with her dictate not to paint her above the neck. He was certain he could do a million portraits of her and never duplicate the same expression. "Strapped in."

She cleared her throat dramatically. "Thirty-something years ago, a beautiful baby girl was born…"

"Thirty-two years ago?"

"Thirty-*something* years ago, a beautiful baby girl was born. She was gorgeous, and totally did not look like a scrunched-up turtle gnome, à la most newborns."

He found himself leaning forward, hanging on to her words. "Of course."

"Her mother wanted to name her Rani. *Rani* means queen. But some fool at the clerk's office made a typo on the birth certificate, and changed that i to an a. Now, the baby's father, he was tickled pink over the accident. Because you see, the stunning infant happened to have a nasty temper, and a forceful, demanding, aggressive personality. One meaning of *Rana* is…king."

Micah laughed, a harsh bark. Smiling felt odd to him, laughing even more so. What spell had she cast over him? "Queens can be as aggressive as kings," he felt compelled to point out. "Haven't you played chess?"

"Stop interrupting."

"Sorry."

Rana's eyes danced. "After much debate, the father persuaded the mother to leave the name, because then the child could claim all the titles of royalty. Rana it was, though they called her Rani when she was young. The end."

He cocked his head at her choice of words. "Why only when you were young?"

"What?"

"Why was Rani only a pet name when you were small?" To his great chagrin, one of his aunts still called him by the childhood nickname she'd dubbed him with. "Mikey" wasn't so precious on a grown man.

She shrugged, as if it didn't matter. "Well, my dad called me that, off and on, until he passed away. I guess, as I grew up, everyone else decided I wasn't ladylike enough to be a Rani."

I'm shallow and vain and blunt and flighty. I've slept with more than my share of men…

He sat back against the cracked red vinyl, attempting to control his abrupt flash of anger. Not at her. With everyone who had ever made her feel like she was anything less than the generous, warm, sweet woman she was.

She called herself QueenofHearts, but he doubted she

considered herself—or at least not Old Rana—worthy of the title. Which was ridiculous. She shouldn't have to become someone else to live up to some idealized feminine alter ego. Hell, if she wished it, he would call her queen right now, as she was.

His queen.

Idiot. You're not in a position to be anyone's idea of a prince consort.

Unable to keep completely silent, he spoke up. "Old or new or king or queen, I think you're exceptional the way you are." He wished his voice could be less gruff. She deserved tenderness, not his clumsy, borderline-growled compliments.

You're so much more than a bunch of scars.

Micah didn't entirely believe those words, but to hear someone say them was a gift. He wanted her to know she was more than whatever she called herself.

Rana stilled, her eyes deep, dark pools. "Thanks, Micah." She cleared her throat, glancing away. "Anyway, that's the origin of QueenofHearts." Her smile was small, but genuine. "Shorter answer to your question: no, it's not technically my name, but it's undoubtedly easier than KingofHeartsHeyFunnyStoryBro, which would have required I transcribe this whole explanation into a profile. I couldn't bank on the perfect man caring enough to read it."

Then he's not the perfect man for you. The perfect man for her would be captivated by her explanation.

Again, he bit back the words he truly wanted to say. It wasn't his place to tell her how to run her personal life. It especially wasn't his place to tell her how to find a mate. His voice was hoarse when he spoke. "It's excessively clever, your choice of a handle."

"It's been a long year. I had to amuse myself somehow."

"Searching for the right man is hard work," he said, ignoring the pang in his chest. And because he knew he needed the brutal reminder, he added, "I must be quite the detour."

Her eyes were suddenly unreadable. "You're my—"

"What?" he asked, when she cut herself off.

"Nothing."

"No. Say it."

"You're my muffin."

He raised an eyebrow. "I'm your… I beg your pardon?"

She exhaled. "When you're on a diet and all you want is a muffin? Like, you would destroy a muffin, you need it so bad. So you have one. And promise to get back on the wagon as soon as you finish." Her jaw hardened. "I shouldn't have you. New-and-improved me shouldn't want you in my bed, and I shouldn't want you to paint me. But I do. So you're my muffin."

She fell silent and sawed a piece of her waffle, sticking it in her mouth. Not ten minutes ago he'd been worrying over the possibility they could be falling for each other. What a difference a few heartbeats could make. Because now he despised the way she was speaking about their relationship like it had an expiration date.

Not a relationship.

That's right. He was the terrible-for-her treat she was indulging in before she went back to a life of turnips and peas. How charming. Micah's jaw tightened, but he said nothing. What could he say?

She poked at her waffle. "This tastes like shit."

His lip twitched. How was she able to make him smile even when he was feeling melancholy? "Does it?"

"You're not going to eat?"

He looked down at his soggy waffle. "I don't really enjoy eating." The words were calm. He wasn't sure why he said them. Because he wanted her to know how imperfect he was? Because she'd made herself vulnerable to him, and he wanted to put them on equal footing?

She wasn't staring at him with pity, so he continued in that same detached voice. "It's common amongst trauma victims. It's not that I'm trying not to eat. I just don't have much of a desire for food. That's why I have the protein shakes." He hesitated. "Your cinnamon rolls were an anomaly. They were delicious."

She sampled her whipped cream and nodded decisively. "I'll make you some more tomorrow, then."

He ought to refuse. She wouldn't be around long enough for him to get used to someone making him sweets. Yet he found himself taking a sip of his coffee, hoping she took his silence as encouragement. He might be nothing more than her *muffin,* but he would take whatever she gave him, for as long as he could have it.

CHAPTER 18

Nearly nodding off in the shower was probably a good sign Rana needed to get more sleep.

She yawned as she turned off the water and got out. Micah's fault. She laid the blame for her current exhaustion solely at his big feet, and not because his insomnia kept her awake. Really, what red-blooded girl would want to sleep when the alternative was tussling in the sheets with a sexy, passionate lover? Not a one.

Rana swiped her hand over the steamed-up mirror, though she didn't need her reflection to tell her she had a silly smile on her face. It had become a permanent fixture since the night she and Micah had spent at the diner a couple of weeks ago.

Her days had settled into a rhythm: wake up, creep across their lawns to her house, get ready, go to work, come home, go to Micah's, fall asleep on his naked chest. In his bed. On his couch. A couple times on the floor. On her days off, she ran her errands or dealt with her other obligations and then came back early so she could stretch out for him in the sunlight pouring into his studio.

"Routine" and "predictable" weren't words Rana had ever been comfortable with. Boredom had always been her archenemy, something to act out against, but she couldn't so much as work up a whiff of worry. In lots of ways, Micah kept her on her toes.

Like the way he'd surprised her last night, when he'd proposed they go out for a late dinner. She'd expected the diner. Instead, he'd driven her to a pretty new Italian restaurant on the other side of town. Rana blotted her face, her smile taking on a dreamy bent.

"The online reviews all said it's quiet on weekdays," he explained gruffly, once they were seated in the near-empty restaurant, and she expressed some surprise at the venue. "And I never was a fan of Italian food, before."

Before his attack, that meant. So the site held no particular memories for him that might intrude on their time together. Her heart had clenched painfully at his quiet admission, but she buried her head in the menu, refusing to let him see it, lest he mistake compassion for pity.

A date. It had totally been a date. Neither of them had labeled it, but she didn't think either of them would have been able to claim that it hadn't been a date. After all, it couldn't get any more date-y than an Italian restaurant. All they'd needed was a chubby man with a mustache serenading them while they shared a plate of pasta *Lady and the Tramp* style.

Dates. Sleepovers. Hell, what was next, him clearing out a drawer for her? Maybe letting her store some tampons under his bathroom sink?

A relationship. This was morphing so fast. Unfortunately, somewhere between him showing her his scars and taking her to a tiny Italian restaurant, Rana had lost the ability to give a fuck about protecting her heart.

This will end poorly.

I don't care.

You're being wholly irresponsible.

I don't care.

He was supposed to be a temporary treat—

I don't care I don't care I don't caaaaaaaaaare.

She dried off her body, the terrycloth feeling too rough against skin that had grown used to Micah's hands. It was like she couldn't leave him without immediately missing him.

Soon. As soon as she got dressed, she would head over there, a promise that had her picking up her pace as she left the bathroom and grabbed underwear from her dresser. A hopeful glance out the window was met with disappointment—the studio was empty except for the huge canvas he was working on. *Her* canvas. Micah was careful to face it against the wall when he wasn't working, aware of her propensity to peek.

He didn't want her to see it, he said, until it was done, which she respected. She didn't like it, because, holy crapballs, she was curious as fuck, but she respected it.

She didn't have to be in to work until the late afternoon today, which meant they would probably spend at least a couple hours in the studio. He would paint, and they would talk. The focus that had so entranced her when she'd first caught sight of him all those months ago was magnified tenfold now that he was working on her painting. Sometimes he would stop and frown, but not once did she catch even a hint of the frustrated anger that used to grip him.

If a little voice inside her head whispered he didn't seem to exactly need her there for modeling purposes as much as he had in the beginning, she ignored it. She reveled in being naked in front of him. There was something dreamy and otherworldly about those few hours, and she wasn't in a hurry to lose them.

After their session was done, maybe he would want to hang out. There was a park not far from their homes. They could take a nice walk. There were usually lots of puppies gamboling about. Was Micah a dog person? She imagined he would be.

Date. Totally a date. Puppy watching is such *a date.*

She drew on her jeans. So it was a date. So the line between boyfriend and employer/lover/bad-for-her treat had faded long ago. So. What.

A tiny part of her stood back, aghast, as Old Rana rode the surge of passion with reckless disregard. The rest of her was buckled in for the ride.

Her doorbell sounded, and she pulled her head free of the T-shirt. Who was that? She'd told Micah when they'd parted ways around dawn she would come right over after napping and showering, and she wasn't expecting anyone else.

By the time Rana emerged from her bedroom, the person at the door had graduated to pounding. Slightly alarmed, she jogged downstairs and peeked through the peephole, her frown transforming into a surprised smile at the sight of Micah. She opened the door. "Hey, what are y—mmmph."

His mouth covered hers, cutting off her speech.

He walked her backwards, kicking the door closed behind him. His hand sank into her wet hair, and he tugged at the strands, tilting her head so he could get better access.

Her heart went pitter pat. His kisses were pure romance.

The wall pressed against her back, his hard body holding her there. He broke off the kiss long enough to run his lips down her neck, planting tiny love bites exactly in the spots he knew made her crazy with lust.

"I'm not complaining, but what are you doing here?" she asked, breathless.

His teeth scraped over the sensitive flesh below her ear. "If it's not obvious, we are definitely in trouble."

"I was coming over, Micah."

He nipped her again, sharper, like a reprimand. "You were taking too long."

That pitter pat sped into a full gallop. She couldn't halt her pleased smile. He missed her! Too. Cute. "I said I would be over by noon."

"That's too long. Come now."

Though she thrilled at his words, she reluctantly levered him away. "I haven't even put my makeup on. Let me go do that."

He captured her chin between his thumb and forefinger and studied her, his dark eyes missing nothing. "I want to fuck you and paint you no matter what you put on your face."

She bit back a laugh at his blunt honesty. "Luckily I don't put on makeup so men will want to fuck or paint me. I feel naked if I don't have at least my eyeliner on."

She waited for him to give her some bullshit about how he was painting her naked and honesty and vulnerability, blah blah, but as always, Micah didn't react like so many other men she'd been with. He looked displeased, but she knew it was over the delay and not over her love of makeup. He gave a short nod and stepped away. "Fine. Go do whatever you have to do. But hurry up."

She rolled her eyes and turned to the stairs. "It'll take as long as it takes, Micah Hale. I don't rush you when you're painting. My face is the finest canvas of all."

"That it is," he surprised her by agreeing. "However, I have lunch spread out on my kitchen table, and it'll get cold."

"You made us lunch?" It was like the guy was trying to figure out ways to claw into her mushy insides.

"I bought lunch," he corrected. "Mostly ready-mades from the grocery. But I did warm them before I came over."

Why that should touch her, she wasn't sure. He had so little interest in food, and between the restaurant and her own love of puttering around the kitchen, her life had always revolved around it.

It was like a vampire forcing down a sandwich so his mortal bride wouldn't feel out of place.

Stop. Just...stop.

"I'll be as quick as I can."

"We can heat them up again." Micah's attention turned to the wall. Absently, he righted a framed picture of her family. They spent far more time at his place than hers, but when he was here, he seemed vaguely fascinated with her décor, her clutter, her colorful cushions and throws. "I would never advocate rushing a work of art."

Yup. That goofy smile was here to stay. She had to consciously banish it so she could apply her lipstick. A light rose today. He liked her various shades of lipsticks as much as she did, though she had a feeling he was always more interested in her lips than the color.

Despite her words, she could do her makeup in under three minutes flat, the result of a lifelong love affair with cosmetics and a chronically late personality, so it didn't take her long to put her face on. She brushed her hair, examined herself quickly, and then thundered back down the stairs. Micah wasn't in the foyer.

"Micah?"

"In here."

She cocked her head, trying to decipher the strange note in his voice, and walked to her living room. She stopped when she realized what he was crouched in front of.

The large painting had been delivered a couple days ago, carefully wrapped. He'd stripped the brown paper off a corner.

Oh dear.

Embarrassment shot through her. "Excuse you, what are you doing?" she asked, mortification making her voice high-pitched. "Get away from that."

"I was curious. And perhaps annoyed at you," he said absentmindedly, his gaze locked on the corner he had unveiled. "It's silly, isn't it? For me to feel like I should have some say on the artwork you purchase for your home?"

She bit her lip, though she knew it would smudge her newly applied lipstick. "It was delivered last week, but I wasn't sure where to hang it." It couldn't go in her living room. That would prompt questions from her family when they came to visit. Her bedroom, maybe…but then she feared it would cause too much heartache if the two of them went their separate ways.

"You didn't say you bought anything that night." All that was visible was a brown elbow and a swatch of yellow from the background, but she supposed he didn't need anything else to identify something he had painted.

"I…didn't want you to know. You would have told me it sucked," she grumbled.

"I wouldn't have."

"I've created better," she intoned in a deep voice, in a fairly decent imitation of him.

A faint smile crossed his face, though he continued to fixate on the painting. With a flick of his wrist, he stripped away more of the paper, so the entire scene was revealed.

She moved behind him so she could look at the couple entwined together, feeling that same gut punch she'd experienced the first time she'd looked at it in the gallery. Lord, had that been almost a month ago?

Need. Desire. Fear.

"It's so beautiful," she whispered, though she wasn't sure why. They weren't in a gallery.

"You didn't have to buy it. I would have given it to you." His voice was curiously flat.

"I didn't want to deal with your whining over how you're no good anymore."

His head bowed. "My whining."

"Yeah. Besides, I don't mind splurging for quality, you know?" She crossed her arms over her chest. "This was worth every penny."

"More than one review of this past show said the paintings were overpriced in terms of quality."

"You shouldn't be reading reviews of your work," she chided. "That's going to get in your head."

"I never did before." He shrugged. "But then, I—"

"I was better before," she finished for him, also in a deep, clipped voice. "Well, I don't believe that." She gestured to the canvas, though he wasn't looking at her. "This is goddamn brilliant, Micah."

He tilted the painting toward him. "You don't have to placate me."

"I'm not." She searched for words. It was heartbreaking that any person as talented as he was could think they were subpar.

Heartbreaking and maddening. She wished she could have a tenth of the brains and talent it took to make something like this. "Maybe you aren't doing the same thing that you did before, but just because it's different doesn't mean it isn't good. I don't know much about art. But this makes me…" she clenched a fist and brought it up to her heart, though it seemed like a foolish gesture, "…feel."

Gently, he leaned the painting against the wall. Slowly, he came to his feet. Which made his sudden, explosive turn all the more startling. He grasped her around the waist.

The room spun. A second later, the soft cushion of the couch cradled her, absorbing her weight and his. He pressed himself against her. "*You* make me feel," he rasped, and covered her mouth with his.

She gave him easy access, her heart pounding even as she thrilled and feared his words. Common emotions now around him.

Had she ever desired someone like this? She ran her hand over his head, removing the tie that held his hair back. She smoothed her fingers through the rough silk. This was quickly becoming one of her favorite sensations, his hair dragging over her skin.

She pulled away. "Micah, hang on…"

His teeth bit at her neck, his tongue soothing the nip. "Why?"

Yeah, why? Rana couldn't remember what she'd been about to say, not with his hand under her shirt and sliding up her side. He strummed his finger along her spine, making her arch her back. Unhooking her bra took a second.

The man was damn good with his fingers. They coasted under her loosened bra, over her breast, and tugged at her nipple. "You're always like this for me," he grunted. "Hot as fuck."

She couldn't deny the accusation. All he had to do was look at her in a certain way, and she'd give him whatever he wanted.

His mouth on her neck moved south, toward her cleavage. Rana tipped her head back, ready to forget lunch, the entire afternoon, maybe everything she had to do that week. Hell, was there anything she had to do that could take priority over this?

She was so lost in the haze of desire, it took her a minute to realize the person calling her name was not Micah. The voice was far too high-pitched to be Micah.

Nope. That was definitely not Micah. That was her mother.

She froze under Micah, who hadn't seemed to hear the other woman, judging by his busy hands. She immediately turned from pulling him toward her to pushing him away. Holy shit. Holy shit. Holy shit.

Not her mother. It couldn't be. Was this a nightmare?

If it was, then the nightmare was her fucking life.

Always attuned to her, Micah sensed the change in her and stiffened.

"My mother," she whispered in his ear. Not because she actually thought she could get away without her mother hearing her, but because she couldn't manage much more than a whisper at the moment.

She could say this much for Micah—he was fast, launching off her like she was on fire. Rana sat up and struggled to get her clothes put to rights. Micah tried to help, but both of their hands fumbling over her body only meant she barely got her bra re-hooked and the cups back over her boobs before her mother appeared in the doorway.

The older woman froze, her eagle eyes taking in the two of them. They were sitting on opposite ends of the couch, but Micah's hair was down and tousled, his lips swollen. Rana could feel how hot her face was. Her shirt was askew. Her breasts were popping out.

None of that mattered. Because her mother could find her and a man playing mahjong, and she'd assume that Rana had been fucking him not two seconds prior.

For good reason. Rana had lived at home until she was twenty-two and Devi was done with high school, and Rana couldn't count the number of times this scene had been acted out—her mother walking in on her locked in an embrace with some good-looking guy.

Frustration and nerves running hot, Rana stood and locked her legs to keep herself steady. *Only this time it's your house. Your couch.*

Why did that not seem to matter?

"Mama," she said, her voice fainter than she would have

hoped. "What a surprise."

"I apologize. I didn't know you had…company." Her mother surveyed her tousled appearance before meeting her eyes. A chill ran up Rana's spine. Fuck it all, she knew that frigid disapproval. She'd seen it since puberty, had even grown accustomed to it, considered it a necessary price to pay for living life however she wanted.

That look had been absent for so long she'd forgotten how much it hurt. Guilt and regret and anger made Rana's hands shake. "I…uh…"

After a long, awkward moment, her mother continued stiffly. "Your door was open. You shouldn't leave it unlocked like that."

It didn't really matter if her door had been locked. Her mom had a key, as did her sisters. Any of them would walk right in whenever they felt like it. Standard practice. Ringing the bell first was optional in her family. "Yeah." Rana cleared her throat. "This is my…" Panic spurted through her. What was Micah? Was there a title that was safe?

They hadn't been able to call their date a date last night, so she sure as hell couldn't refer to him as her boyfriend. Lover or affair was out, unless she wanted to give her mother a heart attack. Rana tried to jiggle her bra strap unobtrusively, in the hopes her breasts might readjust themselves.

"Neighbor," she finished lamely. "Micah's my neighbor."

"Neighbor." Her mother said the word slowly, with a great deal of skepticism. Her gaze dropped to Rana's neck. Since Micah had just been scraping his teeth over her skin, no doubt there were visible marks there.

"Yes. A neighbor." Out of the corner of her eye, she saw Micah stiffen, but she was so consumed with calming her mother, she couldn't pay attention to him right now. "Micah, this is my mother. Mama...Micah."

Her mother scanned Micah, and Rana was certain she had judged him and found him wanting in that single sweep. To his credit, Micah was silent but dipped his head politely.

"Rana. Walk me to my car." Ice dripped off every word her mother uttered.

Of course. Mama did hate to shed blood indoors.

Micah stirred. "I'll go—"

"No."

"No." She and her mother spoke in unison.

"We'll only be a minute," Rana managed, struggling to keep her voice moderate. "Hang on."

She knew in her gut this was not going to be pretty. It was dumb, but she wanted Micah to console her after, tell her she was fine and her mother was wrong and everything would be okay. She needed that.

Silent as a mouse, Rana followed after her mother to the front door. They both stepped outside, and Rana closed the door.

It was her house. Her body. Her heart. She wasn't a child anymore, and she didn't have to listen to her mother or beg her approval.

None of those arguments were worth a damn when Mama turned on her heel and faced her, her words cracking across her nerve endings. "So this is why you wanted to stop looking for a husband? Because you are having an affair with this man?"

Rana let out a long, low breath. “He’s my neighbor—”

“I am not stupid.” Disappointment flashed in her eyes, and Rana felt about three inches tall. “How many times have I walked in on you with a boy? Since you were fifteen years old. I know that look on your face. For God’s sake, Rana.”

Funny her mother should invoke her teenage years, because she definitely felt like she was fifteen again. No, worse, because when she’d been fifteen, she hadn’t had any inkling of what it was like to have her mother’s respect.

Now she knew. She straightened up, for fear she would get down on her knees and beg her mother to be pleased with her again.

“When you said you wanted to settle down, I was so happy,” Mama said, not bothering to moderate the volume of her voice. “I figured you were done sowing these wild oats.”

Rana opened her mouth, intending to apologize, but instead all she said was, “If I was a man, you wouldn’t care about me sowing my wild oats.”

“You’re not a man. You’re a woman.”

“That’s dumb,” she muttered. “It shouldn’t make a difference.”

Silence for a second. Her mother clenched her jaw, hard. “It’s the way the world works.”

“Maybe it shouldn’t work like that.” *What are you doing? Diffuse the situation, don’t aggravate it.*

“Do you even want to get married, Rana?”

“I want love.” She heard herself, and it was like listening to a broken record. She’d said this so many times over the past year, but her mother hadn’t yet picked up on the distinction. Her mother cared about the big ceremony, the fancy wedding outfits, the license itself. Did she?

Not really.

She blinked. She didn't care about getting married at all. Sure, perhaps eventually. But all she'd truly wanted since she'd started this whole process was a guy she could come home to.

"Do you think you will have that with this man? This long-haired…" Her mother threw up her hands. "Is he even employed?"

"He's an artist," she said, her lips numb.

"An artist." Her mother shook her head in disbelief. "I put doctors in front of you, and you wouldn't even look at them, but you think an artist will make you happy?"

Rana could have pointed out that Micah had an income, but she knew that wasn't the point, and it wouldn't matter to her mother. Micah didn't have a steady job. He'd never gotten any kind of diploma. They hadn't discussed his parents' careers in-depth, so for all she knew, he could be missing that all-important successful gene.

Rana twined her fingers together, aware her mother was waiting for an answer. Micah wouldn't be able to give her love and forever. He wasn't suitable for a long-term relationship. He was her muffin. *The man you'd fuck, not the man you'd marry.*

That was the answer her mother was waiting for. "Maybe he could," she said, her voice strong and clear.

Wait. What?

Her mother looked as shocked as Rana felt. "What?"

The words fell from her lips, feeling so damn good she couldn't regret them. "Maybe he could make me happy."

"You are not serious."

A strange sense of calm descended on her, and she felt vaguely disassociated from her body. Like she was watching some stranger talk. "He's a good man. He really is. Kind. Funny. Gentle. His job title has nothing to do with that."

"Rana…"

"He's talented. He doesn't think he is, but he…is. Talented and passionate about his work."

Her mother shook her head, resignation deepening the lines around her mouth. "You aren't seventeen anymore. This isn't some boy on a motorcycle that you're claiming really is good underneath his tattoos and criminal record!"

"I've never brought home a man like that," she retorted, aware her temper was rising. "Never, not once. I might have dated them, I might have slept with them, but I never brought them home. Because I knew none of them would ever be good enough for you."

Her mother's eye twitched. "I think…"

"I've bitten my tongue," she rasped, unable to shut up. "I've gone along with everything you've said this year, haven't I? Looking for the man you decided would be perfect for me." A suitable man. What did that even mean?

"Because I know you can find someone good. A man who knows nothing about your past, one who would be happy to have such a pretty, lively girl as his wife."

Each word her mother said cut into Rana's heart like a knife, while bringing every single action she'd taken in the past year into sharp, glaring focus. *A man who knows nothing about your past.*

That's what she'd been doing. Searching for a man who would only know New Rana. A man who would never know the impulsive, overtly sexual drama queen Old Rana had been. Because if she wanted love, truly wanted it, she had to change. New Rana might be worthy of love from a good man, defined as whatever her mother said a good man was, but she had to hook him fast before her looks faded, because that was literally all Any Rana had going for her.

Or at least, that was the message she'd internalized. It wasn't true, though. Was it? "What's wrong with my past?"

Her mother's nostrils flared. "Rana. Do you think an eligible man wants a wife who has slept with so many men?"

All of the blood leached from her face, and she reeled back like she'd been slapped. Never had her mother come right out and said what they all knew she thought: that Rana had been judged a slut the second her mom had found her letting Gary Peters stick his hand up her shirt when she was thirteen.

Rana tried to swallow. Funny, she'd never minded anyone whispering about her fondness for men. She did mind her mother thinking she was the most disgusting thing in the world.

Like a piece of chewed-up gum. They'd had a rigid, awful neighbor who had told her daughters that, that men didn't want a piece of chewed-up gum.

She'd never felt that way, until this moment. Was this what her mother truly thought of her? After decades of constant disapproval, this shouldn't surprise her. It shouldn't cut her to her heart.

Except this was the woman who had given birth to her and cuddled her when she was a baby and braided her hair and raised her sisters, so yes. Yes, it hurt like nothing else could.

"How can you say that?" she whispered. "That wasn't necessary."

Regret spasmed across her mother's face, but Rana's chest was knotted with too much pain to care.

"I know." Her mother walked forward, and Rana braced herself, but she didn't touch her. That was a good thing. Rana wasn't sure if she would welcome a hug right now. "Rani..."

Rani. No, no, no. Her mother hadn't called her by the pet name since she was ten or so. No one had used it since her father had died.

A part of her yearned for the woman to say it again. *Tell me I'm your Rani, no matter what I do.*

Another part of her couldn't stand how it sounded on her lips. Wrong. Fake. Not her name. She was Rana.

"I apologize. Truly."

Rana didn't want an apology. She wanted to rewind time so she wouldn't have to hear her own mother call her worthless because she loved sex. She dug her nails into her palm, struggling to bring her riotous emotions under control.

"I... Don't you see I'm trying to help you?" Her mother's voice became wheedling. Pleading. "It's not too late. You're still young. This is the time. Didn't we talk about this? Your chance to change your life."

"Maybe I don't want to change my life. Maybe you decided I needed to change my life, and I went along with it because I was so desperate..." She'd been so hungry for love. She would have done anything for it. She could see that now, and her desperation staggered and shamed her.

Get married? Okay. Change herself? Sure. Follow an

arbitrary list of criteria she barely understood to find the perfect man? No problem.

"Parents know what's best for their children—"

That might work for parents who understood their children. Her mother didn't know *anything* about her. "I think you should leave."

Her mother hesitated, emotions playing over her face. Regret. Anger. Disappointment. Always the disappointment. Finally, she sighed. "Very well. You're too overwrought to discuss this properly."

Overwrought. Hysterical. Emotional.

She'd gone numb. Rana watched her mother walk away. Her chest hurt so hard she wondered how her heart could still pump.

As soon as she was able to move, she flung open her door and stormed inside, only to find Micah leaning against the wall in the foyer. His face was expressionless, his dark eyes shadowed.

She slammed the door shut and pressed up against it. Her breath was coming fast, and she was unable to moderate it. His thick brows snapped together, and he crossed to the door, grasping her shoulder. "Breathe, Rana."

She couldn't. It hurt too much.

But slowly, subtly, as he massaged her shoulder in a circular motion and breathed loudly and audibly—for her, she supposed—next to her, she managed to calm herself enough to speak. "I hate her," she sobbed, like a petulant child.

"You don't," he said quietly.

He was right. She didn't. She couldn't. "You don't know what she said to me."

"I heard."

Her head came up. “What?”

“Your door’s not that thick.” His face was harder than ever, unyielding. “I heard.”

“Oh God.” She considered all the things she and her mother had said, and felt a rush of shame. “We’ve never had a confrontation like that before. I mean, I knew deep down I was her disappointment. Her practice kid before she got it right. But she never looked at me like *that*.”

He stroked her shoulder, down her arm, linking their fingers together. Tears brimmed over her eyes, until she felt the splotch of wetness on her cheeks. Inhaling deeply, she fought to get herself under control, but it was of no use. “I used to imagine us one day getting into a fight, laying our feelings out. I imagined I would be so strong, you know? Like I thought I wouldn’t care what she thought about me at all.”

He tugged her closer. “Of course you would care.”

“I feel weak for caring.” The truth was dawning on her, and it was ugly. Had she truly paddled around behind her mother like a baby duck for the past year, craving her approval? Was that who she was now?

He tipped her chin up. With his thumbs, he wiped away her tears. “My parents have always thought the sun rose and set on me,” he said, bitterness coating every word. “For the last two years, all I see when I look at them is disappointment in who I’ve become.”

Rana swallowed, trying to see past her own pain to his. “I’m certain that’s not true.”

“No?” His lips compressed. “I put an ocean between me and my family so I wouldn’t have to see that disappointment anymore.”

"You—"

His tone was harsh. "I'm not saying this so we can talk about me. I'm just saying…I get why you let her talk to you like that. It's hard not to do everything in your power to make sure the people you love keep looking at you with approval. Instead of disappointment."

That sounded surprisingly insightful, actually. Too insightful. How had he been able to see that when even she couldn't? Her chest heaved. "I'm sorry."

"You're sorry?" He ran his hand over his head. He'd retied his hair, and she wished he hadn't. When he had it down, she could imagine she was seeing a part of him no one else did. Like he was hers. "You have no reason to be sorry."

She had so many reasons to be sorry. "The things she said about you…you can't take it personally. She doesn't know who you are." Her voice was scratchy.

He stilled. "She knows I'm no good for you long term. But we already knew that, didn't we?" His lips pressed together, so hard they made a white line. "I heard her. I also heard you. What you said about me."

"I couldn't not speak up," she whispered.

She'd gotten so good at reading his face. A necessity, because otherwise the man didn't emote.

There it was. A softening of his eyes, the relaxing of his mouth. "The things you said were…sweet. So sweet. But, Rana. Maybe…maybe we should reevaluate—"

"Micah." Her heart squeezed. No. No, no, no. Reevaluate? That word was dangerous. She'd been the dumpee and the dumper too many times not to know what was coming.

His Adam's apple bobbed. "That was your condition.

Right? We wouldn't fall in love with each other. Because it wouldn't work."

"You're not in love with me," she rushed out.

He took a step away, and it felt like the entire Atlantic Ocean had come between them. "It…it doesn't matter how I feel about you. You weren't going to fall in love with me."

She tried to force a laugh, but it sounded too much like a sob. "Wow, that's some ego you have, if you think I'm in love with—"

"Tell me you aren't." The words sliced through the air, cutting her off. "Tell me you felt nothing for me when you defended me to your mother just now. Tell me you don't love me, Rana."

She opened her mouth, knowing she was going to lie. Wanting to lie. *I don't.* That was all she had to say. Two words.

And she could go back to his arms. They could forget this awkward conversation, and she could strip naked for him again.

She wasn't in love with him. They hadn't known each other long enough to be in love with each other. They were too different. Neither of them was emotionally stable enough to fall in love.

Two. Words.

"Rana." The word was almost pleading. "Say it."

She had never begged a man, not since she was a young girl who didn't know any better. "Don't do this. Not now."

His forehead creased. He wasn't unaffected. She could see his pain in the way he held himself away from her, in the lines on his face, in the halting way he spoke. "It was your condition. So we could keep this temporary…"

"Would it be so bad?" she blurted out.

He searched her eyes. She waited, breath caught. Then he devastated her with a single word. "Yes."

Well. This hurt too much for her not to be in love with him.

Stupid, foolish, impulsive Rana. This is why I tried to improve you, New Rana chided her. *What kind of dummy falls in love with a fling?*

"I can't give you what you need," he was saying. "You deserve—"

"Stop." She wanted to back away from him, but there was nowhere to go. She was already pressed against the front door, and they were in her house. She couldn't run away from him. "Please don't say I deserve better."

His face was drawn. "It's the truth."

"Uh-huh." She was perilously close to losing it, and she couldn't cry in front of him. Not the way she wanted to, in deep, racking sobs, face down in her bed. "Okay. So. We're done then."

"We have to be."

They didn't have to be, she thought viciously. They'd been happy. This was hurting them, because he was being a butthead.

He's only sticking to the condition you put in place.

Nope, sorry, this was not the place or time for logic. "So, um. You don't need me to model anymore?" The question was almost too desperate, but she needed everything spelled out, every ambiguity cleared up.

He swallowed. "I think I have everything I need. I'll give you a check."

"You can stick it in my mailbox." He knew where that

was. Anything so she didn't have to see him when he came marching over with the reminder of their time together. Would she even be able to cash that check?

Yes, damn it. She would. She'd cash that little bitch of a check and she'd spend every dime on all the silly, frivolous things that made her happy.

His eye twitched. "Very well, then."

She nodded. "Right," she managed. "Awesome." She focused on a point over his shoulder and forced another smile, this one utterly fake and wooden. "Thanks for the sex. And the gig. It was a cool experience."

"When the painting's done, I—"

"I'd rather not see it right now. Maybe later. I don't know."

He hesitated but didn't push it. So solicitous. What a prince. "Of course."

She couldn't do this anymore. She groped behind her until she found the doorknob, and then jerked open the door, standing aside. "You can go."

He took a step, then another, his gaze fixed on her. "You know this isn't easy for me," he said hoarsely. "You're the first woman I've slept with, the first woman I've painted, since the attack. You're the first taste of…normalcy I've had in two years."

Oh, the irony. Rana Malik had had men call her a wild child, a whirlwind, crazy, and slutty, but not one had ever called her normal. She cleared her throat, trying to swallow down her bitterness. "Maybe it'll get easier. Like, the next girl you dump for her own good, you'll barely blink."

He came closer, until they were standing side by side in the doorway, and for a second she thought he was going to kiss her.

She couldn't stand that. Couldn't stand the thought of him brushing his lips over hers and then walking away. She pressed her head against the doorframe, leaving him more than enough room to pass.

A muscle in his jaw twitched. "I don't want anyone else."

She quelled the hopeful leap her heart gave. "That's a fucking lie." Oh, now she was strong. Or at least she sounded strong. Same thing.

"I'm not ending this because I want to fuck other women," he growled, a hint of anger replacing the sorrow and, oh God, pity in his expression.

"Maybe not now, but you will." She nodded so hard, her hair bounced. "You will, because that's what you did before, right? When you were 'normal.'" She made air quotes around the word. "You fucked women and you painted them, and you sold your paintings for tons of dough and you lived in a golden age where everything was perfect."

His teeth ground together. "You're being flip."

"No, I'm basically repeating everything you've said. Your life was perfect. And now it's not. You'll be okay, though." She clenched her teeth. "You had me, right? You said it: I made you feel. I was your first taste of normalcy. Like…therapy. I think you called them *steps* once. That's what I was. A step." A step on the path to moving on from what had happened to him.

You used him for your own purposes too, her conscience whispered, cooling her hurt anger before it had the chance to burst into flames. *Remember the muffin? You don't get to be so self-righteous.*

Ironically, the fact that her hands were unclean only made her madder.

"*You* weren't the step, it was…" He trailed off, and a mask descended over his face. "Yes. Fine. You were a step."

Hurt washed over her, another layer of it. So much pain it didn't even matter anymore. She raised her shoulders. "You'll sleep with someone else. You'll paint someone else," she said, needing to hear the words.

"I'll sleep with someone else. I'll paint someone else." He recited the words flatly. "I'll get back to normal."

Each word was like a sharpened knife against her heart. "Get out, please," she managed. "I need you to go. For real."

Micah's lashes lowered. "Of course."

He had placed one foot on the front porch when she spoke up, unable to stop herself from talking to his wide back. "For the record, you may not think you're perfect anymore, but I lov—I did like you, Micah. From the moment I saw you."

He jerked, but that was his only reaction. Or the only reaction she saw before she shut the door very carefully, mindful that it not slam.

What would New Rana do? New Rana would pull herself together, look at her life unflinchingly, remove all emotion from the equation, and get herself back on track. Maybe she would call her mother and apologize, or reactivate the dating apps on her phone. There were so many things she needed to accomplish.

New Rana got herself up the stairs. New Rana carefully closed the blinds on her bedroom, and pulled the curtains too, shutting out the daylight and Micah's house. New Rana got her clothes off and slipped into her pajamas.

That was about all New Rana could manage. Current Rana curled up on the bed and cried her heartache out in huge, loud, tearing sobs.

CHAPTER 19

A ringing cut through her grogginess, and Rana grabbed at the cell on her nightstand. "'Lo?"

"Where are you?" Leena's assertive voice rang through the line.

Damn it. This habit she had of answering phones when she was half-asleep was going to kill her one day. Rana rolled to her back and stared at the ceiling. "My bed. Why?"

"You missed meeting Devi for the walk-through of the new site last night, and you didn't show up for work today. We're worried."

"I texted Devi."

"In all Emojis. What the hell does sad face, ice-cream bowl, lightning bolt, heart even *mean*?"

Rana pursed her lips. "If I have to tell you, it's not worth it."

Leena made a rude noise. "Why aren't you working?"

She got up, threw her legs over the side of the bed, and cast a glance at the clock's glowing red numbers. Huh. It was six p.m. That was late. Had she been in bed since yesterday?

What was there to get out of bed for? "I'm not working because I don't feel like it." Listless, she stood and staggered to her bathroom as Leena started yammering in her ear, probably about responsibility and leadership and all sorts of other boring shit.

She shoved her toothbrush in her mouth and grunted in response to whatever Leena asked her. A couple of half-hearted strokes on her teeth and she was done.

When she lifted her head, she winced at the person staring back at her in the mirror. God, she looked like crap. *Note to self: avoid your reflection today.*

"This is an important time, and we need you…"

Rana fingered the tangled strands of her hair, which were all knotted up in a rats' nest on the back of her head. She'd always loved her hair. It was naturally thick and shiny, and she'd worn it long forever. Most of her loving, nonantagonistic memories of her mother revolved around her combing Rana's hair.

Micah had liked it too.

"I'm going to cut off all my hair," she blurted out, interrupting Leena's lecture.

There was a long pause on the other end. "Don't do anything. I'll be there in ten minutes."

* * *

"MOVE IT, sister."

Rana stood aside obediently as Leena walked inside her door, unsurprised to see a very worried-looking Devi behind her. "Needed reinforcements, huh?"

"I was concerned, so I tagged along," Devi said in her soft voice.

"Well, you saw me." Rana closed the door with a snick. "I'm fine."

Leena looked her up and down and raised a brow. "Wow, I didn't realize being fine made you look like shit."

"Have you eaten yet?" Devi asked, always the peacemaker.

Rana opened her mouth, and then realized she didn't know. She'd had a bite to eat yesterday, in between crying jags. She thought so, at least.

At her silence, Leena took command of the situation, as was her wont. "Come on then." She swept them all into Rana's small kitchen, and directed Rana to a chair.

Devi began opening and closing the fridge and cupboard doors.

"I don't have much food in stock," Rana said.

"I can see that." Devi's tone was cheerful. "I'll make do."

Of course, Devi could make a gourmet meal out of sawdust and saliva, which she might be reduced to today.

Rana sighed and propped her head on her hands. It felt too heavy to support. "Guys, I'm really not great company right now."

"It's a good thing you don't have to entertain us." Leena's tone brooked no nonsense.

Rana shrugged, too steeped in her own depression to really bother with them. She didn't know when their presence went from unwanted to soothing. While Devi puttered around her kitchen, Leena fetched Rana's brush from her room. At the first gentle touch of the bristles against her scalp, Rana closed her eyes and sat without complaint while Leena patiently removed the tangles and braided it. By the time Devi slid a steaming-hot plate of French toast in front of Rana, she felt slightly more human.

In true form, Devi had arranged the toast in an artful stack, with just the right hint of cinnamon and syrup layered on top. As appetizing as it looked, her mind rebelled at the thought of eating. "I'm not hungry."

Neither Leena nor Devi responded, but Leena set to cutting the French toast into small pieces. A cup of coffee appeared at her right hand. Leena forked up a piece and held it in front of her mouth. "Ahh."

Rana opened her mouth to protest being treated like a child, but the food was shoved in instead. She would have reamed her sister out, but it tasted so damn good, she couldn't. Her stomach growled.

She didn't fight the next bite, or the next. She allowed Leena to feed her until her stomach felt moderately full and the plate was empty. Leena put the fork down.

"Do you want more?" Devi asked from where she sat across the table.

Rana shook her head and took a healthy gulp of coffee.

"Okay, girl." Leena pulled out a chair next to hers. She settled in, careful not to muss her pressed skirt. Her angled hair swung above her shoulders. "Time to talk."

"Nothing's wrong."

"Uh-huh." Leena looked less than convinced. "Come on, Rana, you're no good at keeping things bottled up."

Yeah, Rana loved to talk. That was the saying, right? Rana could talk to anybody. She traced the ring of moisture left by her orange juice glass with the tip of her finger. "Really, I'm just in a bit of a slump. I'll be okay by tomorrow."

"Rana." Devi stilled her hand by settling hers over it. "Please, let us help you."

She took a deep breath. In her mind, she patted Devi and gave a brave smile. "I'm fine, really. I got my period, and it's a bitch. You know how these things are."

With a minimum of fuss, Rana followed her sisters to the door and showed them out, grateful for the opportunity to clamber back into her cave of a bed and disappear.

Of course, things never played out quite like they did in Rana's head. In reality, she took a deep breath, and her verbal filter went on the blink. "I've been trying so hard to be good and loveable, but then I met my neighbor who I was also creeping on and he was so hot and so I slept with him, but I think I accidentally fell for him even though we both agreed it was supposed to be temporary, and now I'm miserable because he called it quits for my own fucking good, and I don't want an acceptable man I want him, and that's why I'm only responding in Emojis because Mama doesn't understand them, but she keeps texting me because we had a big fight and she said I'm a slut no one will ever love." She said the last on a wail, and then threw her head down onto her folded arms to sob her heart out.

Silence reigned for a long moment.

"Rana…" Devi trailed off, her voice strained.

Leena didn't speak. After a second, both of her sisters' chairs scraped against the tile. In the midst of her tears, she heard doors open and close, and the faucet turned on and off. As her sobs subsided to a weak stream of tears, Leena tilted her face up. A soft, wet cloth ran over her heated cheeks, followed by a dry one, the motion oddly soothing.

Rana squinted out of her swollen eyes at a bottle of

whiskey Devi thumped onto the table, along with three shot glasses Rana had bought on vacation in Jamaica. They were shaped like naked women.

"I've been saving that whiskey." Her voice didn't sound like hers, it was so thick.

"I've never seen you need it more," came Devi's emphatic response. She poured three shots and shoved one toward her. "Drink."

"I just ate."

"We'll do it with you." Leena grabbed a glass and pounded it back. "Now down the hatch."

She accepted the shot reluctantly, but the warmth that spread down her throat and blossomed in her chest was the most welcome thing she'd ever experienced. "Oh, I needed that," Rana sighed.

"Yes. You did." Devi sat down and collected the shot glasses, clutching the bottle as if she was ready to pour more emergency liquor. "Okay, Rana, I only caught about a tenth of what you spewed out…"

She sniffled, her misery a living, breathing thing. "Forget it, okay? It's all stupid."

"What isn't stupid is that you're devastated. We're going to help you, like you help us when we're sad."

Rana peered at Devi. "Do I help you when you're sad?" Her lip trembled. "I usually hurt more than help."

"Oh my God," Leena muttered under her breath.

"Leena," Devi snapped, then smiled at Rana. "You always help me. Remember that time that guy stood me up for dinner a few years ago? You spoon-fed me ice cream and watched movies with me so I wouldn't cry."

Leena stirred, reluctantly chiming in. "Or that time I

was certain I failed my accounting exam, in college. You drove down and took me to that god-awful club in Miami."

"You hated that club."

Leena shrugged. "Hating the club and being annoyed with you was better than crying in my dorm room all night."

"So let us help you," Devi said firmly. "Now, what's this about needing to be loveable? We already love you."

"You almost didn't," she whispered, unable to look at Devi.

There was a long pause while Devi processed that, and then she laid her hand on Rana's arm. "Wait. Are we talking about what happened with…?"

"Yes," she rushed out, not eager for that man's name to ever be said again. "That."

"I told you, that's old news." Devi shook her head. "I would never hold a grudge against you based on that. He was an asshole."

"You should," Rana said, blinking hard to keep from crying. "I was an asshole too. I betrayed you as much as he did."

Leena snorted. "Bullshit. Your heart was in the right place. You weren't actually there to seduce that turd."

"My heart's always in the right place. I just…don't think." She rapped her knuckles against the table. "I go off half-cocked and I ruin everything." *I'm sorry, Mrs. Malik. Rana is such a bright girl, but if only she would learn to control her impulses…*

Her sisters exchanged looks. Devi spoke first. "Rana. I had no idea you were still beating yourself up over this. But I'll tell you as many times as you need to hear it: I totally don't fault you for what you did. Was it maybe a little overboard? Yes. But I do understand why you thought you had no other choice."

Leena interjected. "And yeah, you can be impulsive. You don't think everything to death like me—"

"Or fret over rejection and failure like me," Devi added.

"But sometimes those impulses pay off. I mean, hell, you're in charge of hiring for a reason. Because you read people in a split second and can tell whether they'll work out or not."

Rana sniffed. For years, she'd yearned for her sisters to acknowledge she was in charge of something at the restaurant other than filling water glasses, but now she protested. "I'm in charge of hiring because no one else will do it."

"Because we're not good at it like you are." Leena shook her head. "We need your ability to take risks. Hell, if it were up to me, we'd be sitting on the profits from this one restaurant until we all die. You're the reason we expanded to catering. You're the only reason we're expanding to a second site, long after the time we should have. You were the one who pushed us out of our comfort zones."

"Truth." Devi poured three more shots of whiskey. Without protesting, all three of them took the drink. "And you are loveable."

"You seriously thought we would stop loving if you didn't…what? Change?" Leena sounded incredulous.

She lifted one shoulder. "Maybe."

"That could never happen," Devi said.

"I was trying to be better. New and improved." Her fingers played with the shot glass.

"Rana." She looked at Devi. "That new-and-improved

thing...is that what the men were about? The talk about getting married?"

Rana bit her lip, unsure if she could verbalize the mess of emotions inside her to anyone, but needing to try. They felt ugly and huge inside her chest. "I'm beginning to realize maybe it's all tied together," Rana said haltingly. "It's like one day I woke up and I realized how I really only have you guys. I felt...lonely. Leena has had Rahul forever. Then you found Marcus and Jace. I just wanted someone to love. But none of the men I met felt right. And then I met Micah..."

"Wait." Leena held up her hand, stunned realization widening her eyes. "Micah Hale? That's the neighbor you slept with?"

"Yeah. I lied when he came to the office. It was supposed to be a fling and...then it wasn't." She studied the table. "He broke things off with me yesterday. For my own good."

"Asshole," Leena muttered.

"He's not a complete asshole," Rana tried to defend him. "I think he's sincere. He has a lot of stuff he needs to work through. I was just like...a step on his way to recovery, you know? I knew that going in. He said as much when we ended things."

"Then fuck him." Rana jerked her head up to look at Devi, who wore a grim expression. "You deserve way more than being someone's stopping point."

Fresh tears stung Rana's eyes. She had always been an easy crier. She'd spent her life hiding her tears, fearful everyone would think she was even more high-maintenance than they already considered her to be. "Do I though? What do I bring to the table?"

"What kind of a question is that?"

She turned to Leena. "You're smart and ambitious and educated. Devi's sweet and nice and accomplished. What am I?"

"You're not seriously asking this." Devi raised her eyebrows.

"I'm pretty. I have a nice face and was lucky enough to be born with long legs and firm breasts. And that's it. All I bring to a relationship is myself."

"That's enough," Leena said sharply. For a second Rana thought she was telling her to shut up, but then Leena continued. "Who you are is more than enough."

"And when it fades?" Rana was aware her voice was rising in desperation, and she couldn't stop herself. "When I'm not pretty anymore? What's going to be left then?"

"Did Mama say this to you?" Leena's words were deadly quiet, sharpened with menace.

You can find someone good. A man who knows nothing about your past, one who would be happy to have such a pretty, lively girl as his wife. "I've slept with too many men, but at least I'm pretty, so I better trick someone into marriage now," she whispered. "That's the gist of our fight."

"Jesus," Devi muttered. "You have not slept with too many men."

"What the hell does too many even mean? More than one, less than a hundred?" Leena's face was hard, her eyes blazing. "If any man getting between your legs cares what number he is, he's probably a dickwad."

Rana looked at Leena's empty shot glass. It wasn't that her sisters never swore…it was just that Rana usually swore the most. "That's what I used to think."

"It's the truth. As for the other stuff…God, Mama's really done a number on you, hasn't she?" Devi leaned forward in her chair. "Tell me something, when you call Leena the smart one, is that all she is? Is she lacking in kindness?"

Rana swiped at the tears on her cheeks. "Of course not."

"And me? If I'm the nice one, does that mean I'm a dog?"

"You know you're gorgeous." Rana frowned at Devi. "It's not the same. You guys have everything. I have…"

"Your pretty face and body, I know. And nothing else." Devi's lips tightened. "Do you remember what things were like when Daddy died?"

Rana locked her hands together. "I try not to remember."

"Let me remind you. You had barely graduated. I was in middle school, upset over zits and boys. Leena was a junior, stressing about SATs and where to go to college." Devi's mouth curled down. "We had the funeral on Friday. You were in the restaurant on Monday."

Rana made her hands into fists. "I needed the distraction."

Leena's voice was clear and firm. "And you kept that restaurant not only functioning but turning a profit until I graduated from college. Until Devi graduated from culinary school."

"Mama was there—"

"The fact that you did it while Mama was working there is a miracle in its own right," Leena said dryly. "She should have driven you to drink. But you held it together for years. You managed *her* for years, until Devi and I could come.

And all we did was take over Mama's job. None of us can interact with customers the way you can."

"The way Daddy could," Devi added softly. "You're so like him. He wasn't just a pretty face, and neither are you." She glanced at Leena. "And personally, I, for one, am really sorry if I ever gave you that impression."

"Me too." Leena arched a brow. "I don't want to hear about this again, weirdo. You're terrible at brooding."

Rana's smile was wobbly. "I do hate being depressed," she confessed.

"Your emotions are too big for you to bottle them up," Devi said. "That's one of the things we love about you."

A tiny ray of light pierced her heart. "That I'm a drama queen?"

"You are a drama queen, but in a good way. You're not volatile. You're exciting. It's wonderful."

"I don't know if I believe you." But Rana wanted to. Every fiber of her being yearned for her to believe them.

"You should." Devi leaned forward. "The Rana I know, she's confident."

"I am confident. About some things," she confessed.

"You should be confident about all the things. If you want to have a serious relationship, great. If you don't, sleep with as many men as you want."

"It's not…"

"It is," Leena interjected, her voice hard. "It is exactly that simple, Rana. This is the rest of your life we're talking about. Fuck whatever you've been told. Fuck Mama and her plans for you. Fuck whatever it is in your head that's keeping you from doing whatever you want. Fuck this asshole who told you you're just a step. You're no one's step.

You're an amazing person who deserves to have whatever you want."

Rana and Devi were both silent when Leena finished her impassioned speech. It was, without a doubt, the first time Rana had heard her middle sister say such violently critical things about their mother.

Leena grabbed the whiskey and swigged it straight from the bottle, placing it down with a determined thud. She pulled her phone out of her pocket and hit a number. "Preeti? It's Leena. Devi and Rana and I will be otherwise busy tonight. You can close up." She muttered a few more things and then hung up. She looked back at both of them belligerently when they stared at her, still astounded. "What? We can't all have a night off?"

"We've had nights off before," Rana said slowly. "We usually plan them better, is all."

"We're going to have two places before long. We need to learn to delegate."

Devi raised an eyebrow, but her eyes were sparkling. She nudged the whiskey subtly closer to Leena. "Did you say the D word?"

Leena accepted the bottle and took another swig. "Damn right. Let's have a girls' night."

They had never had a girls' night, not that Rana could remember. Devi had always been so much younger, and Leena had always been far too uptight to party the way Rana used to like.

The way Rana currently liked. She hadn't gotten drunk, properly drunk, in a year. She eyed the whiskey and calculated how long it would take her to catch up to her sister. She didn't know if it was the alcohol or their pep talk, but she felt better about herself than she had in months. Even with the heartache of ending things with Micah.

She could handle her too-big, inconvenient feelings for Micah if someone else could help her handle her too-big, inconvenient feelings about herself. She looked down at the table, where the three of them rested their hands; her own longer and bonier with nibbled-away green polish; Leena's, darker with a perfect French manicure; Devi's, a shade in between with short, unpainted nails.

Her smile was small but unforced. "Girls' night sounds perfect."

* * *

"HOW DRUNK," Rana said, with great seriousness, "is too drunk?"

"No such thing," Devi promptly responded.

Rana stuck her hand into the bag of chips on the sofa next to her. Devi had tried to make dip a while ago but had ended up dropping sour cream on the kitchen floor. Leena had staggered over to clean it up but had slipped and fallen, swearing over the sour cream on her shirt. Rana had been giggling too hard to help much at all.

So it was plain old greasy potato chips for them. Rana stuffed another handful into her mouth. They would do. "Why have we never done this before?" she asked her sisters from where she lay sprawled on her couch. They were sisters. Sisters should drink together.

Leena licked the salt off her wrist, took the shot of tequila, and sucked a lemon wedge. "'Cause we're responsible pillars of the community. That's fucking why." Something new Rana had discovered: get a bit of alcohol in Leena, and her potty mouth rivaled Rana's.

"Your turn." Leena nudged the shot glass over to Rana. The sequins on the tank top she had stolen from Rana's closet to replace her ruined shirt glinted in the dim light of the candles they'd lit, the overhead light far too bright for their eyes now.

Rana obediently completed the ritual and groaned in pleasure as the fiery liquid raced down her system. "Christ that's good. Go, Dev."

Devi sat up, drank her shot, and collapsed back in her seat, her legs sprawled wide. "I shouldn't be doing this."

Rana smirked. "Why? It's not like you're pregnant or anything."

Leena shrieked, and they both looked over to find her fisting her hands in her hair, her eyes closed. She looked like a demented harpy. "Please don't say that. You'll jinx her! Who would go to the PTA meetings, all of them?"

Devi's expression took on a disgruntled cast. "I'm not planning on having babies right now, thank you very much. Marcus and Jace and I are still feeling each other out."

Rana snorted. "Feeling each other out. Heh."

"Ew. I don't even want to hear about…"

"Lay off," Rana interjected, noticing the storm cloud come over Devi's face.

"I will not."

"God, you're cynical," Devi said.

"And you're a romantic," Leena shot back. "But this isn't romance, it's lust."

"Leena, stop being such a jerk!" Devi's raised voice caught them all by surprise. "I get that you don't accept my decision about Jace and Marcus, but I am getting damn sick of listening to your jabs. I don't like Rahul, neither does Rana, but do you see us making fun of him constantly?"

Rana wanted to applaud. Devi was so damn easygoing, it wasn't natural. A little annoyance and anger cleared the air, and Leena had it coming for her constant needling of Devi's boyfriends. However, she did need to clarify something.

Rana cleared her throat and raised her hand. "Actually, Devi? I totally make fun of Rahul constantly." Leena's longtime boyfriend was a stick-in-the-mud and a blowhard. The fact that their mother loved him to pieces made it harder to accept him.

Leena stared at Devi and ignored Rana. "I thought you liked Rahul."

"Why should I? He takes my vibrant sister and turns her into a shadow of herself." Devi grimaced. "I can't stand him."

"Well." Leena blinked. "Then it's a very good thing that we broke up a couple weeks ago, isn't it?"

"What?"

"You did what?"

Leena reached for the tequila bottle, as if she hadn't just dropped a bomb in their gathering. "Yes, did I forget to mention it?"

"You know very well you did." Anger gone, Devi collapsed back into the overstuffed chairs. "Why didn't you tell us?"

"You guys know how I hate to make a fuss."

"Um, actually, Leena, breaking up with your boyfriend of many years isn't making a little fuss. Are you…okay?"

Leena took another shot and closed her eyes as she

sucked on the lemon wedge. When Rana was ready to get up and rip it out of her mouth, she opened her eyes. "Yes. I think it's one of the best decisions I've ever made." Her tone was filled with certainty. "After all, I was starting to feel like I was only with him to please Mama." Her laugh was humorless. "Isn't that silly? Oh, God. I still have to tell her. I've been dreading it."

"That's not silly." Rana's lips compressed. "I'm thirty-two years old, and the first time Mama told me she was proud of me was when I said I wanted to settle down. Once I had that approval, I couldn't lose it. I want her to look at me…"

"The way she looks at me," Leena finished. Leena's skin was darker than hers and Devi's, but Rana could have sworn she lost some color in her cheeks. "I'm well aware of what I've had to do to get that look."

Rana's hands trembled. She curled them into fists. Relief. That was what she was feeling. "You are?"

Leena nodded, her face grim. "It was always in the back of my head when I dated a man. Could I bring him home some day? What kind of a son-in-law would he be?"

"That look is the reason I know I'll never be able to tell Mama about Jace and Marcus," Devi interjected. "I mean, I can't tell her the whole story. If she knew I was involved with two men…" Devi's jaw tightened. "I get it too."

Rana swallowed. Of course they got it. Why would she think they wouldn't? They were probably the only two people who would get it.

Micah had seemed to understand too.

Well, he wasn't here, was he?

"Is Rahul moving out?" Devi asked quietly.

"He left on Sunday, with his necessary possessions. I'll box up whatever else is left this week, and he'll come next weekend to pick it up."

Despite her best efforts, Rana shivered. So cold. Slice, slice, cut your significant other out of your life. She didn't know what else she'd expected from a couple whose relationship had always struck her as sterile, but still.

"Okay. Do you want to, um, talk about what happened?" Rana couldn't remember the last time Leena had spoken with her about her boyfriend, any boyfriend. She'd always been so private about such matters.

Sure enough, Leena declined. "Not yet. I'd rather not. Really, guys, I'm okay. Devi, I'm sorry I was sharp about…you know."

Devi and Rana exchanged a look. If Leena was even half-heartedly apologizing, she was more upset than she let on. "Leena…"

She looked up from her empty glass. "Seriously. Enough. You're a person who thrives on getting all of your emotions out there. I'm not."

In Rana's opinion, it wasn't healthy to be as tightly contained as Leena was, but there wasn't too much she could do about it. She shook her head slightly at Devi, who was opening her mouth. "Okay. Hey, maybe you should find some hot young stud to console yourself with."

"There's a gardener at Jace and Marcus's condo who's really something," Devi teased, her good humor resurfacing.

As intended, Leena smiled faintly, and some of her previous alcoholic glow returned. "Maybe I will. In any case, this whole night has gotten off track. It's not about me tonight." Leena poured all of them another shot and nudged them to her and Devi.

Leena raised her glass, and Devi followed suit, looking blurry around the edges. "To the best big sister in the world."

"Here, here," Devi said. "But I've got two, so I'll say one of the best."

Tears swam in Rana's eyes. Damn, she'd done enough crying to flood the place tonight. "Aww, thanks, guys."

They all drank and subsided back into their pillows, silent. Five minutes later, Devi's soft snore filled the room.

"We're a little messed up, Rana." Leena's whisper came from next to her.

Rana rolled her head, the better to see her sister. "Yeah."

Leena contemplated her glass and then placed it back on the side table. "But Mama loves us."

"I know."

"It would be easier if she didn't."

Rana wanted to repeat her *I know,* but it seemed redundant. She settled for nodding.

"When I told you that you wouldn't lose us…that's true for me too? No matter what I do, no matter how much Mama disapproves, I won't lose you guys?"

Rana opened her eyes in surprise at the tortured whisper. Leena sat in the chair, staring at her, with the most honest emotion she'd seen from her unflappable sister.

Suddenly stone-cold sober, she struggled to sit up and make room on the couch. When she extended her arm, Leena wasted no time in coming over to sit next to her. Rana wrapped her arms around her sister's slender body and pulled her closer, uncaring about the crushed potato chips between them. Leena rested her head on Rana's breast, and

Rana stroked the soft strands.

Christ, she hadn't held Leena like this in…forever. Once upon a time, when they'd been children and shared a room, Leena had often crawled into her bed to escape from the Florida thunderstorms that terrified her.

Their father's funeral, Rana recalled. That was the last time they'd embraced. The next morning, Leena had seemingly morphed from a normal teenager into a rigid and controlled young woman.

Rana mourned for that smiling young teenager. The transformation was partially her fault. She'd showered Devi with all her maternal love and care. She should have insisted on taking better care of this baby sister instead of assuming Leena was invulnerable.

Leena's tears dampened her shirt, driving the stake of guilt deeper.

"Yes. That's what it means," Rana said softly, and realized that if she wanted her sister to believe it, she had to believe it too. Rana tilted her head at sleeping Devi. "On that point, you need to make sure Devi understands she won't lose either of us too."

Leena hesitated. "If Mama finds out about those men…"

"What are you doing, showing her what life is going to be like for her?" When Leena looked away, Rana had her answer. Ah. Rana should have known Leena's harshness toward Devi's lifestyle was born out of misguided helpfulness. "Mama's going to think what she wants to think." As she said the words, the truth of them hit home. Rana had no control over her mother's brain. None of them did.

Christ, was that a freeing thought or what?

"I only want the best for her," Leena said quietly. "You

and I aren't immune to needing approval, and she's not as strong as either of us."

Rana was abruptly glad Devi was asleep. "Bullshit. None of us are weak." She straightened. "None of us." She hadn't believed it until that moment, but she suddenly saw what her sisters had been saying.

She had kept her family together after their father died. She may not have a string of degrees after her name, but she played an important role in their business and her family's life.

She'd slept with men and lived her life how she'd wanted to, and she'd enjoyed herself. Surely that took a certain amount of courage.

She had value. A lot of it.

"We make a pact right now," Rana said, her voice growing stronger. "The things we do, the decisions we make, may mean that we won't measure up in other people's eyes. But the three of us, we stick together. That means we support each other."

"Devi's asleep," Leena pointed out. "She can't pact with us."

"I'll tell her about the pact tomorrow. You know she'll be on board."

Leena nodded slowly. "Okay. I…I guess my future's up in the air now too, huh?"

"You need us as much as we need you," Rana said brutally.

Leena looked at Devi, and her face softened. She loved the baby of the family as much as Rana did. "I'll lay off her. I promise."

"Good."

"And if Mama and the rest of the world turn their backs on us tomorrow…"

Two years ago, Rana would have made a face and sneered. A week ago, Rana would have caved, toeing whatever line her mother put in place. Tonight, she considered the possibility. "We deal with it." Rana brushed her lips against the top of Leena's head. "It is what it is. And we…deal. Together."

Leena gave a loud sniff, and then plucked at her borrowed top. "I like this shirt. It's so shiny."

Rana craned her neck. "It's too small on me anyway. You can have it."

"I don't know where I'd even wear it," Leena fussed. "I don't go anywhere."

"Maybe you should."

Her sister lifted her chin. "Maybe I should. I…like the way it makes me feel."

She'd liked the way she'd felt around Micah. Not New Rana or Old Rana, just plain old her. Her chest ached at his memory, for herself and for him.

She pressed her hand to her stomach. That was life though, right? Painful, sometimes. Maybe he had done her a favor, and she'd thank him later. It seemed unlikely, now, but perhaps it would happen.

She'd love again, but only when she found someone like Micah, who never made her feel like she was lacking. The way she felt whole right now, holding her sister close.

This was who Rana was. Drama queen, crybaby, seductress, friend, goofball, sister. She relaxed into the couch, trying to get comfortable in her own skin. It was an awkward fit, and it would take some getting used to, but it felt…right. She'd missed herself.

For the first time in a year, Rana breathed.

CHAPTER 20

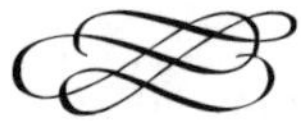

When Micah had been a child, their neighbor had had the saddest-looking pug. Sometimes the pug's owner would dress it in sweaters and skirts, and the poor thing would stare at Micah as if its life couldn't get any more pitiful.

Right now, he was feeling way more pathetic than that sad, whining, bulging-eyed pug.

Micah had a canvas in front of him, but he was sitting there more out of habit than an actual desire to create anything. His agent had called and asked if he would be interested in doing another show in a few months. A bigger publicity push, more guests, larger city.

He had told the other man he would think about it. He should have been delighted another gallery had approached him. That meant someone somewhere thought his latest work held some promise.

Sadly, he was too focused on his own misery to work up much enthusiasm. Or to turn his attention to what he might actually create for the show.

Nothing with Rana in it.

He avoided looking at the right corner of his studio, where all of the sketches of Rana were stacked in a neat pile, along with about three separate canvases. He hadn't been able to continue the one he had started of her when she was here, so he had picked another pose, but that had also been difficult. Same with the third.

It wasn't like before, where he had felt sucked dry of creativity. If anything, he had too many images and thoughts jumbled up in his head, straining to break free. He wanted to do nothing but sketch and paint Rana.

It was simply too painful.

It'll get better, he tried to assure himself. It had only been a couple weeks. The first period after a breakup was the hardest.

As if the heavens were agreeing, a mighty boom of thunder sounded. The rain was coming down in sliding sheets, a late-afternoon thunderstorm. Rain here wasn't like back home. It was violent and hot.

He didn't bother glancing out the window. His studio was always dark now. He'd found brand-new blinds on his doorstep the day after he'd dropped a hefty check in Rana's mailbox. They'd come with a note, scrawled in feminine handwriting. *I'm sick of having to keep my curtains shut.*

He'd installed them within the hour. They'd been closed ever since. An apt punishment for him. She was right, she shouldn't have to be the one to close herself off. Not when she'd been so open and welcoming.

He might be miserable, but he was well aware he was the problem. Any other man would have clung to the promise of Rana's love with both hands, not shoved her away.

For her own good. She deserved better than him. She deserved everything.

That didn't stop him from loathing himself for not being everything she needed. Or from worrying over whether she was okay. Had she fought with her mother again? Was she still upset over the ending of their affair? Christ, the way she had looked at him. Like he had broken her heart, seconds after her mother had done the same.

Without her his days were bleak once again. He had little to look forward to. He kept wanting to talk to her, tell her things that would make her laugh.

He slept better with her. He ate better with her. Most importantly, he felt better with her.

How had she wormed her way into his life in such a short period of time? How was that even possible?

His phone's tiny ring filled the air, and he jolted. He wished he could throw the damn thing away now that he and Rana were over, but he couldn't. His mother would have a heart attack.

He fished the phone out of his pocket and glanced at the display, mostly out of some perverse need to assure himself Rana wasn't calling to tell him she lov—

Nope. Definitely his mother. Who had called the previous night. With a sigh, he picked it up. "Mum."

"Micah," she said, and he could hear the trace of relief that was never far. *Oh hello, dear, I'm so happy you're not dead.*

"What's going on?"

"Nothing much. Just thought of you, figured I would call and say hi."

Micah nodded, though she couldn't see him. "Wonderful."

"Have you called back George yet?"

He leaned back on his stool. He had told his mother about the possibility of a new show. "Not yet. I'm still thinking."

"Well, don't think too hard, dear. This is an excellent possibility for you."

His mother had never so much as had an opinion on his career before the attack, recognizing that a nurse was probably not the best person to tell an artist how to run their life. Now… "I said I'll think about it," he said, with more bite than he'd intended.

His mother paused. "Did I call you at a bad time? Are you painting?" Her voice dropped, though why, Micah wasn't sure. "Is that sweet girl there again?"

Micah had managed to avoid speaking about Rana with his mother, generally by changing the subject in response to her heavy-handed hints. This was far more than a heavy-handed hint. He couldn't ignore a direct question. "No. We, ah, finished our sessions."

"Oh. Does that mean… Well. Micah, it was fairly obvious you were otherwise involved. No model would be at your home at all hours. Are you…not?"

Micah massaged his temple. "No. We're not."

"Oh." Disappointment. So much of it.

His jaw clenched, and he tried to hold back the rebuke, but it came out anyway. "Stop it."

"Stop what, Micah?"

"Stop thinking of it as a setback. It's not."

"I didn't—"

He ignored her flustered words. "Relationships end all

the time, and no one considers it backsliding. It's not another signal that something's wrong with me."

"Micah, I never said—"

"You were thinking it. Every time you call me, I know you're thinking it. About how I'm not who I was before, and the person I am now is some beast that needs to be placated or pacified. Well, I'm not. I'm not who I was before, but I'm not weak. I'm not broken."

She was silent for a long minute. "You're not weak," she whispered. "But sometimes I feel like I am."

He ground the heel of his palm into his eye socket, hating the regret. Maybe the words had been building up for a while, but he could have articulated them better. "Mum, I apologize."

"Don't. You're right. Your father's been saying this to me for a while, that it's not healthy how obsessively I call you, that I might be smothering you. I—I figured you could stand a little smothering. I didn't think my worry would hurt you so much." Tears clogged her voice.

Great. That was two women who cared for him who he'd recently made cry.

He opened his mouth to apologize, but she wasn't finished. "Sometimes I think I'm going to burst with my worry. I never felt like this before the attack. You know that. I raised you to be independent, but now all I wish is for you to be back here, in our home, where I can keep you safe."

He gentled his tone. "No one can keep anyone safe, Mum."

"I could try. I could see you every day. I could make sure you eat. I could cut your hair for you. I could make you go to therapy."

He winced.

"You think I don't know you're lying to me about going? I don't even know why."

The white canvas was blurry in front of him. "I don't either."

"You know it would help you."

"I know." He licked his lips. "Maybe because I know it would help me."

"That makes no damn sense, Micah."

His mother so rarely swore. How could he explain something he didn't even understand? "It's like…I had no choice in anything that happened. The attack. The hospital. The therapy." He swallowed. "How all of it made you and the rest of the family and all my friends feel. All of that was out of my control."

Her breathing was loud. "But you could control where you moved. And what you ate. And whether you went to therapy."

He rose from his stool, suddenly restless. "I'm sorry, Mum. I really am."

"I don't think you're broken. I miss how blissfully oblivious I used to be, is all. And I miss how happy you were with your life."

He rubbed the back of his neck and paced to one end of the wall. "I miss that too." But now that he thought about it, life wasn't complete misery now. Why, when he'd been with Rana, he'd been downright blissful. Even with all of his hang-ups and baggage.

"Your father's been pestering me to go to some group-therapy thing. Maybe I'll go."

"That sounds good."

"And...maybe I won't call you as much. Would you like that? Would that make things easier for you?"

He shut his eyes. "Maybe we could be like we were before. Where we called when we had something to talk about."

"Yes." Her laugh was nervous but real. "I only want you to have someone you can talk to, my dear. That's why I've always pushed therapy. I just know it helps to have someone who understands. If I didn't have your father..." She trailed off. "Well, I don't know how I would have managed."

His eyes were drawn to his blinds. "I'll—You may have a point. I'll think about it."

He expected her to pursue the topic, but surprisingly she retreated. "Very well. I—I'll let you go then."

"I love you, Mum," he said hoarsely.

"I love you too, dear. I'll call you...in a few days. Or next week."

He smiled. "Sounds good."

After she hung up, he leaned against the wall for a while, trying to marshal his thoughts. They were too chaotic and jumbled for him to get a solid hold of them.

He frowned down at the phone when it rang again in his hand. Hadn't they just talked about some distance—?

The sight of the international number stopped him cold. He recognized it because he'd gotten rather good at avoiding it.

His finger hovered over the decline button, but he hesitated. She would only keep calling him until she got a response. Especially since he knew who had directed her to call him.

He picked up the phone. "Paige."

There was a shocked silence on the other end. “Micah,” the caller finally said. “I didn’t expect you to actually pick up.”

“You called me though you assumed I wouldn’t answer?”

“Yes. So I could tell everyone that I tried.”

That pulled a small smile from him. “My mum called you, didn’t she?” Of course, the woman might say that she would back off, but her worry and nurturing ran deep. It would take time for her to learn that he didn’t need her smothering to survive.

“I’ve been sworn to secrecy.”

Yeah, his mother had told her to call him. *I only want you to have someone you can talk to, my dear.* Who better than the woman he’d shared his trauma with?

“How are you?” he asked, his voice automatically gentling.

“Well. And you?” Her voice had softened as well.

Skittish horses. That’s what they were, circling around each other.

“It’s been a while.” He had seen her and answered some of her phone calls in the aftermath of the attack. She’d been justifiably upset, certain he hated her, and though he had been battling his own demons, she’d been his model for years. They’d been good friends, often grabbing a pint together when they weren’t working. He hadn’t wanted her to feel that way.

After the first year or so, he’d slowly stopped responding to her. It hadn’t been personal. He hadn’t really wanted to respond to anyone. All his friends did was remind him of who he wasn’t anymore.

He could imagine her sitting in a chair now, her muscular legs curled up under her. A competitive swimmer all her life, she had a unique body he'd loved painting. The last time he'd seen her, she'd lost a bit of weight, but she'd still looked strong.

"It has." She paused for a beat. "How do you like the expat life then?"

"America is…different."

"I imagine it's like the Wild West. No one cares where you're from."

"Americans are surprisingly nosy, for all of that Wild West heritage," he said dryly. "But it is easier to be…lost."

"I bet. London is small."

Yes. That had been the problem exactly. Sometimes it felt like everyone knew him and what had happened. "It's always warm here. Even the rain is warm."

"Now you're trying to make me leave too."

Micah didn't laugh, and neither did Paige. They both knew she couldn't leave—her elderly mother depended on her greatly, and he was certain that hadn't changed. "There are things I miss about London," he said instead. "But this is what I didn't know I needed."

"That's good, Micah. I—I'm so happy you like it there." She paused again. "I'm getting married."

He flinched, doubling over slightly as if he had taken a blow to his solar plexus. He recovered at once, breathing shallowly through his nose, holding the phone away so she wouldn't hear. "Congratulations."

"My therapist said…well, I wanted to call you and tell you personally."

"That's kind of you." The words scraped out of his

throat.

"I felt like I owed it to you..." She trailed off.

He shoved his thumbs into his eye sockets. This. This was why he hadn't been able to speak with her, though he knew he ought to. Her pain was a raw, gaping wound, far too similar to his. He wanted to run from it, even as it scraped over him, releasing all of his demons.

"You owe me nothing, love," he said gruffly, slipping back into the casual endearments he'd once traded so easily with his friends.

"If I hadn't been dating that monster, you wouldn't have been hurt," she whispered.

Shrill screams rang in his ears. He had been so in shock, he hadn't even felt the final blow cutting across his face. But he could well remember seeing Paige through a veil of red as he watched her deceptively small boyfriend haul her away.

He focused on his blank canvas to ground himself, tearing himself away from that memory. She needed reassurance. "If that monster hadn't been a monster, I wouldn't have been hurt," he responded.

"I had no idea he would snap like that. I could have made it clearer you and I weren't sleeping together, I..."

Micah raked his hand through his long hair, abruptly annoyed with its length. It felt far too thick and heavy on his head, stifling him. "You saved my life. You were the one who got away from him. You were the one who called the police. If that ambulance hadn't come in time, I would have been dead."

"You wouldn't have been in that position if it weren't for me and my terrible choice in boyfriends."

He stopped. Nothing he said would make her believe

she wasn't to blame. Maybe she would carry this guilt with her until her dying day. And there was nothing he could do about it.

Nothing.

She was talking, but he couldn't comprehend her words. "Will we ever be like we were?" he asked abruptly, interrupting her and unable to care. He had a feeling he already knew the answer.

She hesitated. "Before…he did what he did?"

"Yes. Will we ever be like that again?"

"I…I don't think so. It doesn't feel like it."

He wasn't a talker. But the words were pouring out of him, spurred by the one person who might possibly have a solution. "I feel like everyone's waiting for me to snap out of this."

"Snap out of what?"

"Snap out of…this." He gestured his arm around him, though she couldn't see. "Like I'm on some sort of quest to get back to human and I just have to collect enough points or golden coins, and one day I'll wake up and everything will be as it was."

"Ah. Baby steps?"

He breathed out at her sardonic tone, the one that matched his mental monologue in counseling sessions. "Yes."

"I had a therapist who kept talking about those. I switched to my new one. She explained that maybe it wasn't steps back to who I was, but steps to being happy. Functional. Content."

"And you're okay with that?"

Her tone softened even more. "I am. But then, I'm not

like you, love. I was always aware of how imperfect I was."

"I never thought I was perfect."

"No, but you were a perfectionist. And you were good at everything you wanted to be good at. Micah, you never really struggled for anything you truly wanted, did you?"

He opened his mouth to protest, but he couldn't. Not really. He had enjoyed being the best at anything he did. If something had proved difficult, it had been an easy matter to avoid it and find something he excelled at and was rewarded for. His talent had been nurtured at an early age by doting parents; he had easily gotten into the art school of his choice; he hadn't been a starving artist for long before gaining critical and commercial acclaim.

He had worked hard, yes, but the rewards had always been there. He pursed his lips, for the first time realizing that maybe his life hadn't been quite so amazing before the attack. Just…easier. "I suppose not," he admitted.

"And then you were in the wrong place at the wrong time and almost died," she said with a heavy dose of self-loathing. "So, yes. I get why you might be less resistant to the idea of settling for a different life."

He ran his hand over his hair again. *What if I'm never able to get my hair cut again?*

What if I'm never as successful an artist as I once was? What if I'm never able to go out in crowds? What if I hate going to pubs forever?

What if I'm always weak?

"A lesser life," he said, barely conscious of whispering the words out loud.

"No," Paige said immediately. "I never would have so much as dated my Derek before all this happened. I would have been too shy or insecure. Nor would I have had the courage to think of getting a law degree back then. I'm starting a full-time study program soon, you know. I'll be a solicitor." Her eagerness and pride was apparent in every syllable she spoke. "So, no. This doesn't have to be a lesser life, love, I don't think so. Just a different one."

His heart beat so hard he had to place his hand over his chest. Though he knew it was impossible, he could swear the scars on his back throbbed.

He thought of his barren home, the home he had purposefully chosen not to furnish. Rana was next door, probably curled up in her too-big bed, listening to the rain pound against her windows.

What if I'm always different?

What if he was?

For the record, you may not think you're perfect anymore, but I did like you, Micah. From the moment I saw you.

Rana had liked him. As he was.

Perhaps…perhaps he could learn to not mind himself either.

"Are you sure?" he asked hoarsely, feeling stupid for the need for affirmation.

"Yes," she said, her certainty making him shake. "I'm sure. Same way I'm sure I'll always feel terrible about what happened to you, like I shoved that knife into your back myself. But I'm learning to live with it."

"I suppose it doesn't matter how many times I tell you it wasn't your fault," he ventured.

"No. It should, but it doesn't." He heard a smile in her voice. "That doesn't mean I don't like to hear it."

His laugh was rusty, but she laughed along with him,

though the joke wasn't that funny. "Will you send me your mailing address?" he asked, mentally flipping through the paintings he had stored in England. There were canvases there with Paige's face on them. His agent had been supremely agitated when he had refused to sell them. Other works with Paige as his model had instantly quadrupled their already hefty price tag in the months after the attack, driven by sensationalist, hungry collectors. *This painting is of the girl whose boyfriend went mad. Delicious.*

Something about people being excited about owning a piece of the drama surrounding a near-fatal attack and kidnapping made him want to smash something. He imagined the vultures inspecting the canvases for bloodstains, and he wanted to throw up.

Paige could have them and do with them what she wished. They'd fetch her and her new husband a tidy nest egg if she sold them. Or they could destroy them.

"Sending me a wedding present?"

"Yes." He'd imagined one day he would be able to walk into that warehouse and peruse the works he had previously done without feeling a pang that he was now subpar. Now, all he wanted to do was get rid of all of them. The ones without Paige could be sold, the money put in an account for a rainy day.

Because he wasn't subpar, necessarily. He looked at the canvases sitting in the corner of his studio, all works in progress of Rana. He couldn't call anything with her face or body on it subpar.

Different. He was different now.

A small vein of excitement opened within him, a creative surge he hadn't felt since he'd walked away from Rana.

Hell, he could do anything he wanted now, couldn't he? The world was his oyster. Long after he was dead, maybe collectors would divide his life's work into periods. No one period better than the other, but all different.

"I'll email it to you."

"Thanks." He paused. "Paige. Still not your fault."

"Still love hearing it."

He grinned at her cheeky reply, his heart lightening. "Be happy."

"You too. Love you."

"I…" No, he couldn't say it, even if it was the love of a friend for a friend. He couldn't say it to Paige, when he hadn't been able to say it to Rana. "I'll talk to you soon."

The phone went dead in his hand, and he carefully placed it on the bench next to him. Then he walked out of the studio and down the stairs, not bothering to take an umbrella with him as he left his home.

Not weak.

Not less.

Different.

He was almost to Rana's front stoop when he stopped, finally able to think past the instinct guiding him.

Wait.

He looked up at the house. Lightning illuminated her home, thunder following a second later. The warm rain whipped around his body, plastering his clothes and hair to his head.

No. This wasn't right.

I was your first taste of normalcy. Like…therapy. I think you called them steps once. That's what I was. A step.

He didn't want her to think that. She hadn't been his

therapy, she'd been his...well, his love.

If he rang her bell now, she might let him in. She might even listen to him or take him back. Yet what would he say? That he had changed his mind? She deserved a grand gesture. Not a waterlogged fellow rapping on her door in the middle of a storm.

His own words echoed in his ears. *It's not enough to give someone the answer. You have to show the work, so the person can figure out if that's the right answer for them.*

Lightning lit up the sky, the rain soaking his clothes and hair. He backed off, until he was in his yard, his jaw firming.

Yes, he was a perfectionist. He couldn't be perfect for Rana, whatever perfect even meant anymore. But if he was going to offer her his battered heart, he could damn well ensure he gave her the best possible version of himself he could. She deserved to be with someone who was certain of what he was and what he wanted. Not an impulsive madman drunk over an epiphany.

What if she finds someone else while you figure things out?

He swallowed over the pain of that thought. Maybe she would. He would suffer. But if she was happy, that...that would be okay too.

He went inside, uncaring over the water he was tracking over the kitchen floor, and went to the old-fashioned corded phone hanging on the wall. As little as he used his cell phone, he had never so much as touched this thing, something he had connected for emergency purposes only.

His therapists' after-hours answering service picked up. "Hello," he said rather simply. "I'd like to make an appointment."

CHAPTER 21

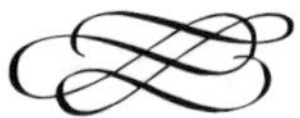

Rana's heels tapped on the pavement outside of the new restaurant's location, a sense of satisfaction rolling through her as she admired the sign that had gone up yesterday. *Royals.*

It had been Leena's last-minute idea not to use the same name as The Palace. Rana had jokingly suggested it be named Royalty, after her rather regal name.

She'd almost cried when Devi had squealed out *Royals*, and then hugged her, claiming it was perfect. She *had* cried when Leena had agreed, because, "Well, the whole thing was your idea to begin with."

The Palace's little sister was less than a half-hour drive from their original restaurant, nestled in a bustling strip mall anchored by a busy supermarket. The windows were covered in butcher paper, since the interior wasn't quite ready for public consumption. Next week, the three of them would rip it down and let the world take a look at their risk.

A stir of excitement rose in her belly, sneaking past the low-level depression that came and went. This place had been good for her. Something productive to get her mind off the man next door. She had thrown herself into preparations for their grand opening, gaining more confidence in offering her opinions to her sisters and demanding their attention. She'd even stood up twice to her mother, when the older woman had decided to poke her nose in.

Their relationship still hadn't recovered from the hurtful things Mama had said to her that day on the porch six weeks ago. It lay between them like an ever-present silent bomb. Yet Rana could tell her mother was genuinely sorry. She was quiet in her presence now, her cutting remarks absent, a subtle sadness in her eyes when she looked at her. That sadness was terrible to see. Rana knew eventually her soft heart would cave and she'd forgive her mom. Maybe the other woman would revert back to her critical words and pressure to get married, Rana didn't know.

What Rana did know was that she wouldn't give in. She wouldn't go back to believing she was worthless. She'd grown too strong for that shit.

She resisted the urge to make a silly face and admire her guns in the reflection of the door. This was their new place. She needed to show some decorum. So she sedately juggled the bag Leena had insisted Rana had to bring over here tonight, unlocked the door, and went inside, flipping on the lights.

Where she promptly dropped her bag and yelped.

There, in the center of the room, on an easel, sat a massive painting. And on that canvas was…her.

Only it was a her she'd never seen before. Rana walked closer, heart pounding hard. Micah—of course it was Micah—had remained true to their agreement and hadn't painted her face.

His other work had been abstract, dreamy. This was harsh, almost hyperrealistic, like she could touch the canvas and feel warm flesh.

He'd painted her on a bed, on her side, her breasts plumped, her arm outstretched toward the viewer. One leg was crossed over the other one, hiding the place between her legs. Sunlight gleamed on her skin, burnishing it with gold. Her hair covered her face, revealing only the curve of her cheekbone, her stubborn chin, and a glimpse of red lipstick-stained lips.

She had never posed for him like this. Is this what she had looked like, sleeping in his bed?

No, it was her bed. She recognized the embroidered flower on a pillowcase peeking at the top. Now that she studied it, she realized the sunlight cascaded over her in a subtle pattern. Like it was streaming through half-open blinds.

Her chest physically hurt, she was so overwhelmed. God.

Vulnerable and erotic. A well-loved sexual being. That's what she was.

She was unable to stop devouring the painting with her eyes. When she was within arm's reach, she realized the lower left-hand corner of the painting didn't hold Micah's customary bold signature.

Queen of My Heart

Rana clapped her hand over her mouth to stifle her cry. There was more, in smaller print. She bent over.

Curtains, door, arms, heart. All open. Only for you.

Please.

Love,
Micah

Well. Talk about making her feel.

She straightened up and looked at the painting again. Odd how it was suddenly wavy.

She dashed her tears away and read his signature again. *All open. Only for you.*

Was there really a decision that needed to be made here?

While she wanted to take the painting with her, it was so big and her hands so clumsy, she feared damaging it. She'd have to simply come back. Maybe with Micah and his big SUV.

Her heart leapt with hope, and she struggled to contain it. Not yet. She wouldn't be putting the cart before the horse.

How she managed to make it home, she wasn't sure. When she did turn onto her street, she didn't bother with her driveway but slid into Micah's.

The sun had just set, and the evening sky was dusky blue. Rana got out of her car and craned her neck. Sure enough, she could make out flickering lights in Micah's studio window. Since she'd bought him blinds, the room had been closed off.

She swallowed as she neared his door, her heart thudding. The knob turned smoothly in her hand.

She came inside and shut the door behind her. The house was quiet, still. Rana wiped her hands on her jeans.

Was he home? Had she misunderstood the painting?

The stairway light was on, though, and from around the corner she could see the soft glow from the kitchen. Plus the lamp in the living room.

She did a double take at that. The floor lamp was new, as was the leather sofa it was sitting next to. Same with the modest flat-screen TV.

Still sparsely furnished, of course, but a change was a change.

"Micah?" she called out uncertainly.

When she received no response, she made a quick decision. She was here, right? She hadn't imagined what that painting had said. She had to see, for both their sakes.

She mounted the stairs slowly, drawn to the studio. She pushed the door open and blinked.

Candles.

Dozens, maybe even a hundred of the buggers, all over the place. But they weren't what truly shocked her.

She was what shocked her.

Every available surface had a canvas leaning against it. Huge newspaper print covered the walls. She was everywhere. Her hands. Her breasts. Her face. Her legs. Her butt. All of her.

In the middle of the empty room was a large sculpture. She stumbled closer. It was rough and lumpy, half-finished, but she could recognize herself in the clay. The pose matched the one in the painting in the restaurant.

She knew he was here—he had to be. Still, she jumped at the slight clearing of his throat, and swiveled around. He stood leaning against the doorway, wearing his standard jeans and a white T-shirt. His hair was wet, and the T-shirt clung to the damp spots on his chest.

He looked good. A little paler, a little skinnier, but good.

She said the first thing that popped in her mind. "You know, this room makes you look like a stalker who has never heard of a camera."

His eyes warmed before he gave a small laugh. She clutched the sound close to her heart, letting it warm her. It had been so long since she'd been able to pull that sound out of him.

"Not a stalker," he said huskily. "In love."

She was gaping, she knew that. He'd signed his name with a "love" on that painting, but that could have meant anything.

But in love? In love was different. That could only mean one thing.

He shifted on his feet. "I meant to be in here when you showed up. Your sister, Devi, was going to call me when you left for the restaurant."

Ah. There was one mystery answered. Devi had helped him. "I left early, without telling anyone but a couple of the staff. She may still think I'm in the back looking at new apron designs."

"Or she wanted to keep me on my toes. I don't think your sisters care for me very much."

"You hurt me."

His flinch was obvious, but he nodded. "Yes. They made it clear they were unhappy with me when I went to them yesterday to beg them for help."

"You…begged them."

"Yes." Micah grimaced. "Leena wouldn't talk to me at all at first. Just glared and swore at me. Your youngest sister? Devi? I thought she was nicer. But then she insisted I eat before we talk."

Rana stifled a laugh, humor winning out over everything else. "Pakora? Fried fritters that almost kill you, they're so spicy?"

Micah rested his hand over his stomach. "I thought I could handle spicy food. Until yesterday."

Rana coughed to hide her laugh. God, she loved her sisters. "She did the same thing when she was fourteen and this guy came over to ask for my forgiveness for some terrible sin."

"Yes, well." He shrugged, his intensity unwavering. "A little discomfort is nothing."

She knew her sisters. They were aware she'd been melancholy without Micah. He must have passed whatever test they'd laid out for him.

"They like you," she said. "Or they wouldn't have helped you at all."

"That's good. They're a big part of your life."

She bit her lip. "What is all of this?"

His shoulders lifted, then fell. "I want you back."

Her heart raced. Her impulsive instincts urged her to throw her hands around him and hold on, but the part of her that was older and wiser hit the brakes. "I want love, Micah."

The candlelight gleamed on his high cheekbones, deepening the scar on his lip. He walked forward until he was barely a foot away from her. "Are you seeing anyone else? Someone who…someone you could love?"

"No," she whispered. "I haven't dated anyone since we broke up. I needed some time to think. Readjust my search filters. The ones I had in place, they weren't reflective of what I'm truly looking for."

He took another step. "What are you looking for?"

She pressed her lips together. "You."

His body jerked.

"Funny how that happened," she said with a lightness she didn't feel. "The perfect guy slipped through all my filters for the perfect guy. It's like my heart knew what I needed better than my mind." She took a deep breath. "But taking a break doesn't mean I don't want someone who will love me and adore me for as long as I live. I do. I want forever. And I'm not going to settle for whatever scraps you throw me, and I'll handle it really poorly if we get together and you dump me again for my own good. Like, I'm talking burning-this-motherfucker-down, handling it poorly." She looked him dead in the eyes. "I don't want to be someone's step, Micah. I want to be someone's destination. I want to be their ending. I…I deserve that. I'm worth that."

"You do." He took another two steps, until they stood so close his wide chest brushed against hers. His dark eyes were warm as they rested on her face. "You are. I was an idiot. You said I saw you as a step, and maybe I did. A way to get back to where I was, to who I was.

"I went back to therapy." His smile was sardonic. "I don't like it, but I'll keep going. I don't want you to feel like *you're* my therapy, because you're not."

"I—"

"Let me finish. I realized something when I didn't have you anymore. I always thought my life before the attack was perfect." His brows met, and he looked terribly, adorably confused. "But how could it have been? You weren't in it."

"Oh," she managed. How. Utterly. Romantic.

He cupped her cheek, calluses and healing scars rubbing against her skin. Some familiar, some new. "My life was easy. But easy doesn't always mean better. I don't want to go back to a world or a time when I don't have you."

She couldn't speak. He'd killed her vocal cords dead with his cuteness.

Mistaking her silence as hesitation, his jaw tightened, his eyes sharpening. "I told you we had to break up for your sake, but that was a lie. I broke up with you because I was a coward. I was scared of failing and disappointing you eventually. I don't want to be scared anymore. I want to put the work in, because I know the rewards will be wonderful." His thumb rasped over her lower lip. "You said once that you see me. Not only my scars. Look around you, Rana. I see you too."

She did look around, and he allowed her to, releasing her so she could turn around in a complete circle. Though the paintings were in various stages of completion, each one conveyed something different: excitement, lewd invitation, vulnerability, impish mischief, seriousness. All the things that made her up, neither Old nor New, but her.

Her stomach lurched with excitement. She placed her hand on the head of the rough sculpture. "I didn't know you sculpted."

"I don't. I haven't, not for the past ten years." He came to stand next to her, shoulder to shoulder, and covered her hand. His skin was nicked, covered with healing scars, some a few weeks old, others fresh.

She examined his fingers. "You injured yourself."

"Learning curve. Relearning curve. As soon as I started working, I remembered how much I loved it." His lips quirked. "I shoved sculpting aside. Because it was too hard."

She eyed all of the paintings and the budding sculpture. "Have you been sleeping at all?"

"Not much." He stroked his finger over the sculpture's flank. "This was supposed to be a cast. I was going to do it in granite, and it was going to be my grand gesture to win you back. But it took me so long, I couldn't wait for the finished product." He shook his head, a sheepish smile forming on his face. "God, it's awful, isn't it? It's going to take me forever to work all the kinks and imperfections out of it."

"I like the imperfections." Rana inhaled, thinking over his words, his declaration that he loved her. "For how long?" How long did he want her for?

He didn't miss a beat, somehow understanding what she was asking. "As long as you'll let me."

"I'm selfish." She lifted her chin. "I might let you forever."

He didn't shy away. "Forever would be quite ideal."

"I demand the sex remain amazing. You'd still be my muffin. Only, like, my permanent muffin."

His lips twitched. "I would be honored to be your long-term sweet."

She gave a decisive nod. "No other models. Unless I'm in the room. I'm that selfish."

"I don't particularly want any others. I'll use my brain. Or you."

Relief ran through her. She understood that he hadn't

slept with models as a regular course of events, but, well...she wasn't perfect, and jealousy happened.

He hesitated, looking bashful for a second. "I actually have some ideas. For sculptures. They're...nothing like what I've done before. I want to think about them. Maybe learn the craft better. If I sell the paintings I have in storage, I have lots of time to figure that part out."

"That sounds fine." She pulled his head closer. "Now you kiss me?"

"Gladly," he murmured. His lips sipped at hers, tentative at first and then pressing against her with more surety, his tongue stroking hers.

She tilted her head back when they separated for a breath. He ran his thumb over her lower lip. "Coral, today," he murmured. "I do love all your lipsticks."

"I'm glad you say that. Because after I used my modeling money to buy your blinds, I blew the rest on makeup."

He blinked. "That was a lot of money."

She puckered up her lips and laughed. "Honey. This isn't cheap."

His answering grin was foolish. "Then I suppose you'll just have to model for me again."

She twined her arms around his neck. "We haven't known each other long. People are going to say this is crazy." *Wacky Rana. Jumping into everything feet first.*

Yeah. It was part of her charm.

"What are you talking about?" His smile was brilliant, a flash of white, prompting an answering smile from her. "We've known each other forever. Since you first started peeking in my window."

She winced. "Stop. We should stop talking about that.

It definitely was not my finest moment."

Micah wrapped his big arm around her waist and hauled her close. The candlelight flickered over his face, playing with light and shadow. He dipped his head, until his lips hovered over hers. "You're right. It was mine."

A NOTE FROM THE AUTHOR

Thank you so much for reading Serving Pleasure! I hope you enjoyed it. If you would like to know when my next book is available, please visit me at www.alisharai.com or follow me on twitter @AlishaRai.

If you haven't yet read Devi's story, you can check out Glutton for Pleasure. If you're looking for other books of mine that are similar in heat level/genre to this book, I recommend The Bedroom Games Series or A Gentleman in the Street.

Finally, for any readers who may already follow me on twitter and know of (and have laughed at) my (many) online dating mishaps: while I may have taken some inspiration from real life scenarios, everything in this book is purely fictional. Similarly, Mama Malik is nothing like Mama Rai.

...Except those two ladies do share a fondness for scoping out potential sons-in-law on Indian matrimonial websites. Yes, friends. Those are all too real.

GLUTTON FOR PLEASURE

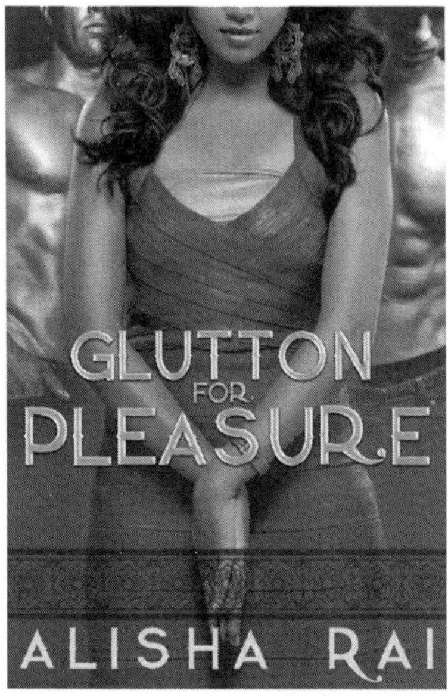

Still hungry? Devour Glutton for Pleasure.

They're craving something sweet. She likes it spicy.

Devi Malik knows how to heat things up. She does it every night as head chef in her family's Indian restaurant. Her love life, though, is stuck in the subzero freezer. Now, with a chance to fulfill a secret fantasy with her long-time crush and his brother, it's time to put her desire on the front *two* burners.

For Marcus Callahan, a love-'em-and-leave-'em attitude isn't only a necessary evil of their kink. It's a protective device. Lately, though, his brother Jace has been making noises about craving something more.

Jace's dissatisfaction with their lifestyle grows with every glimpse of sweet little Devi. Yet Marcus is too haunted by the pain of their shared past to give love a chance.

Despite their reputation for vanishing with the dawn, they discover one night with Devi isn't nearly enough. And Devi finds herself falling in love with two very different men.

It'll take more than explosive sex to light up the shadows surrounding the Callahan brothers' secrets. But Devi's never been afraid of the dark.

OTHER BOOKS BY ALISHA RAI

Pleasure Series

Glutton For Pleasure

Serving Pleasure

Campbell Siblings Series

A Gentleman in the Street

Bedroom Games Series

Play With Me

Risk & Reward

Bet On Me

The Karimi Siblings

Falling For Him

Waiting For Her

Single Title

Night Whispers

Hot as Hades

Never Have I Ever

Cabin Fever

Made in the USA
Middletown, DE
05 December 2015